MATU

# The
# Body of Dancers

### A Novel by

## Candice Leigh Brown

BASKERVILLE
PUBLISHERS, INC.
DALLAS • NEW YORK • DUBLIN

BASKERVILLE Publishers, Inc.
7540 LBJ/Suite 125, Dallas, TX 75251-1008

Library of Congress Catalog Card Number: 93-70996
ISBN: 1-880909-07-3

Manufactured in the United States of America
First Printing

*For my mother, Maxine McAlister Brown–and for Bill*

Remembering is an ongoing process of discovery. It involves going back and excavating the early years of your life–piecing together and reinterpreting things you already know, starting to connect feelings with images you've always had, experiencing unfamiliar body sensations. At times you may experience flashbacks in which you relive aspects of the abuse or reexperience the feelings you had at the time–terror, extreme physical pain, tremendous isolation. These experiences can be disruptive and terrifying. You may respond with shock, horror, or disbelief. You may feel panicky and suicidal, or relieved to finally know the truth about your life.

–Laura Davis, *The Courage to Heal Workbook;*
*For Women and Men Survivors*
*of Child Sexual Abuse*

Perhaps it was the German expressionists, perhaps it was Martha Graham, but someone decided that time in dance didn't have to be only a matter of speeding up and slowing down depending on the tempo of the music and its permissible *rubatos*. Theatrical time has never been the same as literal time, and the drama's various devices of narrative condensation and heightening had taken hold early in the history of ballet. But Graham departed radically from these conventions by introducing flashbacks, memories, and the simultaneous visualization of more than one time at a time as a character confronted events of the past–not in a dream, but in a "real" action. In a Graham dance it's not always possible to tell where in time a character is–past, present, or future. The narrator figure can be at one moment telling how she feels now, in her old age; at the next moment she may be acting out events in her past . . . Instead of being something that's supposed to enhance or vary the look of movement, time can actually convert the movement into another thing, or can impose an entirely different stylistic gestalt on it.

–Marcia B. Siegel, *Watching the Dance Go By*

# *Act One, Scene One*

If you are lucky enough to last through to the final tryouts, the management will keep you standing in line for as long as half an hour while they discuss your relative merits. During this ordeal, try not to lose your faith in God, and remember: if you are a girl, you can always marry and have children.

–Agnes de Mille, *To A Young Dancer*

The mind thinks crazy things before it plunges the body into the unknown. It is San Francisco; I am a sixteen-year-old apprentice in the ballet company; Henry sleeps over on weekends. We lie across my bed, naked. A candle throws its flames on the white brick walls of my flat. I lift my arm slowly, pale and long, imagining it's a feather. Then I let it fall, a snowflake drifting aimlessly. Henry's arm, veiny and weathered, traces mine. Together we choreograph an *adagio* of arms and fingers and shadows. Often this is what we call sex: hours of slow movements, reflected against the wall, until the candle dies out. My floor is caked with different colors and layers of wax. I have not scraped it off during the four months we've been together.

# THE BODY OF DANCERS

The little room is lit only with candles when Henry is there. Still, even in the half-dark, the courageous dance of time moves through his body. He isn't well: his skin is smoky and transparent, his eyes an unhappy blue. He forgets things, repeats himself, reads and re-reads the same passages from the newspaper. He is slipping away from me, dancing inside a music only he can hear. "Damn it all," he will say, again and again, "we should go to a small town, somewhere trembling with heat and life. I'll sell the school, you can leave the Company. We'll read Shakespeare and take early morning walks. This is all so unnecessary, old heart." Only then will I notice the purpling lips and tearing eyes, the inexorable shriveling of a man reaching toward seventy. But the moment will pass, melting away like candlewax, and we will sleep bound together by our differences.

I found him in the daylight, before I was ready to know, but after, I realize only now, I had begun to look. It was a Sunday in June 1980, a week or so after I flew in from Indianapolis to join the Company. Through the cracked windows of my one-room flat in the Tenderloin, I could see a dented street sign, a boarded-over liquor store, a porno shop with flashing neon nipples strung over its entrance. I was poor, scared, ambitious, and lonely. I was also young, very young, and I didn't think I knew much about anything except ballet. So I took a bus, then the BART train, clutching a sheet torn from the Yellow Pages. Henry's studio was just outside the city limits, surrounded by a clean circle of shrubbery.

I knew what I'd find before I even went in: the rhythmic hiss of a gasping heater, the anxious boredom of stage mothers on scratchy sofas, a scarred piano, a shiny hardwood floor, a wall of mirrors. Scuffling slowly among the adolescent limbs and bunheads, correcting and frowning, frowning and correcting, was Henry, his gaunt tempered frame fleshed out by suspenders and baggy pants. I did every combination twice through, at full speed, but he ignored me. Only afterwards, when the rain came and the girls packed up their make-believe tutus and pink ballet boxes and slumped into the back seat of the family car, did Henry come over and ask who I was. Just like that. "And now, my dear, who are you?" I should have expected this question, but I hadn't. Lost in a familiar routine, I'd momentarily forgotten where I was and how far I'd already come.

So I told him what he'd probably already guessed, about my apprenticeship in the Company, how ambitious girls sought outside coaches. The rest I left unsaid, but perhaps he guessed that too. He listened attentively, his thick white eyebrows creasing his face like a snowplow. "Why me?" he finally said. I kept looking at him, then offered the truth. "You were right on the BART line." He gave me a worn smile. " 'I have anticipated thee, Fortune,' " he said, " 'and entrenched myself against all thy secret attacks.' " I must have looked puzzled, because he quickly added, "A classical allusion. Your dancing inspired me. Come, we must keep this old ship afloat." As the rain fell harder, flooding the waiting room, we placed buckets beneath the leaking roof and he told me about his "salad days"—partnering Dame Alonso, two seasons with the Ballet Russes, a tightlipped compliment from Balanchine. Then he asked me to come back, promised to work with me. I'd get into the Company; I was good, perhaps very good; I just needed some direction. He didn't tell me that he needed me. I didn't notice.

I longed to rest, but I couldn't afford to stop moving. I think I knew this then, but I'm not sure. I lived on the Company subsistence money, $597.47 a month, a pale blue check with the Golden Gate Bridge in the background. There was an occasional bit of charity from back home, but they didn't have anything either. They assumed, or prayed, that I could take care of myself. Just before I left Indiana, my father came home to die. He spent most of his time in bed, coughing up blood. It was hot, but his one good hand clutched the sheet tightly to his throat. He was too sick to touch me anymore. "Grow up, Natalie," he said, and then said it again and again. The vodka bottle was still between us, on the night table my mother had picked up at a yard sale. On the other side of the torn yellow window shade was the Indiana summer swelter, pulpy and gelatinous, palpable and perverse. Cherries rotted on the trees and the yard grew up thick with wild strawberries. When I walked into town with my suitcase and dance bag, to catch the bus to Indy, my mother didn't come out on the porch to wave goodbye. I left her framed in the draped front window, rocking back and forth, picking imaginary lint from her $4 Salvation-Army dress.

The previous January I'd gone to Chicago for the audition. San Francisco's Bay City Ballet was holding its annual Midwest tryout. "Tell them whatever they want to hear," Mrs. Pike, my ballet teacher, advised me, tightening her hand around her thinning neck, one last gesture at defining her role as mentor. So I took a bus up the interstate through the fallow Indiana farmland, my dance clothes folded neatly in an oversized black bag, the toe shoes sponged with Calamine lotion to make them an even paler pink. The address of the audition was paper-clipped to a torn fifty-dollar bill—a gift from Mrs. Pike. No one saw me off. I was fifteen but ready to lie about my age, as long as they gave me a chance. I couldn't even picture who these people were or what it was going to be like; somehow that made it easier to imagine being someone else.

Before I left for the audition I experimented with my hair, wrapping it in fat cinnamon rolls, small knots, and woven braids. I studied glossy pictures from the few dance books in the public library: faded ballerinas with buns secured at the napes of their necks, rounded faces and rouged cheeks, tragic eyes peering through long lashes. In contrast, my own face was all angles, as though pieced together like a children's puzzle. My eyes were too big, I didn't have much of a nose, and lipstick only made me look younger. Finally, I decided to wear my hair as I always did: pulled tightly and centered in the back. I took only a standard black leotard and pink tights, a pair of frayed leg-warmers and a sweater. I knew nothing about marketing myself, about the deceptions of make-up and marine-blue danceskirts and all those other things you can suggest just by wearing the right attitude. Perhaps this was to my benefit.

I saw Chicago from the window of a cab. Bulky winter coats crawled the grey-lined streets, disappeared behind snowbanks, reappeared framed against billboards. The air smelled of bad cheeseburgers and old snow, and the cabbie grinned gold through his rear-view mirror. He stopped in front of a narrow brown building with glass doors and ornate shining handles. "Ya got a pickup time?" he shouted out the window. "No," I said, feeling defensive and exposed, as though I should have known when things would end. He thrust my change into the cold air, then slapped the meter with his gloved hand. An old lady coiled in fur and wearing orange lips got in the other side. They slipped into the traffic, choking the street with black fumes.

I mounted the icy steps of the famous ballet academy quickly, slipping and sliding, dance bag bumping against my side. But, just before the glass doors, I stopped. Fifteen is the age for dramatic gestures impulsively conceived, surreptitiously enacted. I removed a hairpin from my centered bun and buried it carefully in a mound of snow piled against the stair railing. I wanted to leave something of myself behind, some trace, I suppose, that would be there when Spring came.

Inside it was warm and almost familiar, like one of the old photographs I'd studied. A clean well-lighted place: gold carpeting, padded wooden benches, dark panelled walls with discreet groupings of old photographs and performance posters. Beneath a bulb-lined display case filled with brand-name dance merchandise—T-shirts, sweatpants, leg warmers, earrings—was a small desk. A fat woman sat behind it, ruffling papers, pencilling cryptic notes on forms. I waited for her to notice me. She didn't.

"The Bay City audition. Where should I go?" I finally asked. The woman didn't look up. She pushed a form toward me with a ringed hand white as dough, and continued writing. "You'll need a number," she said dully. "Fill out the form and clip your picture and resume to it." She still hadn't seen me. I had neither a photo nor a past. I stared at the empty white spaces on the form. "Excuse me," I said, "I've never taken an audition before."

The receptionist lifted her eyes and looked at me for the first time. "You're too late for the school audition," she said. "It started three hours ago." The sweat beneath my clothes was making me nauseous. The school cost money: you paid them for a year or two of instruction and a shot at making the Company from the inside. I had to aim higher. "I'm here for the *company* audition," I said. The receptionist's eyes widened slowly. She shook her head. "Just fill in what you know."

I didn't know much then. I made myself eighteen, figuring that was old enough to suggest responsibility but not too seasoned. I considered inventing a last name, something French and romantic, but decided one lie was already risky. When I returned the form, the receptionist tilted her head as she glanced at it. Her eyes mocked everything she chose to acknowledge.

"Here's your number," she sighed. "Don't lose it or they won't know who you are." Then she momentarily softened. "Pin it to your leotard strap, dear."

I took the square white paper and stared. "How many people are here?" She pressed her fleshy lips together and patted the thick stack of glossy photos and forms. "Could be double that," she said. I was only number seventy-six. Mrs. Pike had told me they might take three. The receptionist stared at me with tired

6

eyes, and I realized she was much older than I had first thought. "Dressing rooms are down the hall to the left," she said. "The large studio's by the restroom, that's where you wait." I wandered off in the direction she'd pointed, clutching my number. "Make sure you stand in front," she called after me, as though offering a gift.

I avoided the crowded dressing room and changed in the bathroom. The long dark corridor leading to the large studio was uninhabited and shadowy. As usual, I'd stumbled on to the least-travelled path. I felt as if I were a little girl again, wandering the town park late at night with my mother. We'd play a shadow game with the trees, pretending they were bad men with rifles or swords. We'd bolt through the blackness, hide behind bushes, bury ourselves in piles of dead leaves. In the milky transparent light of the moon my mother's face would hollow out until only two crazy flint eyes remained. And then she'd be gone, running off by herself somewhere in the dark, and the park would begin to crawl with nightlit secrets. I'd call to her, terrified that one of the bad men we'd imagined had come to life and taken her away. She wouldn't answer me. I'd hold my breath, try to feel courageous, but I was a secret coward. I wanted the game to stop. Somewhere, I hoped, my mother was hiding, crouched on all fours.

I think I actually held my breath as I walked nervously up that shadowy hallway toward the audition room's metal-studded swinging doors. Perhaps I half-expected my mother to leap out at me and block the entrance, her hair slapping her face, those crazy grey eyes darting from side to side. But she wasn't there, not this time. Maybe the bad men finally had come to life. In any event, I was going through this door alone.

The huge room was almost empty. At the front was a long low table of adults, their fully clothed backs sweating against the mirrors. These, I knew, must be the judges, the Company reps. They whispered among themselves and smoked cigarettes. They weren't paying any attention to me, but I crept along the wall anyway, until I found a *barre*. The rounded wood felt smooth and secure. I had known only one place: a shallow windowless room with a portable metal *barre* for the taller girls and low wooden ones for the children; two rusty mirrors that broke your body into waves; an unused upright piano in the corner. This mirrored room was as large as my high-school auditorium. The only other person in it besides the judges and me was the pianist. He had two dots of rouge on his cheeks and a purple scarf around his neck. He didn't notice me either. He was slumped over a black concert grand, staring through heavy-lidded eyes at the vacant dance floor.

Suddenly, a carnival of bones and colors and voices exploded into the room. Ghostly young women appeared in electric colored Danskins and transparent skirts, lambswool sweaters and glittering princess earrings. Some had fake flowers in their hair. The men were mostly barechested and wore tights cut above their knees. One of them, heavily made-up and wrapped in hot pink elastic, *pirouetted* up to me, then dropped to the rosin-covered floor and clapped his hand tragically across his heaving breast. I'd never seen anything like that, but, somehow, I already knew the feeling. I sat down next to him and began to stretch.

A long-limbed body in black warmers cut through the tangle of writhing torsos and stopped in front of me. "Shit," she said, rising to point, "my shanks are too soft." I looked at her beautiful feet, bound in black satin, and wondered what she meant. "Could you move," she said; it wasn't a question. I pulled in my legs and scooted closer to the wall. Hugging the *barre* with her body, she swung her head down so that she was looking at me. "Kiddie audition was earlier," she whispered, nudging my leg with one of her feet. She startled me. "Fuck you," I said. It just came out. Her white skin colored perfectly. "You're nasty," she drawled. Then, with a wink, she moved off to a different place in the room.

Yet nothing had really prepared me for this moment. I had studied with one teacher in a smalltown school hidden behind an oak tree. Mrs. Pike stuffed her blouses with tissue paper, wore clunky black-laced ankle boots, and complained about hemorrhoids and a dead husband. When, finally, she told me I was very talented, beyond her scope, she offered little choice. Work hard and get out of town, or go to beauty school and marry a drinking man. She'd done what she could; I was on my own now.

A small taut figure in burgundy stretch pants and a forest green sweatshirt stepped out of the mirror and came to life. Bringing his hand up to his brow, he peered into the crowded room. "Attention, dancers," he barked. There was an immediate silence, as though the lights had gone out. He cleared his throat, then swivelled around to face the judges. A communal murmur broke between them. He faced us again. "Groups of twenty in a line. Quickly now," he said. "We're behind schedule." *Barres* were carried to the sides by the male dancers, while the women clustered in groups. I was gathered up by a knot of elbows and knees and propelled across the floor. When we stopped, I felt a hand on my shoulder. I turned. It was the apparition in black warmers. She smiled; it wasn't friendly.

The first group of people moved to the center of the room and stood facing the table of judges. I watched uncertainly, not understanding what was going on. The judges sat there immobile while the barking man paced up and down, occasionally pausing in front of a dancer, shaking his head or grunting, then moving on. After a few minutes of this, he pivoted on his heels and faced the judges again. I couldn't hear what was said, but I suspected bad things were happening. I wondered when we would actually dance. "Number thirty-two, you can go," he said sharply. "Numbers one-forty-two, seventy, twenty-four, twenty-five, twenty-six, twenty-seven . . ." A female protest drifted from the table. "Sorry. Number twenty-seven, you stay." The wall-length mirrors mercilessly doubled the rejected numbers, and the smoke thickened above the judges' table.

# THE BODY OF DANCERS

By the time they reached my group, I understood that dancers got eliminated right from the start, on body type alone. Broad shoulders, wide hips, short waist, large breasts, thick arms, flat feet. I stood to the right of the black-clad woman, whose sleek and muscled body suddenly scared me. Next to her I lost form. She gave me a side smirk as the man in burgundy crept closer to us. He stopped before her and put his finger to his lips, as though appraising property. "Dallas Ballet," he said triumphantly. "Company's going under," she explained in a quiet voice. He nodded and moved on down the line, skipping me entirely.

Then the *barres* were returned to the center of the floor and we took our places, left hands curled around the metal, heels pressed together in first position. Each time the barker passed my place at the *barre*, I would begin to tremble, lose my concentration, forget the combination of steps. I was having a difficult time following the music or even understanding how the steps were put together. Mrs. Pike had given the same class for eight years; I'd never learned to think on command, only to memorize and perform by rote, dragging my obedient body through the movements like coloring inside the lines.

The numbers dwindled as my panic increased. The barker would demonstrate a basic move, then crawl around the room, muttering insults, touching bodies, calling out numbers. He kept returning to me, staring right in my face, trying to break me down. I wobbled once or twice but managed to keep my balance. Once he grabbed my leg, pulled it up high to the side, then ordered me to hold it there. He stood beneath the extended leg, both arms folded smugly across his green chest. I knew if I lowered my leg I'd thump him on the shoulder, and yet I lacked the strength to maintain the height. Sweat ran down my face and I could feel myself reddening as I strained to keep the weak leg from falling. He snorted when my poor limb finally crashed on his shoulder. He ignored me for the rest of *barre*.

The second half of the audition was spent in the center of the room, unsupported by a *barre*. Those of us who were left, maybe sixty, were placed in groups of seven or eight and given longer, more complex combinations to perform. I was usually better in the center, freer to give myself over to the music. Rising on point, I *bourréed* in quick small steps diagonally across the floor. More eliminations. Now we were moving in groups of four, *entrechats*, *grand jetés*. I looked over my shoulder. The soft, almost boneless, black-slippered dancer shadowed me, her limbs extended from her torso with practiced restraint like a figure from a textbook. I knew I had to get beyond the mere steps, to somehow break out of the group and stand alone. I smiled at the judges, counted the music, and forgot my limitations. Some of the rejected dancers had returned in street clothes and gathered on the sides to watch. The room was tired with sweaty bodies and used rosin. We kept going for over an hour; the *enchaînements*, the dance phrases, became progressively less restrictive, more expressive. I kept waiting for them to call my number.

Finally, the barker clapped his hands. About thirty left. We were not allowed to leave the room. I rested against the wall and felt my body sinking into exhaustion from the inside out. All around me dancers visibly collapsed. Chests rose and fell, wet hands rested on knees, faces sweated eyeliner. Only the woman in black remained untouched. She stood apart from the others, her small head posed securely atop her thin long neck. She barely seemed to breathe. I was watching her through the mirror when the barker started calling numbers again. This time, however, the called numbers gathered in a small group on the right. The rest of us were dismissed. I gathered up my courage and began walking to the exit. I had stopped breathing. I wanted to die. "Number seventy-six, you stay," the barker said. He motioned irritably as I turned around. "Pay attention," he chastised me. The shadowy woman in black had disappeared.

Four of us remained. The piano player packed up his tired eyes and left. There was to be no more dancing. They just wanted to talk to us now—the final *enchaînement*. They came to me last. I had returned to the wooden *barre* where I had begun. Holding my audition form, the barker walked over to me. He was frowning at all the empty spaces on the page. Without even looking up, he said, "How old are you really?" I flushed, then subtracted. "Seventeen." "No," he said quietly, still reading the form. I hesitated. How much would the truth hurt? "Fifteen?" I finally conceded, as if questioning it myself. His eyelids flashed up and away from the paper. "Yes," he said, and walked back to the table of judges. They conferred, then he returned, moving slowly through the mirrored room. He leaned across the *barre*, hand on his hip. Now what? "Company apprentices don't make much," he said. "Do you have help?" Were they offering? Or was I? I didn't know what to say. He leaned in closer. "Rich parents? Trust fund? Friends in the Bay area?" A lie was all I had. "Yes," I said. He straightened up. "No," he corrected, and returned once again to the judges. When he came back the last time, I had peeled off my leg warmers and was putting them in my dance bag. The judges were filing out from behind the table. He rested his chin on his fingertips and studied me. "Do you *really* think you're ready for this, Miss Barnes?" I had run out of answers. I slipped my shoulder into the strap of my dance bag. "No," I said. It was the quickest and steadiest response I gave. Yet he continued to stare at me. He looked like he was praying. Finally, he lowered his hands. "Yes," he said, correcting me one last time.

They saw then what Henry saw later. I was good all right, but that's never enough. Many of the other dancers there were also very talented, and they had already internalized all those unearthly roles a dancer spends her life inhabiting, had been fashionably trained to look like sylphs and faeries. Behind those practiced bodies were the best schools, years of over-priced lessons and extravagant recitals. Their confidence came from a generation of mothers with expensive faces who sat on cushioned sofas in carpeted waiting rooms, reading self-help articles in the ladies' magazines, tapping heeled feet to the strains of Chopin, casting sidelong glances into the dance room. Meanwhile, their fathers had written out the monthly checks, shouted *bravo* during recitals, and gifted their princesses with glass ballerinas twirling tinnily inside Nutcracker-Suite jewelry boxes. They were all acting out the fantasy life of middle-American girlhood, living confidently and simultaneously inside and outside the ballet. In a way, they needed no audition. They'd joined the Company long ago.

So why me? When I was five, maybe six, my father accidentally set a grease fire in the kitchen. I remember the sickening howl, the blistered pockets of skin on his hand, his dull grey eyes promising "this is your fault," although it wasn't, couldn't have been. Running after him into the night-filled front room, I grabbed his wrist and plunged the hand into a bowl of ice. "I'm sorry, Daddy," I cried over and over, watching the ice melt to slivers around the dying flesh on his fingers. He went away for a while after this. Next time he came home he hit me across the face. My mother didn't say anything, not then, not ever. She'd stand before the bathroom mirror, rock from her heels to the balls of her feet, brush her greying hair, hum to herself.

That's what Henry and the Company reps saw in that terrified girl straining to maintain the precarious height of her extended leg. My difference, something to define themselves against, someone willing to exchange her darkness for theirs. They knew I'd be a good girl, an obedient apprentice. That I'd eat only grapes and rice and throw up between classes; dance ten hours a day on bloody feet and dislocated hips; learn every role in every ballet and go to every rehearsal. They knew that my dance soul was unprotected by money, family, costumes. That I'd learned how to make myself invisible long before I'd worn my first pair of second-hand ballet slippers. They even knew, in some way at some level, that I'd spent a lot of my childhood hiding inside a musty canning shed next to a mortuary, keeping watch for my father, waiting for my mother to come home from the swing shift. They saw all that—and they knew, as if they were looking into their own abandoned souls, how willing I was to plunge my body into the unknown.

I slept with Henry before I even began menstruating. It happened in his empty waiting room, after only one month of Sundays. He rested his hand on my shoulder, then pulled my leotard down. He was gentle, kind, patient, but I stood there a long time, not moving, hardly breathing, humiliation spreading like a fan across my naked chest. I was remembering the Mason jars of canned tomatoes and pickled rhubarb, the sunlight refracted haphazardly by the shed's cracked planking, the cold steel of my father's belt buckle pressed against my bare stomach, his hand wedged between my legs. "You like it," he'd insist, but I never said anything and I always kept my eyes on the broken sunlight. Here too was loneliness in silent performance and I held fast to it, to the flawed beauty of the ancient dance. Henry couldn't have known, of course, although I never resisted and I never closed my eyes. When, months later, I did bleed, he bought me a box of tampons. He didn't say anything, and I accepted his gift in silence.

# *Act One, Scene Two*

Be simple. The least effort, the least motion for a given effect, is what is wanted. All of ballet training is an attempt to strip extraneous tension, nervousness, and fidgeting away from the pure line. A great dancer seems to move more slowly through any given exercise, because there is no wasted motion whatsoever, and, therefore in fact, there is more time for the movement.

–Agnes de Mille, *To A Young Dancer*

*I* am standing on a cement block in first position, waiting, as usual, to be told what to do next. The San Francisco day is already sinking into the low fifties. The *corps* and apprentices are posed in front of the Civic Center, mocking art. Inside, a throng of ballet and symphony subscribers attends a modern-art exhibit. If they buy—and they will, they always do—some of the proceeds will dribble down into the Company's account. The string section is strolling the galleries. We're the outside entertainment, frozen and freezing facsimiles of the pricey sculptures inside. My cracked and dirty pedestal is riddled with large flaking gaps.

15

# THE BODY OF DANCERS

I've tried to conceal my small breasts with a strip of surgical tape, but the nipples are still visible through the sheer white material of my unitard. So I fold my arms over my chest and stare straight ahead, avoiding the constant parade of strangers. I know this place well. During the past two months Henry and I have come here nearly every Sunday, thrown stale bread to the pigeons, waited out the threat of rain. He will hold my hand, call me "old heart," tell me stories, always different, always the same. After a while, I will stop listening and watch the street artists sketching five-dollar portraits, fondling scarred guitars, unrolling braided rugs. Ocean breezes sharpen the reedy notes of the sandpipe players. We drift like this through the unhurried Sabbath afternoons. A shallow line of acacia trees and boxed yews protects us from the wind.

But today is a workday. Raincoats and briefcases swarm along Grove Street. Windows blink, doors swing, ruined choirs of voices, bells, alarms, and drills rattle and drone. Desperate faces whiz by me at a windy speed: some glance and shake their heads, others stop and stare and eat cold sandwiches oozing with mayonnaise. Henry will probably be teaching an Adult-Ballet class now, ministering to the sad fantasies of overweight women. For an hour a week, in the shaded greylight of his studio, they come to worship and adore. Smiling, whispering, posing, he passes among them; receptionist or executive, mother or grandmother, Mrs. or Ms, they will blush and giggle and be healed by his touch. I torture myself thinking about these half-dressed women arriving early for class, lingering afterwards, sprawling on sofa and chairs, listening to his stories. I want him to myself. But he flashes me a partial smile, as though my jealousy amuses him. "It's part of the job, Natalie."

In the middle of the square, a circle of *corps* dancers in sweatsuits stands next to a dead fountain. Rising and falling from *relevés* into *pliés*, they warm their arches. Miss Carabee, the Company watchdog, waddles along the edge of my cement block, issuing instructions to the unposed dancers. "Over to the edge. That's it. Keep it straight. C'mon girls." The defiant rolls of fat spill authoritatively from her big sweater. A miscalculated dye has transformed her once grey hair into a bunch of raspberries covered with white fuzz. "Two-hour standings," Carabee continues, "that's the order. And girls, there are no full bladders here." Carabee sucks in her breath until her chest swallows her neck, then dabs at the corner of her mouth with a contemplative finger. Squeezing her eyes into worried slits, she jabs my goose-pimpled arm. "Straight away from the torso, like so."

I use her for a mirror and thrust my arms out. Mrs. Pike would pose us in her weekly variation class, trying to demonstrate famous solos from the great ballets. But she hadn't actually seen a ballet in years and her memory was never much good. Striking attitudes in long skirts and buttoned blouses, she would suck in her rouged cheeks and tilt her head sideways, as if listening for her cue. It was a quirky routine, and the other girls mimicked her mercilessly in the dressing room. But, as I walked home after class, I would practice these poses, tilting my head expectantly into the gathering darkness. "Like this?" I ask Carabee. Her cheeks hang in loose tired folds, a bulldog's jowls. She's been in charge of galas and auctions and fundraisers too long. "Just do it," she says wearily. She lives in a walkup in the Sunset District. Tonight, when she goes home, she'll cook greasy rice and listen to Johnny Mathis. She sighs loudly. "Now here I am wasting words again. Swallow it, honey, hold your center, and get those arms out."

"There are rewards for the good girls," Henry used to say. I wanted to believe him, I needed to believe him. Every Friday, tacked next to the rehearsal schedule on the bulletin board, were the apprentices' special instructions: clean the studio mirrors, sweep the dressing-room floors, crack and grind the rosin, head the lower-level classes. There were only eight of us, living on the edge of the Company like orphans, waiting for a position to open. I had the least seniority and the longest wait for a place in *corps*. If there was a place. You could wait forever, they could demote or fire you tomorrow. They never justified and we never questioned. It was an economics of scarcity and we were the reserve labor force. Sometimes the uncertainty was even more exhausting than the work.

I learned to rest on the express train to Henry's studio. I'd close my eyes and pretend I was weightless, just a bodiless spirit rising from a cracked leather seat in a dark subterranean space beneath San Francisco. I always returned to him late Friday afternoon, dusty and damp, prepared to work, longing to share my week with him. He knew how competitive it was, but there were things I couldn't tell him. The other girls resented me: partly for my youth, partly for my talent, but mostly just because I was there, a foreign body invading their space. Most of them were from the Bay area, had grown up together in the Company school, knew each other's strengths and weaknesses, had worked out their pecking order long ago. I could change everything. And so they clustered together on the other side of the dance room when I walked in, or my point shoes mysteriously disappeared, or I was bumped off-balance at the start of a combination. Trivial stuff, especially when packages of black beauties exchanged hands every day in the hallway between classes and empty laxative boxes cluttered the dressing-room floor, but it hurt anyway, and I knew Henry didn't want to hear about it. He would have said, at any rate, "Ignore those things, they're not important." He was right, but still I longed to curl up in his arms and cry.

I did tell him about Mr. Himmel's Apprentice classes. Himmel hated me on sight. The very first class he beelined over to me, poked his finger in the side of my leg, and announced that I was fat. He wore a red kerchief to conceal his neck wrinkles and sucked in his stomach so that the bare strip of flesh between his shirt and jazz pants rippled. He sneered, slammed his counting cane into the floor, made nasty comments. He always singled me out. "Long line is what you want, not this squatty, lumpy look, Miss Barnes." I'd try to lengthen my body against his granitic gaze, but usually he'd just turn on his heels and march away. "It's always wrong, never what I ask."

"Politics," Henry said, flattening his hand against the center of my back. We stood at the *barre* of his unlit studio, recreating Himmel's class. "He's just playing a game." I pressed my stomach into my spine, searching for the ballet dancer's center. "What's the point of it?" I asked. He pulled my leg out to *seconde*, massaged the arch down so that my foot was better positioned, then let go. He counted with his fingers as I held the extension. "Break you of any differences, so you'll fit into the *corps* like all the others." I gripped the floor with my supporting leg and watched the other one tremble. "Hold it from under the leg, Natalie." He motioned for me to lift out of my hips. "We'll beat them at their game," he said sadly.

I was never certain that Henry wanted me to make it. Emotions flowed through his pale eyes at a frightening speed. He viewed my body as an instrument that could carry his own ideas, somehow redeem his past, his failures. Some days he'd torture me with slow *adagios* and endless balances, or make me do everything double-time. Other times he'd stop our private lesson half-way through. "This is all so unnecessary, old heart," he'd say. On those days we'd lock up quickly and take the early train into the city. We never stayed at his place during those first six months.

I dreaded these aborted sessions. The silence between us was unbearable and, though I tried not to think about it, I knew that we were moving away from my dream and closer to his. I wanted to hear the sad French singer on the Wharf or wander among the warm smells of cappuccinos and buttered croissants; he wanted to return to my apartment. We'd climb the steps, insert the key, push our weight against the peeling door. The radiator rasped and roaches scurried out from behind the old pipes. I tried to make it easy for him. I'd light the candles, remove my clothing quickly, crawl under the cold sheets of the sofa bed. Often he would sit in the sagging chair by the window, look out, study his hands. He remained apart from me.

My first fundraiser was a cocktail party up in Hyatt Tower, a weeknight early in August. I drank ginger ale, lifted my spine up straight, tried to look sophisticated. The apprentices and *corps* were to stand gracefully in corners, perch upon sofas and chairs, move vaguely about the room as though ready for flight. We were not encouraged to eat—or talk. I found a corner and watched the swirling finery: the sleeve of a woman's red-velvet jacket; the steaming clams and escargot nestled on white tablecloths; the translucent silver-studded chandelier; the mauve drapes framing an off-center view of the Bay.

Lincoln, the only male apprentice, joined me. He was a kind of universal token: male, black, and gay. He held up his hand and stared at the clean white moons on each nail. "They're still arriving. Look at 'em." The patrons formed restrained groups, sipped champagne, murmured approval at the appropriate moments. "See that suit over there, the one in tight stripes? Wants some ballerina ass. Comes over to me stinking whiskey and asks what girl has the best chance at a career. Sleazy closet bastard."

I stared at the suited man. He was talking with Suzie, a pale woman who rarely smiled and often knitted leg-warmers for the other dancers. The man placed an arm around Suzie's back and squeezed. I whispered, "What did you say to him?"

"I said a *corps* girl is a *corps* girl." Lincoln's voice dropped. "Shit. Might as well be Suzie. Been stuck in the line six years." He tore at his finger then spit the nail into the carpet. "Hell, what could I say? Not even front row?"

But all of us were playing at being dancers. Some of the girls, like Suzie, had been at it longer. First, they'd starved themselves into the Balanchine ideal of transparent yielding flesh—until their legs could go past ninety degrees, above their heads alongside their noses. Then they'd enlisted in the *corps*, one of thirty in *Swan Lake*, hopping back and forth across the season and the stage, eyes glued to the floor in search of curling tapemarks. Only a few, a precious few, would ever stand before the abyss, facing an audience that had come specifically to see them. The others were washed away in the background, peering through eyeliner and fake lashes, their careers reduced to diets and swans and bunions.

I could see Suzie's head wobbling elegantly atop her neck. It was as though all her training had prepared her for this moment, posed in the Hyatt Tower like a statue, waiting for someone to breathe life into her. Perhaps some kind of miracle would sweep her up and carry her to center stage. Suzie leaned in closer to the man by her side, turned her head up to him, and froze. Her face was aglitter with the soft lights of the room, and the twenty years she'd put into her work disappeared beneath an unrehearsed smile. She'd found a spotlight, if only for a moment.

One of my daily duties that summer was to clean the studio mirrors. No matter how often I'd circle them with the damp cloth, hand smudges would reappear. I'd wipe and wipe, smearing my reflection, watching myself recede behind suds, only to appear again not quite whole and not yet clean. After a while, the mirror began to reflect alternate images. I was never quite sure what I'd find beneath the soapy water. My arms became knobby branches, my legs dead roots. My leotard was a space suit, my feet swollen sausages, my face a Cubist collage. When it got too weird, I'd stretch out flat on my back along the sweat-stained wood and stare at the ceiling. Wistful strains of practice-piano Vivaldi would drift through the vents from a neighboring room, and I'd turn off my mind and drift with it. But then the tune would end, or a bell would ring, and I'd have to go off to class or crack the rosin or clean the mirrors again.

One weekend Henry bought a full-length mirror for my closet door. It took him an hour to nail it up. When he finished, he told me to undress. It was the only time I cried about our sex. But he was determined, almost angry, and so I stood naked before the mirror, tears running down my face, my reflected flesh bunched between his gnarled hands. I tore down the mirror after he went home. It shattered in a thousand pieces and slivers of glass got lodged in the soles of my feet.

By late summer, Henry and I were in a routine. We talked over the telephone Monday through Thursday, worked in his studio on Fridays, spent the weekends at my flat. Saturdays were half-days. In the afternoons I washed tights, lifted weights, cleaned lettuce, soaked muscles. Henry read history books and listened to radio Sinatra or one of his Stravinsky tapes. Often he fell asleep while reading. I'd take the book from his lap, crawl into bed and read the passages. The facts and numbers confused me. So I'd drift off into a mythical class, one where I pulled off multiple turns, executed perfect *jetés*, struck breathtaking balances. I wore beaded gowns with slim pink straps, shiny sequined bodices, rose satin tutus. My crowns were always inlaid with red stones.

It was mid September before I got Henry to go to the Wharf. He was always difficult to move, as if by holding the day still he could prevent the unwavering passage of time. Yet we held hands, bought crab cakes, sat on the pier and watched brawny-muscled fishermen haul in clams and rusty beer cans. The air was bitter and wet, the wood planks creaky beneath our feet. We crept along Beach Street and joined the tourists. An organ grinder and his monkey performed for a tour-group of senior citizens; a clown circled the group on a bicycle, juggling tennis balls. The street was lined with easels, jewelry stands, pretzel vendors, street dancers and singers. For a quarter, we listened to the Human Jukebox whistle an off-key Beatles song through the narrow slit in his cardboard costume.

I wanted to stay the rest of the afternoon, see, smell, and hear everything. I strained at Henry's arm, but he hung back. He wasn't just tired. "You mustn't get so carried away," he said. I turned to him, still excited. "Oh, why not, Henry? It's fun. They're artists!" He stopped now and the crowd flowed around us. "Not real artists," he said firmly. "They perform for quarters. To buy a meal." I let go of his arm. "I get paid," I reminded him. "So do you. And they're so free!" He grabbed both my arms. His hands were trembling. "Freedom is not mindless activity," he bristled. "Artists are responsible to ideas, to history." I must have drawn back, because he released his grip and softened his voice. "Listen, old heart, the money, the attention, the happiness . . . if it comes, it comes. But it has nothing to do with art." I reached up for his trembling hands and took them in mine. Then we turned around and walked away from the street carnival, against the crowd.

I returned to the Wharf whenever I could. I didn't tell Henry. I'd huddle on the fringes of the street artists' random life, drop coins in their guitar cases, buy their hand-dipped candles and the powdered incense that crackled when it burned. They began to recognize me. The thin Kearney-Street magician, waving to me, would pull a rabbit from his hat and cry: "Hey, placid angel, look!" Or the Cannery French singer would smile raggedly and call me "little frog." After a while, I began to smile and wave back.


"You've got to be more of a politician," Henry was saying. This was only a few days before the posing at the Civic Center.

# THE BODY OF DANCERS

That morning I'd been cleaning the mirrors in the studio room when one of Himmel's gofers, a perpetual level-7 student named Gebba, had kicked open the door. "Himmel wants you in the four-o'clock class, says things are going to change around here." She paused, then added with obvious pleasure, "Says you aren't being cooperative." I spoke doggedly into the mirror: "I've got *rehearsal* at four." Gebba was a gawky girl with short limbs and a barrel chest. She inched her body along the wall, eying me suspiciously, then plopped a hand on one of the clean mirrors. "Doesn't matter what you say, he wants you there." Before I could respond, she chirped, "You'd better change your attitude," and strutted back out of the room.

Henry sat on the edge of the bed watching me. I was stretched out on my floor doing sit-ups. He knew as well as I: when they started scheduling you against rehearsals, you were becoming expendable. Next they'd reduce my subsistence salary, then maybe knock me down to level 7. I'd be just like Gebba, kicking doors in frustration. "You need to cut out the backs of your leotards," Henry counselled, "emphasize the spine." The rocking motion of the sit-ups was slightly disorienting and his voice seemed to fade in and out. I was up to a hundred and twenty-six, and sweating. Henry continued with the list. "Drop five more pounds . . . wear a bright lipstick . . . keep the strands of your hair tucked in . . . count the music." I collapsed at one-fifty. "You've got to hold your own, old heart."

But it didn't seem to matter. Himmel missed nothing. He saw my safety pins coming undone and my bra sticking out the sides; he saw the loose cinnamon roll atop my head and my too-eager feet a half-count ahead of the music. I hadn't gone to that four-o'clock class and now he was taking his revenge. He picked up his cane, marched over to me, and hammered the tip of his stick into the floor, just barely missing my foot. "Miss Barnes," he snarled, "you will lead the Brahms variation." I lurched forward but kept my eyes lowered. "Look at me when I speak," Himmel whispered. My eyes darted upward. "Haven't you mastered it?"

"I'm trying," I said.

"*Umph!*...we don't try, we do." He threw his head back and folded his arms across his chest. The cane dangled from one of his clenched hands.

I couldn't do this variation, and he knew it. The whole class was to perform the *allegro* for the Director of the Company, two girls at a time. Lincoln had his own lively piece to dance— full of steps that were impossibly fast, movements that didn't accommodate his long athletic body. He'd been moaning about it in the hall for a week, but, like the rest of us, was resigned to his fate. The little demonstration was our offering, our hope. Perhaps it would reveal technical proficiency, bring at least one of us closer to the *corps*. Yet each time we rehearsed the variation, cut with multiple beats and leaps, Himmel corrected me viciously. My jumps were too quick, my interpretation too singular.

I waited from the center of the room for the pianist to strike the first dreaded chord of Brahms. Himmel faced me, a smug smile stretched across his pasty skin. Just then, the door flung open, and the Company's ballet mistress, Magda, flew into the room. She was dressed in her usual flamboyant mixture of green zippered leotard, rose and dark blue scarves, canary yellow dance skirt, black leather pumps, and a dozen or so bracelets that embraced her slim arms. She and Himmel were notorious for their marriages—they'd married and divorced one another at least three times, and no one was sure whether they were, at present, on or off.

"Darling, I'm so so *so* sorry to interrupt your class," Magda sang out. She arched her pencilled eyebrows and puckered her burgundy lips. "An emergency, I believe. Some sweet little thing was sent to replace poor Harry. Well, you know how it is, darling. A *mess* at the front desk!" Magda glanced at the class and shook her head, fluttering her hands and twisting her mouth into strange shapes. "Such a business!" she gasped.

Himmel dropped his cane and clutched at the scarf around his neck, then stalked over to Magda. "They're doing Brahms," he mumbled. Then, grasping her by the elbow, he warned, "Tempo's slow. Don't take them through it fast."

"Mr. Himmel! Really!" she mocked in a high-pitched voice, "I would *never* do anything like that."

I backed up until I was next to Lincoln. "We're going to have to do this for *her*?"

"Whatever that worm says, she's gonna do the opposite," he said. "Shit."

Himmel disappeared through the door, muttering. We dropped our tense postures and waited to see what Magda would do. She threw her head back so that the white of her throat showed, then clapped her hands together and ran with small steps across the length of the floor, kicking up her skirt, bursting with a kind of sadistic pleasure.

"Well, darlings, let's see where you are. We'll have ourselves a *good* time. Now, Jerry," she spoke to the pianist, "let's just up that tempo a wee wee bit. Brahms is like a flash of lightning." She widened her eyes and sighed, "Ah, look at all these leggy girls."

I guess I should have known that my career, my life, would turn suddenly and unexpectedly on another woman's vindictive and ironic whim. Magda found me almost instantly. "No, no, no, no, *no*, Natalie," she chastised. "Everything is quick, quick, quick. I want little steps, light and little and quick."

I *pirouetted* from fifth position, then leaped to the side, carrying my arms before me like a bouquet of flowers. I could barely breathe; I had repeated the variation three times consecutively. My feet felt stuck to the floor.

"Little, little, little...well, that's closer, I suppose." Magda's voice lifted again, "You *must* dance Brahms from the center. My dear," she paused, "does Mr. Himmel have you dance through mud?"

I stopped moving and threw out my hands. "I don't know . . . he always wants it slow. I can't do it slow either." I ran my tongue over my upper lip and then pressed both lips together.

It was no use. The other girls stood about the room like vultures, glad to see me singled out like this, each hovering a little higher as I fell once again to earth.

Magda walked over to me and rested a cool hand on my arm. She smelled of Indiana gardenias, like the ones my mother grew outside her bedroom window. "Natalie," she drawled, "what *are* we going to do with you if you can move neither slowly nor quickly? It's a bit of a problem, you can surely see." She brought her face close to mine. "You're very stubborn, aren't you, dear?"

I fought with the images of myself doing the variation: every movement was supposed to come from below my navel. I couldn't find my center, that was the problem.

"There's really only *one* solution that I can see," Magda intoned.

I looked at her painted face through my own tear-streaked one. "Let me do it again," I pleaded.

"No," Magda shook her head emphatically. "It's quite enough for today."

Perhaps Henry felt, too, deep in his own dancer's soul, that Magda's appearance was an omen. He broke routine and came into the city on a weeknight. He sat listlessly for a long time in the faded chair by the half-opened window, listening to a stubborn autumn rain, the folded *Chronicle* on his lap.

"Well," he said, his eyes directed away from me, "we can always go off somewhere, a better place." He pulled the blinds on the window. "Maybe you'll be happier in something else." I was already in bed, the blanket bunched up around my aching body. "I don't want to leave, Henry." He turned his eyes on me, as if searching for some give in my face that would settle everything forever. I shifted my eyes so that I wouldn't have to look at him. "Of course not, Natalie," he said. His restless fingers tapped against the paper, paused, then started up again. I rubbed my calves beneath the scratchy wool blanket, avoided his gaze. Suddenly Henry's hands stopped flat across the print. "You'll get through, old heart."

The next day was the posing at the Civic Center. Carabee put me into an *arabesque*, even though she knew it was a fleeting pose that normally lasted only a few counts. I balanced with one leg on the cement block, held the other in an arc above my waist. As the cold air settled in my limbs, the muscles in my lower back began to resist. Carabee had placed two and three girls on each of the other blocks in various poses, but I was left without a partner. At first, she'd wanted to pair me with Lincoln, but, thinking this a bit radical, had put him alone on his right knee a few feet in front of me on another block. "You've gotta be kidding!" he'd said when Carabee had pushed at the nape of his neck, indicating, rather forcefully, that he was not to display any pride.

My leg was already beginning to wilt from its dreadful *arabesque*. I closed my eyes, felt myself getting dizzy, opened them again. A few drops of rain were falling and the city landscape was becoming a still photograph. "Thought this was a liberal company, then they go and put me on my knee," Lincoln was muttering. "Gotta pray too. Shit." It was usually easier for the men. They romped through the Company like puppies, partnering the women on stage and off. If they attended rehearsals, classes, and fundraisers, sold tickets, wiped down floors, threatened no one, they almost always became soloists. And then, whether they deserved it or not, they could get a principal role, the chance to slip themselves into a part. In the *corps*, the girls were indistinguishable from one another.

"Living statues, girls, living statues. Don't blink," Carabee snapped. Looking out to Grove Street, I tried not to think about what Magda had said. It was impossible, of course, and so I clung desperately to Henry's soothing insincerity. "You'll get through, old heart." Really, I had no idea where I'd go once the door to the Company had closed.

Two women loomed in the doorway of the Center, wrapped in fur, clutching programs in their gloved hands. "Shit,"

Lincoln said under his breath. "Linc!" Carabee admonished, before whipping around herself and pointing a finger at me. "Your arms, dear, your arms!" The air snaked itself in rings about my fingers and I let them flutter briefly before my elbows locked into a bend. I looked down at my wrists. They seemed wrong but I couldn't remember why. The two women were still lolling just outside the door. They glanced to the right and left, then brought their frosted heads together momentarily. Abruptly, the woman wearing a green hat pushed her hatless friend toward me. "Shoot me in front of this one!" she breathed. She thrust a camera into the other woman's white-gloved hands.

"You'd almost think she was the real thing," her friend said. Her tone was dry, nasal.

I kept my eyes locked on Lincoln, who was conspicuously being ignored by the patrons. Pigeons had gathered at the bottom of his block. They fought over kernels of popcorn, rolled lumps of dried chewing gum around like marbles, turned endlessly in tighter and more frenzied circles.

The hatted woman touched my foot, then ran a hand up my leg, stopping at the knee. I tightened my jaw. I wasn't going to move, no matter what.

"Well, she's certainly holding her pose!"

The other woman was pursing her lips into a compact mirror. "They're always *moving* on stage, so you can't really tell what they're doing. I take the opera glasses."

"Ours cracked last season," the hat spoke, removing her hand from my leg, "during intermission. The second act looked positively Braque!"

I felt my leg slowly losing force. My arms had gone numb. "Do you think this color suits me?" the other woman murmured. "Something happens to your lips as you age, lose the color or something." She put the compact in her handbag and backed away from the cement block. "Just push that little button in the center," the hat said, "a bit of magic!" The women's laughter was light like bubbles escaping in the air as my leg crashed behind me.

## THE BODY OF DANCERS

The two women, still laughing, hurried off to a group of living statues who were posed in a circle, their hands interlocked, heads tilted to the sides. I recovered my broken *arabesque*, but held it at a lower, more manageable height. A knot of men followed after the women. Two of them broke away from the group and strode over to me. I held my breath, though the men didn't seem to be looking at me. They stood apart, hands thrust in their pockets. The younger voice spoke first. "Wonder what it takes to score with one of these tutus?" The men laughed. The same man pointed his chin at me. "You think she talks?"

"Oh, hell, Garrison, leave her alone. Thing's probably bored out of her skull. Cold too."

"Hey," the man called Garrison yelled at me, "you alive in there?" He waved his hand in front of my face, then abruptly pulled it away. The old nausea welled up and I began the internal search for the broken sunlight. Then his voice hardened, changed direction. "Look at that big queen on his knee." It returned to me, still hard, but now almost a whisper. "Bet you know a lotta faggots, honey. Ever met a real man?"

"Cut it out," snipped the other voice.

But Garrison pushed on, his voice louder and angrier. "Well, I fucking don't get it. Bunch of gals running around half naked, tits bouncing all over the place, and these guys are doing it to each other." He paused. "Doesn't make any goddam sense."

Garrison cast a flinty look at Lincoln and then me again. He was trying to stare me down, but I desperately held my pose. Finally, he shook his head and the two men walked away. I let out my breath and lowered my leg. Both arms hung at my sides, tears burned my eyes.

And then, because we were not to be spared anything, a pigeon landed on Lincoln's shoulder. It rolled its miniscule head about and gently pecked at his hair. Its grey and white body shuddered with the movement. Lincoln remained still, but the whites of his eyes were turned accusingly on the bird. "Goddam pigeon," he muttered. "Gonna get myself a real life. Shit."

Carabee had installed herself by the hotdog stand; a blotch of mustard stained her sweater. She didn't notice the crowds and the cameras gathering around Lincoln's block. The pigeon roosted, Lincoln muttered, shutters clicked. My body now lost to the day, I too just stood and stared. It was as if there were nothing else to do. Suddenly, the pigeon fluffed its back feathers and ducked its head down into its plump body. Lincoln yelled out, "Stinking bird just shit on me!" The pigeon ballooned in the air, then fell to the ground with a thud. It cocked its head, then waddled away. Carabee dropped her hotdog and started waving her arms. But there was no stopping Lincoln. "Shit!" he yelled again.

"Linc, calm down!" Carabee ordered. "We'll clean it off."

"Don't you be telling me what I gotta do, Carabee!" Lincoln broke his pose and stood straight up on the block. "I've taken enough shit. This statue is coming to life."

He leaped from the block and landed on the pavement as the pigeons hopped to the side. Marching over to the fountain, he pulled his jeans over his hips, dug his feet into two worn shoes, and zippered his jacket. As he grabbed his dance bag, he gave the finger to a dismayed Carabee and threw a kiss to me. A few pitiless cameras clicked away.

Carabee motioned for us to get off the blocks. We were just under two hours, but the sky had started weeping heavily—and really—no one was interested any longer in the living statues. With the other dancers, I huddled under the roof of the Civic Center. Very little was being said. Lincoln was off by himself, pulling loose threads from his purple leg-warmers, cursing Carabee under his breath. I sealed my clothes around my body and waited silently for her instructions. There was no way to avoid returning to the studio. I would have to face the barred door.

When we arrived, I reluctantly crawled past the bulletin board, and headed down the hallway to the dressing room. One of the principal dancers, Simon, stood by the vending machines, drinking from a chipped mug. His face was shadowy beneath a thatch of damp curls. "Long day, huh?" I paused, turned my head, reddened. I wanted to move quickly, cover myself, apologize for being so graceless. It was unlike a principal to speak with an apprentice. Apparently, word had already gotten out. "Well, give my regards to Magda," Simon added sardonically, then strolled in the other direction, toward the rehearsal room.

I watched him go, then retracked my steps. The other apprentices were gathered around the rehearsal schedule, speaking quietly. I felt ashamed and lumpy. The chattering ceased and several pairs of eyes turned to stare at me. I worked my way self-consciously to the front of the group. I couldn't find my name on the rehearsal list. I raised my eyes to the top of the board where the important messages were tacked. My name stood out like a fresh blister. I studied Magda's signature. The girls behind were very still. I turned away from the board and looked at each face. I didn't know what to say to them, and, really, there was nothing I could say. I put my head down, pushed my way through the group, and, fighting back the embarrassment, ran up the long hall. But there was nowhere to go, no one with whom to share the news.

Though my place was unearned, I'd made it. Magda, with a perverse gesture aimed more at discomfiting Himmel than rewarding me, had put me in the Company. Not the *corps*, into which I could never fit, but a soloist dancing apart. I stopped at the end of the hall and glanced in the door at a level-2 class in progress. The young girls were working on their *pliés*. They wore pink leotards, pink skirts, and white headbands. The children peered out the door at me, their small bellies protruding, their backs swaying behind them. Their faces, already set in competition, were sewn with frowns and stitched with fear. As they struggled to close their feet in fifth position, their eyes grew hard.

"Ladies, remember, you must always work to keep your center," the teacher was saying. "Then everything is possible."

So I went to the only place I knew to go. The street artists had already gone home. I stood in the curve of the Bay with my back to the boarded-over deserted Wharf. Across the water the red light that used to be Alcatraz blinked intermittently. Once upon a time they had ferried prisoners across to the Rock from this pier. Go much farther west and you could fall off the edge of the earth. It was a calm night. No wind, no waves, just the red blinking light and the lamblike bleat of a foghorn. They were oddly syncopated. I stood there a long time peering into the darkness until, finally, I got inside their music.

# Act One, Scene Three

> Think of your body and arms and legs not just as things to lift and put down and move about, but as the percussive part of an instrument whose sounding board is the air and all space. You move, ringed with echoes and extensions. Your body is in fact the heart of extending and overlapping cycles of movement.
>
> –Agnes de Mille, *To A Young Dancer*

I look down into the plain old brown casket, no fancy lining or bedding, just pine with a close-fitting top. My mother thinks this will keep the bugs out. I start to touch my father's tightly masked face, then pull my hand back and jam it into my dress pocket. He's been dead in my heart for a long time. Now we can bury him. "Pickled himself in vodka," my mother says. I don't look at her, but I feel her pain circling above us like she's gone and died herself. "Bled like a pig." She's crying now. Her sobs are muffled. I can't touch her either, though I want to. I just keep staring. He looks dead, and I want him to stay that way. "Died same as he lived."

I imagine his death more easily than I do his life. I see him lurching on the front porch, his once-boyish face now knotted with veins and flush-red patches. He knocks over the rocking chair, swears, blows rings in the snow-grey air. He calls to my mother but she's busy inside, stuffing his old undershirts in the gaps along the floor where the front room is caving in. She's talking to herself, pulling fistfuls of crumbled plaster from the wall, cramming those rags into the rotted floor to keep winter out. Something's gurgling down in his throat, hot and cold simultaneously. He's gone too far this time.

"Been out drinking with them other damned fools," she says, after she finally looks up from the rags and sees his shadow wedged in the doorway. Then she hears the rattling in his throat, sees the broken-yellow eyes rolling back in his head, smells the decaying flesh filling that cold room. She drags him to the bathroom, but the pipes are frozen over and ice clogs the drains. He's dripping blood all the way. At the end, it's just the two of them, after all, in death's embrace. He's seeing black shadows crawl across her face, drop to the unswept floor, finally, come after him. He's got nowhere to go.

Or maybe it's easier. He turns over in the night and reaches for the bottle, one last drink before curtain. Drugged with sleeping pills, my mother hears only a whistle. She pushes his hand away, thinks half-consciously it'd be the first time in years. She doesn't want anything from him now. His hand finds the bottle but it slips from his fingers, falls onto the pillow next to her head. He thinks he's choking, that his stomach is coming apart inside, that nothing makes any sense . . . not this woman with the prematurely grey hair by his side or the Pacers getting blown out before halftime, not the farmers complaining about another bad harvest or the boys stealing money from him down at the garage. Nothing can quiet him as he reaches for that bottle on her pillow, his teeth aching at the roots, a taste of metal blistering his parched mouth.

I'm too tired to nurse her pain. I've got my own. It's Thanksgiving. Winter's coming on. *Nutcracker* opens in two weeks and I'm missing rehearsals. I now owe Henry $616 for a bereavement round-trip coach fare. My father is dead. I wander around in the front of the funeral home where Fred displays the new coffins. Some of the boxes are handcrafted hardwoods, lined with satin. My father's is unupholstered pine, but his death is an event, a herald of winter, something to mark time by in a cloistered small town where nothing really happens between harvesting and planting. It seems like everyone is coming to say goodbye.

Fred waves his plump arms like a conductor, says, "funerals are for the living." Spitting into her white handkerchief, Aunt Hazel tells me Fred is just drumming up some business. She's smeared her lips and now wears a faint pink moustache, which she points in Fred's direction. "Takes every paper from Roachdale to Maple Grove." Her scratchy voice drops to a hoarse, confidential whisper. "Keeping the death watch." She wraps her hand around my upper arm. "Going to be cremated myself. Already bought the urn." We're interrupted by my mother's sobs. She's found her way into the showcase room and turns in bewildered circles. Fred hovers over her. Aunt Hazel makes a clucking noise with her dentures. "Woman oughta control herself more. Turned herself grey worrying over that man." Then, suddenly realizing whom she's talking to, she adds, "Good Lord takes care of us all . . . "

Black winter dresses settle into pews, dark-suited shoulders bend over worn Bibles, the preacher's solemn manicured hands clutch the stained pulpit. His white throat emits a muffled drumroll, and the congregation bow their heads. I don't listen to the prayers, the eulogy, the march of false grief. My insides have turned to wire. I was always afraid of him. There was no resting place, no safe time, even when he was dead sober. He couldn't bring himself to touch me then, yet still I was afraid. For some reason I keep remembering one particular moment. Perhaps I dreamed it; probably I didn't. Doesn't matter. There's nothing really special about it. Maybe that's why I remember it. I enter a lightless room where my father watches a rolling Zenith screen, flickers of grey bobbing up and down, casting shadow-stripes on the walls. Static crackles from the television like the voice of God. His back is to me, but I am lost in my own terror of what will happen if he turns around and sees me. I hold my breath, balanced there on the edge of the chasm, between the warm safety of the kitchen with its baking cornbread and the flat silhouette of my father's head imposed upon the screen. I turn and bump my way along the wall, reaching for the other room, panic weighting my legs. I know I can never get away. In the kitchen I take the hot half-baked cornbread out of the oven and stuff it into my mouth. I don't stop eating until the pan is empty.

Now, I trudge through the snow to the boneyard, a small figure in a vast deadwooded landscape. I must go through with this, I must watch them lower the coffin into the hard ground. My mother rides in the funeral limo next to Fred, wringing her age-spotted hands, perhaps sipping from the convenient flask he offers her. The others—and there aren't so many who stray beyond the funeral home—crawl along in old Fords and Chevys, bumping over the snow-cleared mourners' road. I've been away five months now and, already, I've forgotten how different the landlocked air is.

"You've got to breathe through the music," Henry said over the telephone, when I called him from the studio after my first rehearsal. As a new soloist, I'd been given lead Merlitone in the second act of *Nutcracker*. The six of us were to carry fake reed pipes and hop blithely to an upbeat tempo. I was to stand in front of the others, hop alone, turn with a few counts of brisk *piqués*. The part was unchallenging, but for Henry's benefit I made it more difficult. As if really playing an instrument, I tried fluttering my fingers inside the rhythm while the rest of my body moved on top of the counts. It was a small detail and probably no one but Henry would notice. That afternoon I'd also started rehearsals with Simon for a discordant *pas de deux* set to Stravinsky. It wasn't clear why Simon chose me to dance with him, nor why I didn't tell Henry right away. I just leaned against the dressing-room wall, idly snapping the payphone's little metal change door, half-listening as he reminded me to lock my leg in *coupé* and take the force of the *piqué* turns in my inner thigh.

Simon had sauntered up behind me during Company class the morning after I'd made soloist and run his finger down my spine. "Nice back," he'd whispered. The Company Director, craggy-faced and gracefully fleshy, was marking out a combination at the front of the room. Class was basically relaxed: dancers drifted in and out, bundled themselves in sweaters and plastic pants, worked hard but at a slow pace. If you were a principal like Simon there was no pressure to perform. I shivered when I felt his hand on my back, but he just touched my shoulder and grinned. "Loosen up, babe." He paused, then added impishly, "Simon says." He worked out next to me for the whole class, but I concentrated on the Director.

The next day Simon stood behind me at *barre*. Each time we turned to the other side, he'd give me an insidious wink. The more I tried to out-balance him, so that I wouldn't have to meet him when I turned around, the longer he held his own pose. Finally, I smiled back. His eyes widened as though he were mocking me, then he laughed. The Director loped over to our *barre*. "Watch that hip," he said to Simon, "it's working against you." I didn't look at Simon through the rest of class, though he continued to dance by my side, showing off his beautiful turns, leaving sweat puddles on the floor.

Outside of class, Simon had nothing to do with me. He moved in the fast circle, he had important rehearsals, he always seemed preoccupied. I'd be sitting along the corridor wall, sewing ribbons on my shoes or taping my feet, waiting for the rehearsal studio to clear out, when Simon would walk through dressed in powder blue or various attitudes of red. I'd look up and see him pushing quarters into the soda machine, his bulky athlete's body slumped down into two over-arched feet, curls pulled into a short ponytail. Sometimes, he'd see me and flash a crooked line of white teeth or another wink. The other hallway girls, mostly members of the *corps*, said he was just cute enough to get away with anything.

He continued to pester me during Company class. "Want to partner?" he'd say, then grab my hand and take me through finger-turns or experimental lifts. "Just relax," he'd coax, as he dug his fingers under my rib cage and lowered me down the length of his body to the floor. His hands left bruises on my arms and inner thighs. One morning, during a break between *barre* and center, he asked me to work with him outside of class. "A *pas* that will knock their socks off," he promised. "Partner me, babe, you'll see. Simon says." I couldn't resist, I didn't know how.

I told him I wanted a blue dress for my thirteenth birthday, something with puff sleeves and a gathered waist, like a costume from *Giselle*. He sat on the back porch with slitted eyes, waiting until the flies rose in the humid air, then smacking his hands over their tentative bodies. "Gotcha," he would growl. I was feeling restless. I'd been *pirouetting* for days on the soft give of the kitchen linoleum, 'spotting' a grease stain on the wall above the old furnace. Mrs. Pike was having shoulder surgery; the school was closed. "Why a blue dress?" he finally asked. A garter snake slipped through a hole in the weed-covered fence. I didn't say anything. Suddenly, he slapped his hands on his knees. I jumped. "Little birds lose their wings," he said, and went back inside to watch TV.

Mute-faced men are lowering his casket into the pit. My mother stands next to me, leaning against Fred's stout form. I half-expect her to throw herself on the grave, but I know nothing so dramatic will occur. Instead, we will behave ourselves, good girls through to the end. Her sisters whisper behind handkerchiefs about death and marriage, how the two things are a god-awful combination. They reach out and encircle my mother with their grief, not over my father's death (good riddance to that bad rubbish) but because they know what it is to be buried alive. They are only vaguely interested in me.

I sit at Aunt Effie's kitchen table, avoiding the chips and Hershey Kisses and pink-mint jars. "All that smog's enough to kill a person," she's telling me. It's no use trying to explain that I don't live in Los Angeles. The north and the south are unmoving blurred points to which she stubbornly clings. She lifts her legs, bound in elastic bandages, and thumps them on the floor. Something rattles down in the cellar. Probably Uncle Eugene, a senile dweller of household caves who dabbles with oils and stiffened brushes, surfaces occasionally with a new Crucifixion painting. Aunt Effie stores her dead cats' bones in labelled cookie tins on the dry-goods shelf behind me. "Go on," she urges me, "eat something." I resist.

Shafts of cold grey light slipped through the trattoria's three small windows. I pushed the cheesy green strands around on the plate. Henry folded his napkin to a neat square. "Talk to me, old heart." I forked another strand into my mouth, chewed slowly, tried to swallow. I was thinking of rehearsal with Simon, the gale force of strange uneven notes and counts swirling around me, his stomach pressed into my spine, the tiny room's mirrors reflecting the hardened angles of our straining bodies. The pasta tasted like glue, would not go down. Henry glanced at the full plate. "I'm not hungry," I said. A blond waiter hovered in the kitchen door, picking at his moustache with gnawed fingernails. Henry methodically sipped from his water glass. "Perhaps this is good," he finally offered. "A dancer must get beyond the blood and bones of the physical."

Simon had already pushed me through a frenetic two-hour rehearsal, snapped his fingers in my face, molded me into his own cerebral movements. His sweating hands had gotten stuck once inside my dance skirt, but, instead of disentangling himself, he'd grabbed my thigh and squeezed as hard as he could. "Flesh," he'd said. I didn't know if this was a compliment or not. "I can't eat this," I repeated, covering my plate with a napkin. Henry tapped his finger on the rim of his glass, and the waiter raised his eyebrows. At the end of the rehearsal, Simon had bent down to where I sat on the floor and kissed me on the back of my neck. "Melted butter," he'd said.

I stared at Henry, calculated how far I could go. "A principal asked me to dance with him." Henry didn't miss a beat. "That's something, old heart." He nodded his head contemplatively. "When do you start rehearsal?" I looked down at the covered plate. "Last week." Henry was silent, toyed with the edge of his napkin. "Well then," he said finally, "how is it?" His lips had disappeared. "Oh," I shrugged, "Simon says *I'm* doing fine. It's the choreography." I grabbed the edge of the table to keep myself from sinking. "Stravinsky's hard to count." Henry leaned forward as though he were about to speak, then pulled back. I thought of Simon's hand riding up and down my thigh, the damp pressure of his lips on my neck, our bodies trapped between the furious music and the hidden images in the mirrors. Henry's voice was steady, measured, professional. "Tell him to temper the music like a channel conducts water." He closed his eyes and folded his palms together. "Is he a good partner?" I didn't know how to answer this, so I said whatever I could. "His hands slip." Henry opened his eyes. "He musn't treat you delicately. He's got to carry you with him." Henry unfolded his hands, placed them on the table, and leaned forward again. "What else?" he asked eagerly. I looked around for the waiter but his back was turned. I tried finding something safe and truthful. "The movements are off-center." Henry smiled. "Patience, old heart. Good choreography and a solid principal can pull you up."

I knelt before him on the splintered floor of the shed. His trousers were down around his ankles. "Get up," he hissed. I got to my feet, faced him, and stared boldly into the dark. My body had floated upward to some other place. I felt numb. He lit a cigarette and, for a moment, in the brief flash of light, I saw his pale drunken face, closed to me forever. "I won't do it anymore," I said quietly. He spat on the ground. "What'dyou say?" I struggled to find my voice. "I won't do it anymore." I thought he was going to hit me, but he didn't. Instead, he walked past me to the door of the shed, opened it, and flicked the cigarette into the blackness. Then, over his shoulder on his way out, he spat again. "You disgust me," he said and slammed the door. So I stayed in the shed the rest of the evening, fighting the mosquitos, reading by flashlight. My mother wouldn't be home for hours. She was still at the nursing home, serving meals, turning old bones, emptying bedpans. When the porch light finally went out, I crept back into the house and fell asleep on the living-room couch. I didn't hear her come in.

Aunt Opal says, "Amen," then raises her fork and stabs a heap of Thanksgiving turkey onto her plate. Brown gravy runs down her chin as she shovels mashed potatos, then peas, then strings of rhubarb into her mouth. Her napkin has fallen to the floor. Charlene sits to her mother's right, her pudding face framed by red-permed curls. She's still praying, eyes closed tight, lips moving silently. Charlene's always praising the Lord for something, so today she's thanking overtime. We'll serve her last. I sit between my mother and Aunt Effie. They're talking about poor Great-Aunt Gussie, who only last month finally went to join her only baby Eloy. He'd been killed under a tractor at twelve. That was forty years ago and, as Aunt Effie used to say, "His Momma's been bereft ever since." Well, Aunt

Gussie's happy now. Aunt Hazel leans over and taps Aunt Effie on her dimpled arm. "Just like Fred said, death is for the living." Then she elbows Uncle Eugene, who's fallen asleep in his stuffed dress-shirt of indiscriminate color. "Gotta die to be a famous painter," she warns him. Food and conversation no longer interest Uncle Eugene. He belches gratefully and goes back to sleep.

I flex and point my feet beneath the table, nibble at the tomato salad, inhale and exhale. Aunt Effie points to my plate. "You're too thin." Charlene, for whom every diet is really a fast, rises to the occasion. "Ballet dancers don't eat," she says solemnly. My mother sighs, and I think I hear bones rattling beneath her rumpled mourning dress. She begins to cry. "Never would eat much." Aunt Effie pushes her napkin into my mother's hands. "There, there, Sallie, you got enough to think about." Her voice is accusing, but I'm not sure why. I pick up a turkey leg and deliberately gnaw on the greasy flesh. When they're not looking, I spit the meat into my napkin, roll it into a ball, and excuse myself. Aunt Effie watches me with suspicious eyes. I go off to the utility room, which is also my bedroom. A Raggedy-Ann doll is propped on top of the overturned wash bucket. She's missing an eye. I throw myself on the cot, hold my doll, press my hungry stomach into my back. I reach down and feel my hipbones, then pull the skin away from my stomach. I decide the worst that can happen is Charlene will say a prayer for me.

I offered my hand to Simon and stepped into *arabesque*. He placed one of his hands under my extended leg, the other around my waist, then lifted the leg up from the hip socket as I curled it around his neck. I dropped my torso and stretched across my supporting leg. "Shit," he muttered. "It's not working." He pulled me up and patted my bruised leg. "Simon says do it again." He draped his arm across my back and started walking us over to the corner. Doubling over, I rested my hands on my knees, searching for air. Simon bent over with me. "Listen, babe," he said into my ear, "I got a new breathing method. Developed it myself." I spoke to the floor. "What's that?" He placed his hands around my waist and lifted me to an upright position. I started to fold over again. "C'mon, kid. Stand up." I straightened and he moved around in front of me. "Push the air out for three counts . . . like so." He opened his mouth and showed me the roof, then choked out a trio of quick stubborn bursts. I followed him. "Good. Now you inhale three counts." I did what he said. "Swallow, babe." I tried to swallow but only gagged. Simon shook his wet curls. "Keep doing it. Make the swallow a movement. Y'know, throw your body into it. Then inhale, exhale." I tried again. "Do it three more times." I did. When the air finally came rushing back into my chest, I found that I was smiling. "It really works," I said. His face furrowed between two thin eyebrows. "Sure, babe."

I started to walk over to the mirror again, but Simon grabbed my wrist and hauled me back. He dropped my arm, put his mouth on my ear, then whispered, "Simon says, gonna work real hard." He paused. "Gonna do what Simon says." I spoke in a low secret voice, as I repeated the words. He pressed his lips tightly against my ear. "Gonna make this a fucking-A *pas de deux*." I gave myself over to jumpy giggles. He kept on. "Fucking-A, fucking-B, fucking-C . . ." I inhaled, exhaled, laughed, swallowed, repeated the words, then finally pulled away and turned in a circle. "Yes! Yes! Yes!" I shouted, turning faster and wider. Suddenly, I stopped.

Henry stood in the doorway, his face unmoving, still as marble. I wondered how long he'd been standing there, what he had seen. "Natalie," he said, "I need to speak with you." Henry never came to the studio, I didn't want him there. I ran over and pushed him through the door, then closed it quickly behind us. In the hallway, dancers milled around us, lounged against the walls, looked at Henry with calculating eyes. His face was stony. "Your father died." I leaned my head against his chest. His breathing was shallow, impatient. "I'm sorry, old heart. Your mother called." I'd given his number for emergencies, and now regretted having done so. "I'll have to go home then," I said. Henry misinterpreted the reluctance in my voice. "Don't worry," he comforted me, "I'll give you the money." He put his arm around me and we walked down the hall. "Was that Simon?" he said. "Yes." He squeezed my shoulder. "Well, you can use the rest."

My mother digs through the wrinkled heap of secondhand clothes on the floor of her disordered closet. She's on her knees searching for something: a stuffed animal comes flying out, a piece of paper, a flowered scarf, some loose change. "It's here somewhere," she keeps saying. I stand helplessly behind her, waiting for this burrowing chaos to end. She finally emerges, crawling backwards, a yellowed photo dangling from her teeth. "You'll want this," she sputters, and hands me the picture. I turn it over and stare at the curled edges. I don't need to look beyond the white border framing the photo. "Hated having his picture taken," she says. She turns her grey eyes on me and the tears start running down her face. "Weren't no damned good, was he, Natalie?" I get on my knees and put my arms around her, wanting to make all the pain disappear, like rubbing out fresh blood before it stains, but there's nothing I can do or say. She feels small in my arms, but her body is unrelenting. She's been holding herself together for a long time and it's made her hard, like a washboard.

She pulls away from me and rubs her face. "No use crying about what can't be helped," she comforts herself. I keep trying to find my voice, pull it out of myself, tell her the truth. I imagine this voice of mine is ugly, monstrous, something beyond my control. I need to keep it quiet, down inside my body, locked away where it can't hurt anyone. My mother tilts her head and looks over at me, her eyes full of injury. "Oughta come home and finish school." I scan the cramped room, inhale three quick counts, let out my breath. "I can't." She stands up, pats down her dress, shakes her head. "This is where you belong," she says bitterly. I get up and back away, discreetly crumpling my father's picture in my closed hand. "I'm a soloist now," I insist. She glares at me. "Tall stories." She softens her face. "But I don't blame you, honey." I feel the voice working its way through me, fighting to get out. I must keep my mouth shut. "Your father was always spinning lies. Couldn't live in this life." She knows, but she doesn't know. Cannot separate me from him, from her. Stay here, she is saying, live inside this lie with me, and we will make it the truth. But I know, and she knows, that we've been bereft too long. We'll not enter the Kingdom of Heaven together. "I have an early flight," I say. She tugs at her hair, rocks back and forth, hums a little to herself. "Then you'd better get some sleep," she says quietly. I hand her the crumpled photograph. As I go off to the utility room, she is smoothing it out.

Technical rehearsal for *Nutcracker* was like a circus. The first act was bloated with mice and soldiers, dancing sugar canes and mechanical dolls, walk-ons and walk-offs. It took hours to mark the stage floor, pace the children through their parts, coordinate the lighting and the music. Most of us in the second act waited downstairs in the dressing rooms or next to the stage door in the green-room. The hallway was littered with cigarettes and browned apple cores, Band-Aids and dirty point shoes, leg-warmers and gnarled ointment tubes.

I was in the main dressing-room with the *corps*, wardrobe, and seamstresses. Bulb-framed mirrors dimpled the bright orange walls, washing the room in a garish surreal light. Some of the dancers had tried to humanize the mirrors with personal mementos: postcards from sweethearts; photos of baby brothers, parents, their own children; an occasional good-luck charm or old point shoe. Portable radios and cassette recorders were everywhere; rock anthems, country ballads, jazz riffs swirled aimlessly amid the girls' anxious chatter. I had my feet up on the counter, applying Vaseline to my toes. The skin around each toe was swollen and my callouses had rubbed off; open wounds marked each joint. I wrapped some gauze around the two small toes and eased tights over my feet, then began massaging the boxes of my shoes to soften them. The other girls rarely spoke to me, I was isolated within their dressing-room intimacy. I'd moved quickly, but really, where did I belong? The established soloists dressed next door, the *corps* herded together here. No one knew which complaint to share with me, and I wasn't sure what to complain about.

Miss Carabee bustled by, thread hanging from her mouth, a stiff red tunic under her plump arm. Following her was a trail of older ladies, their arms full of tights and bits of fabric. "Can't take my eyes off nobody," Carabee complained. The seamstresses marched on. Carabee pushed through a cluster of half-dressed women, who squawked nervously. "Out of my way, Arabians and Flowers." Carabee and her soldiers disappeared behind a costume rack, but I could still hear her barking orders. The woman next to me was talking to herself in the mirror. "Another *Nutcracker*. What's that? Fifteen? Twenty? A million?" She was dressed in different shades of purple. She adjusted her lavender scarf, then wetted the few strands of hair hanging down on her forehead. She spoke to the mirror again. "Keep cool, girl, just pick up your check and soak your feet." A Flower walked by, sighing loudly. "I'm always cast as vegetation or an animal." My neighbor never looked up from her mirror. "Sounds like every woman's theme song," she muttered to her reflection.

The willowy sweater-wrapped Snowflakes from the closing of Act I drifted through the room. They had been standing around on stage all afternoon. "What a royal screw-up," the leader said. "Flake machine got jammed and dumped the whole box on us. Then the mice got excited and one of them peed her pants, started bawling." She pulled a flake from her mouth and spat. "Kids oughta be outlawed." The four small Chinese dancers scurried past the Snowflakes toward the exit door; they wore black point shoes and carried fans. One of them had headphones and was listening to a Walkman. The edgy Snowflake grimaced. "Little Miss Anorexia and her traveling dope band." Carabee peered around the side of the costume rack. "Costumes are bleeding, programs are late, symphony is upping the tempo. You got problems?" The Snowflake threw out her hands. "Not me. I'm history. Getting married next month." Carabee motioned her away. "Get on," she said irritably, then added, "Lose one, gain one, it's all the same to me."

Miss Anorexia had returned and now leaned over the fold-up chair next to me. Her cheekbones jutted out beneath a thin layer of white skin. She still wore her headphones. She yelled something at me, but I missed it in all the confusion. "What?" I shouted up at her. Her little head and bony shoulders were moving to a private acid-rock beat; her eyes were closed. I tapped her arm. She opened one eye slowly. "What?" I shouted again. "Partner," she yelled back. "Outside."

Simon leaned against the stairwell, smoking a cigarette. His curls were flattened down by a green bandana. "Hey, babe," he said. He held the cigarette out to me as an offering, but I shook my head. "Simon says there's gonna be a sweet little party after dress-rehearsal tomorrow. Big kids only." He shifted his brown elf eyes and blew smoke. "Wanna come?" I didn't even think. "Sure," I said. He wedged the cigarette between his lips and looked at me sideways. "Big debut, huh?" I wanted to share things with him—the excitement of a first performance, the fluttering finger movements I had added, the fear of losing my balances. I had questions too. But we'd never talked like this and I held myself back. "I like the part," I said. Simon ground out the cigarette with his slippered foot, then gazed past me. Looking over my left shoulder, he flashed one of his disarming smiles. I started to turn and see who it was, but he leaned over and kissed me on the mouth. "Sweet," he said, retreating up the stairs. "Simon says, real sweet." I watched until he disappeared. When I finally turned around, there was no one behind me.

Dress rehearsal was messy. The flake machine broke again, one of the Toy Soldiers fell off stage and smashed his kneecap, the musicians were testy and off-tempo. I lost my reed pipe, found it on the top step of a ladder, then misplaced it again. A dancing bear from Act I disappeared somewhere in the theater. Carabee finally found him in the empty control booth during intermission. The little boy had fallen asleep on the lighting console; one of the switches had ripped a hole in his costume. Waiting backstage in my short peppermint-green tutu, I concentrated on breathing. The lights were a dusty yellow and clouds of rosined sweat choked the cold theater air. I could see Simon on the other side of the stage in the wings, stretching his legs, one hand grasping the red velvet of the curtain. He was the lead Russian in one casting of *Nutcracker*, the Snow King in another. Tonight he wore his Russian outfit: a crimson cummerbund was wound securely about his waist, white silk pantaloons encased his legs, a black astrakhan hugged his head. He looked restless and menacing, like a real Cossack.

By the time we were finished with the run-through, the dressing room was littered with used costumes and discarded make-up sponges. The *corps* cleared out quickly; they only wanted to eat, soak, have some wine, sleep. I went over to Simon's dressing-room door and knocked. "Yeah?" he said. "It's just me," I said through the closed door. I heard a low murmur, a vaguely familiar female voice, then silence. "Hey, kid, go around front." There was a pause, another muffled protest. "Simon says, be there in a sec." I backed away from the door, and moved off to the stairwell. Ten minutes later, though it felt longer, Simon emerged. "C'mon, babe," he said, putting his arm around me. "Let's get some air." I wanted to ask a question, but I figured he wouldn't answer it, or would lie if he did. As we pushed through the heavy safety door into the starless night, I knew that the answers, if there were to be any, would have to come later.

We walked up Geary Avenue and into Golden Gate Park. Simon was still restless and brooding, still a Cossack. I felt as if any second he would leap on a horse and ride away furiously across the shadowy park lawn. I found a stone and began kicking it idly between the trees. Simon strolled beside me for a while, then suddenly dropped to the ground next to his dance bag. He rested the side of his head on his upturned wrist. "Come here, babe," he commanded. The city lights flickered across his face, as if the shadows were coming to life. I dropped down beside him. "Aren't we going anywhere?" I asked him. He laughed, then rolled over on his back. "Wherever you want." He reached over and grabbed my wrist. "You hungry?" I could feel his grip tightening. "I'm always hungry," I said truthfully. He pressed his thumbs into my wrists, then brought one of my hands up to his mouth. "I'm going to eat your hand," he said, "then you will never hurt poor Simon." He wrapped his tongue around one of my fingers and licked it. I watched him with curiosity, tried to suppress the desire to laugh, then offered him the other hand. "What about this one?" I said. He shook his curls violently. "Always save something for later."

The bushes behind us rustled. We both swiveled and looked at them, as if they were watching us. Simon smiled. "C'mon, babe, let's dance." He pulled me up and turned us around in a clean circle. We left our dance bags sitting on the ground and began weaving in and out of the trees along the lighted edge of the park facing Haight. A few cars crept along the drizzling street, a horn cut the air. We *jetéd* over rocks and broken bottles, *pirouetted* on grassy clearings. At a break in the joggers path, Simon placed one hand on my back and waltzed us in quick turns back to our original spot. I was laughing and full, acquainted now with the shadows. Throwing both our dance bags over his shoulder, he squeezed my hand and led me quickly through the narrow end of the park.

His apartment was all palpable shadows, broken only by the flashing red digital numbers of a clock radio. It was already after two. We undressed separately, in silence and darkness. I could just make out Simon lying on the carpeted floor, draped in some kind of fur cover, leaning on a couple of large pillows. A match flame momentarily lit his eyes and a sweet smell like incense filled the room. "Want some?" Simon held out a joint. "No," I said quietly and sat down cross-legged next to him. In the intermittent red glow of the joint's tip, I searched for his face. His forehead was smooth like a child's. As I reached out and touched it, I thought of Henry for the first time all evening. He would've waited until midnight or so for a phone call, then poured some milk and gone to bed. He slept slowly, needed more time. I removed my hand, retreated into myself, stared at the clock radio.

"Hey," Simon whispered, rolling over towards me, but I got up, found the window, and pulled back the curtain. A fog had moved in and there were no lights outside either. "It's so dark," I said. Simon's voice was impassive. "What's getting you, kid?" I remained at the window, staring into the swirling mist. "I need to know," I said. I waited for him to respond, though I knew he wouldn't talk. Then I said it again. "I need to know why." I pressed my upper body against the cold glass as if beckoning the fog. "What's there to say?" he finally asked. It almost sounded like a sincere question, and I was tempted to answer it. But then he came over and stood behind me. "Talk makes me tired," he said. I laughed uncertainly. "C'mon, little bones," he breathed into my neck. "Relax, okay?" I gave in just enough and rested the back of my head against his chin. "Things could be real nice, real easy." I nuzzled against him. Then he slipped his arm around me and returned us to the bedded floor. "Nothing complicated." He leaned me back into the fur cover. "Just like dancing." He began to touch me, but I took his hand. "Now what?" he whispered. I brought his fingers to my mouth. "You haven't said 'Simon says.'"

He was still asleep when I dressed and let myself out the door. I'd waited for the sun to rise most of the night, but the weak morning light was hidden in the fog. Theater call wasn't for hours, so I took a bus to the Wharf. As the fog cleared, I walked along the Bay, climbed the metal bleachers behind the Marine Museum, wandered up to the Cannery. The street artists were already unpacked, their weather-cracked hands imploring the tourists. The French singer wrinkled his face at me. A wilted rose stuck out from the rim of his stained felt hat. He patted his guitar, plucked at a few strings, adjusted his microphone. "For my American friends." And then he began to sing "This Land Is Your Land," except he used the original words Woody Guthrie wrote, the ironic dust-bowl Depression lyrics nobody sings anymore.

It was odd to hear that song in this place; the tourists wouldn't pay for those words. When he finished, he slid his fingers along the loose strings, then pulled out a harmonica and blew a few plaintive notes. I put a dollar in his case. His smile seemed automatic. "Nice American lady." He pointed to a display of cassettes in a box by his stool. He wanted me to buy, but I said that I had no more money. He grunted and started to sing another tune, a sad French love song. I stayed to listen, lingering over his broken street voice, his strange gnomic face, the row of rings studding his ears. When he finished, he stared at me with narrowing dark eyes. "You come back," he whispered. "I give you something next time." The intensity, the intimacy, of his tone surprised me, and I left without acknowledging that I'd heard him.

After the curtain that night, I returned my bunch of green carnations to one of the stagehands. They would be recycled for the next day's matinee. I initialed my name on the sign-out sheet posted on the stage door, then went out through the back to meet Henry at the parking lot. He waited for me on the outside landing, holding a single red rose in his hand. "You did just fine, old heart." He touched my face, then held out the rose. "It's awfully pretty," I said. He gave me a half-smile, then held the flower over our heads. "If this make us speak bold words, anon," he said, "'tis all under the rose forgotten." So, he really had liked my performance. He was rarely mischievous and never allusive with me unless he was pleased with my dancing. "You are a dear man," I said, and kissed him on the cheek. " 'I take her for the flower of womankind,' " he sighed theatrically. He gave me the rose and I took his arm.

We began gradually to descend the cement steps. "That was a nice touch," he said. Directly across from us, in the parking lot, Simon leaned against a car, talking to another figure. I couldn't see who it was, her back was to me. "What?" I said distractedly. "Your fluttering fingers," Henry said. We'd reached the bottom of the steps and I was stalling. "I've lost something," I said nervously. Henry leaned against the railing, while I bent down to search through my bulky dance bag. As I fumbled with the zipper, I kept glancing up. Simon was gesturing into the dark. Then I heard his voice, rising and falling, wordless by distance. Magda reeled around, flung an elegant hand into the air, and started walking toward the stage door. "It doesn't matter," I said. "Let's just go." I straightened, then steered Henry to the side of the theater, safely out of Magda's path. "Slow up, old heart," he gasped, but I forced the pace until we were through the alley and had turned the corner by the front of the theater. The marquee's running lights were still on, chasing themselves in an endless circle. I stopped to stare at them, then turned to Henry and held up the rose. "I'm a soloist now," I said. Then I pressed my gloved hand into his and we walked home slowly through the holiday crowds.

# *Act One, Scene Four*

Observe the people around you, not just the dancers in the rehearsal hall, but everyone you meet in
life. You will find a clue here and another there,
some detail that will illuminate a personality, a
way of life, an approach toward style or revela-
tion.

  –Agnes de Mille, *To A Young Dancer*

*L*ost on the fog-curtained edge of Lake Merced, I
climb a mossy flat stone, slip under the surge of mist, call to
Fran, my guide through the formless region. "Where are you?"
I stay close to a streak of light cutting through the dark haze, but
it's just an illusion. There is only the mist. "Fran?" Her cold
hand grabs my elbow. "We've lost Toby," she cautions. He has
three hound legs, doesn't manage his balance easily. I'm
grateful for Fran's touch: I've only known her a few weeks, but
already she seems solid, real. A quivering nose nudges my
hand. I breathe in the blind odor of wetdog fur. "I've got him."

I feel for his leash and the three of us cluster together, scraping against each other. Monstrous shapes form, deform, reform; smoke-haze tentacles rise from the ground, wrap clotted fingers around our ankles. Fran's voice is slow-bubbling tar oozing through the pockets of fog. "If we can only find the bridge."

We begin moving again. Toby staggers ahead, dictates our crazy progress: two loping steps forward, a pause, then an uneven jerk to the side. "Men and machines." I've missed the transition. Fran begins sentences without warning, brackets off her thoughts, speaks in fragments. "What?" I'm remembering all the ballets that call for dry ice and cold smoke. My stomach is hard with pebbles; I don't want to think of ballet; I want to forget. She's looking for a light, a familiar post, something to lead us out of the fog. "The boys'll be worried about their ride." She means the band, the boys in the band. I hang on to the leash, try to center myself over two sinking feet. The night is palpable, grasping. "This is as far as we can go now." She puts her arm around me and squeezes. "Better just sit down and wait for the clear." Toby barks, slaps his grateful tail against my leg, hovers close to us.

Somewhere behind us, hidden in the mist, is the dented green van, a mandolin player, several back-up guitars, a chipped keyboard, and Armand, the French singer from the Wharf. They're probably on break by now, eating greasy chicken wings on a glassed-in veranda. I imagine Armand's irritated dark eyes piercing the window, scanning Urbano Drive, wondering where the hell we are. Fran has the keys to the van. Another two sets and they're out of here, pocket the cash, divvy up later. He'd like to do some folk-rock, but the doctors' wives, inhaling bacon-wrapped olives and warm candlenut cakes, keep requesting the French ballads. He's mad at Fran anyway. She's taken me away from him again. He'd throw her the hell out if he didn't need her to pay most of the rent and drive the band around. Someday he'll hook up with a sharp lady, a real looker who can talk her way past the agents. He figures that's all he needs: a mouthpiece and a break. Then he'll have it all, any time, any way. Armand's seen a lot of late-night movies. He believes them.

I waited a long time before returning to the Wharf, weeks after the *Nutcracker* costumes were put back in storage. Simon and I were still working out the *pas*, still spending an occasional late night in his apartment, but, he insisted, neither of our partnerships was ready to go public. I didn't like it much, but I got used to it. Then Henry cancelled our routine weekend. He wasn't feeling well—"an ancient malady, old heart." I sensed he wanted me to take the BART and come to him, but he didn't ask and I didn't offer. As I hung up the phone, I was already thinking about the Wharf.

The mid-winter waterfront: writers haul wine-stained manuscripts to the Eagle Cafe, longshoremen load cargo into thick-bellied freighters, conventioneers wedge token loaves of sourdough bread under their arms. The weather is always cloudy and grey, with a threat of rain. I found the French singer on Hyde, talking to the street painters. I approached him slowly, working my way down the line of easels. When he saw me, he narrowed his eyes and beckoned to me with one of his ringed fingers. I pretended to ignore him, absently watched the artists caricature the tourists in smeared charcoal. Then he was beside me. "I play inside the Cannery now," he whispered. Up close, he smelled of old newspapers and frankincense oil. "It's better inside."

We were standing next to a wool-bundled woman pencilling shadow figures on a canvas. She wet her thumb, rubbed it across the paper, then glanced over at us. Her eyes moved quickly, saw everything, forgot nothing. "Sit for me," she urged, and motioned me to the wood stool beside her. She pulled out a ragged scarf from her quilted bag and wound it around my neck. "There, you look just like one of us." I giggled and tilted my head. The French singer snorted, rubbed his stubby hands together impatiently. "I leave early today, Fran." She smoothed the paper with a chafed hand, gave a habitual nod, reached for a piece of charcoal. Hovering over me, he dropped a plastic ring in my lap. "A little gift for my American friend." Fran shook her head. "Armand, you're in my light." Armand moved around behind her, directly in my sightline. His dark narrow eyes were oddly familiar. Numbly, I returned his stare, held my pose. "Later, you bring her to me," he said to Fran. As he walked off toward the Cannery, I slipped the ring onto the little finger of my left hand.

The summer I was eight, a community of snakes came to sun on the flat rocks along Sugar Creek. The town council put up six feet of chicken wire around them, but I wasn't afraid. I pressed my nose into the fence, watched the sinuous warm serpents coil themselves around each other, wished that I could touch them. Each day that summer I camped by the fence with a couple of hard-boiled eggs, some leathery green apples, a piece of crusty cornbread. I'd sit in the shade, dig for worms, build forts out of oak chips and maple sap, or wade out to one of the rocks and watch for catfish. That's where I met Robin and Batman. They were the only black kids in town; Robin's name was given, Batman's taken. They lived in a crumbling house on the county border, beyond the creek and across a field of oily dandelion weeds. Toting paper bags and slapping at mosquito-bitten legs, they spent their afternoons picking wild onions, bitter greens, and mushrooms caps in the woods surrounding the creek. Robin's cotton dresses were always caked with mud. Her brother was tiny and asthmatic. He wore a tattered black cape that had once been a shawl; between wheezes, he claimed to be the world's greatest crime fighter. He often rested along the chicken wire and threw pebbles at the sleeping snakes. He didn't have much of an aim.

Sometimes they took me home with them. We'd meander through the humid field, scratch at our stinging arms, wait for Batman to get his breath. He'd buckle over, shake his head like a wet dog, wheeze, gasp hungrily for air. "OK," he'd finally say, straightening up, and we'd know that his lungs had cleared. The house smelled of burnt molasses and camphor. Granny, who wore her silver hair in a low knot at the nape of her neck, was usually bent over pots of boiling waxbeans and rhubarb in the kitchen, or outside in the chicken coop, shaking her lumber-like arms at stubborn hens. First time I saw her, she raised her old woman's body from the porch rocker, hissed "white trash," and bared her yellowing teeth. Robin jutted out her jaw, put her hands defiantly on her hips, then shook her dangling cornrows. "Her's my *friend*." Granny rolled some spit around in her mouth, then sent it flying. Batman put a frail hand on my shoulder. "Gonna have some of your frybread, Granny." Retreating behind the screen door, she peered out at us like we'd put a curse on her. "Like hell you is." I figured whatever lay behind Granny and that closed screen door had to be a lot better than going home.

I followed Fran down a long matted corridor, past a dented row of closed steel-grey doors. A naked ceiling bulb dripped anemic light on the peeling plaster walls. Winged roaches crawled along the baseboard, over the limp leg of a woman with orange spiked hair slumped against the fire exit. She was either stone dead or dead stoned. Fran rattled the loose door-knob of Number 8, then pushed her arm through a small square hatch and rotated the knob from the inside. The disembodied walls of the dark candlelit room pulsated inward, groaned deep and low. Gusts of cold air blew in the half-opened windows. The bitter wind passed first through the hollow eyes of African masks dangling from bare valances, then rippled among beaded curtains, fringed shawls, fake animal skins. Piquant odors drifted aimlessly: rose petals, curdled cream, incense. A bald man with doughy skin and slick eyes offered me a sugar cube. Fran waved him away. "She's Armand's." As we snaked past tangled mounds of speakers, legs, wires, and arms, voices knifed the air. "Comes up from the sewers." "Swallows 'em whole." Fran tucked a few strands of grey-streaked hair behind her ear. "You can wait in my room," she said, kicking open a green flaking door.

Fran's room was cooler, quieter. Canvasses were propped against the bare walls, a draped easel dominated the center space, a long narrow window lay concealed behind an Indian scarf. As she pulled back the scarf and hooked it to a nail, scattered grey light shadowed her face. "You want tea?" She sounded agitated. "Sure." My voice slipped quietly through the shadows. She moved a bowl of floating lemon rinds and plugged a tea kettle into a wall outlet. "Getting late," she said. I twisted the ring on my finger and stared at the covered easel. Fran took off her tattered black wool coat, started to throw it into her closet. "Out, out of here!" she growled. Two hooded figures scrambled across the floor on all fours. She herded them out of the room and slammed the studio door behind them. "No privacy," she muttered in a flat voice, then scuffled in her clogs back across to the kettle and poured the tea. She handed me a blue ceramic mug. "He'll be here soon."

As Fran squatted against the closed door, I walked over to the window. Three floors below was a desolate alleyway thick with gnarled leafless branches. A green heap of battered metal was parked against the back of a rotting shed. "Who are these people?" Fran didn't say anything. I turned away from the window. "Do all of them live here?" She was still crouched like a cat. "They come and go," she said finally. "I don't keep track." She got up from the floor and began digging through her charcoal box.

Sipping my tea, I wandered over to her easel. "Can I look?" She glanced up briefly, shrugged her shoulders. I lifted the drape, then backed away and stared at the canvas. A vague body part floated amidst a swirl of dark colors and violent brush strokes. "It's beautiful," I said. Fran ignored me, scooted the charcoal box across the floor. "I feel that way sometimes," I said. Running a hand through her hair, she tilted her head and stared at me over her shoulder. "How's that?" I sat down on the floor in front of the painting and hugged my knees. The formless form on the canvas altered constantly—a fractile geometry of changing patterns and rhythms. "The tempo's suspended, repressing the notes." She brought her hands together, rested them under her chin. "Who *are* you?"

"Nobody," I said. "A ballet dancer." Fran slid over next to me and hugged her knees too. She looked up at the painting. "You can see music?" she asked. I leaned back, thought about it. "Sometimes. Usually I feel it." She looked over at me. "Trying to get inside it?" I nodded. "I know what you mean," she said softly. She stared into my eyes for a long moment. Her own eyes were large and brown, like horse chestnuts. Then she reached out to me, gently pressed her fingertips against mine. We met at an imaginary point halfway between us. Touching and being touched, we held the pose, two suspended tempos feeling the notes together.

Suddenly, the house was rattling with strange metallic sounds. I could hear Armand's voice winding through the front room. She dropped her hands. "He's coming," she whispered urgently. "What can I do?" I said. At long last I was afraid. Fran took my left hand again just as Armand opened the door. His earrings glinted in the half-light and two black street eyes cut the distance between us. "Come, little frog," he beckoned. "I have something to show you."

Fran put her other hand on my leg. "No, Armand. You go away."

He paused on the threshold, held out his arm to me, flashed a dark face. "Come." I didn't know what to do or say.

"Leave her alone." Fran's voice was hard, unrelenting. Then she held up my hand, slipped the ring from my finger, and threw it at his feet. "She's *my* friend."

I was racing up the stairs, two at a time, late for another rehearsal with Simon, when I almost ran into Himmel. He blocked my path at the top of the staircase. "Miss Barnes, you're moving too fast." I backed down a step and pressed myself against the wall. At that moment, Lincoln appeared behind Himmel. He'd been about to bolt down the stairs, three at a time as he usually did, but now he stopped and leaned over the railing. This was too good an opportunity to miss: he had a preoccupied victim and a captive audience. He stuck his thumbs in his ears, then wiggled his fingers. Himmel tugged at the kerchief around his neck. "You're going about it all wrong." I nodded, though I wasn't certain what I was agreeing to. Himmel studied me with cool eyes. "Simon's bootstrapping." I tried to ignore Lincoln, who had now resorted to wagging his tongue. I was confused. "What do you mean?" Himmel stepped down so that he was level with me, then brought his face up close. "Why don't you think about it." But I couldn't think: Himmel scared me, and now Lincoln had put his little fingers in his nose. I sat down on the step. As Himmel walked past me down the stairs, he said matter-of-factly over his shoulder, "Keep working on your *port de bras*, Mr. Freeman. It could stand some improvement." Lincoln rolled his head. "Shit," he mouthed. Then he looked at me. "Hey, bunhead." I was still trying to think. "What?" He rested his elbows on the railing. "What's going down?" I shook my head. "I don't know." He vaulted over to the landing and cupped his hand under my chin. I looked up at him. "They'll hurt you," he said. "That's all they know."

# THE BODY OF DANCERS

I wrapped the sunflower-yellow sheet around my body like a mummy and shuffled across the floor. "How's this?"

"Better than yesterday," Fran said. Sunlight folded sharply about her arms like aluminum foil. She daubed at her palette. "But it still leaves a lot to the imagination."

"That's how I want to be remembered." I wiggled on to the green-crushed divan, then fell backwards against the headrest. "Just head and feet."

Fran peered around the side of the easel and shook her paintbrush at me. "I oughta give you only one eye. Right in the middle of your forehead."

"Why's that?"

"Center you."

I stared up at the ceiling. A crack snaked from the top edge of the wall to the base of the floor. "Where do you go when you're not here?"

"Another planet," she said, shifting the easel so that she was facing me sideways. "That's good. Keep looking down."

I raised my eyes, persisted. "I'm serious."

" So am I. You're looking up again." She stroked her paint-covered trousers with the brush, leaving a dark smudge on the knee.

"What's it like?"

"The planet? Very strange. Only men and machines."

I lowered my eyes. "How do they survive?"

"Asexual reproduction. Mothers' names are assigned arbitrarily. Okay, *now* move."

I hung over the side of the divan and traced my toe on the bare wood floor. "Simon says women have all the power."

Fran laughed. "Another perceptive observer of social behavior. What else does Simon say?"

"That I'm really good in the *pas*. That it wouldn't work without me." As Fran silently rubbed the canvas with a turpentine-stained rag, I pointed my toes and wagged a foot at her. "Something wrong?"

"Not sure." She got off her stool, stepped back from the easel, shook her scarved head. "Maybe I'm losing perspective." She screwed up her face, then darted her eyes back and forth across the canvas.

"Simon says you can't get ahead without a partner. Men jump, women are lifted." My body was casting a shadow against the white wall. I looked like a hot dog in a bun. "I'm hungry."

"But you never eat. Bad angles." Fran scooted her stool a little to the right, contemplated me for a few moments, then returned to the painting.

I ducked down and watched the shadow slip behind the divan. "Why do you take care of Armand?"

Fran grimaced. "Need a bit of shoulder." I tried to shimmy a little out of the sheet and started to slide, off the divan. "Really, you're impossible. Always moving. You get one eye, that's it."

By the time I stopped the slide I had bared both shoulders. "What do you get out of it?"

Fran raised her eyebrows and shrugged. "Better light." She applied even strokes to the canvas, her body falling and rising with each wide movement. Another way of dancing, of tracing patterns. She glanced over at me. "Are you going to rehearse forever? When do I get to see you dance?"

"When I learn the roles."

"Ah, the roles. Well, you can teach them to me. I never seem to get them right." She lifted her brush and stepped back from the painting. "This is as far as we can go now."

She shifted the easel around so that I could see it. Amidst the swirling blue and yellow brushstrokes floated one unattached brown eye. "Living is a desperate art," she said.

The crayons were lined up in a tattered yellow box. She was obviously proud of them. "You take Blue." I put the crayon in my mouth and started chewing. "Just the tip." It tasted greasy, like the candlewax she'd made me eat the week before, or the dead sun-baked worm. I watched her peel the paper away from Orange, slip it between her lips, roll her chocolate eyes impishly. Granny suddenly appeared in the doorway, a bucket of water gripped between her hands. As if outside of time, I watched her lift the bucket above our heads, the dirty suds at first trickling slowly over the brim, then falling in a frightening fast rush. "Big hump-back bugs is gonna get you," she warned.

Most of the time we were left alone. Their mother worked in a fast-food diner, mopping floors, scrubbing runny eggs off plates, rubbing down counters. She kept six transparent green bottles full of pennies on her bedroom floor—"dream money," she called it. The three of us would haul out the thick Monkey Ward's catalogue, spread the pennies on her white fringed bedspread, then pore over the pictures. We wanted to buy Batman a glass greenhouse so that he could breathe better. He was always talking about lungs and good air. Restlessly flipping through the glossy pages until he found the musical instruments, he'd point to a jeweled steel guitar and get a dreamy look in his eyes. "Gonna be a rock star and ride around in a black limo." Robin couldn't decide what she wanted. Sometimes she'd get mad, flounce out of the room, go cry in the kitchen. She said it wasn't no fair, all them pretty things, and who was we with our bottles of pennies. I tried to tell her it was only a game, that what really mattered was making a mud pie and looking at the snakes. But she'd get to sobbing so hard that I'd know there was something deeper inside her, a small hard lump that nothing could ever get rid of. After a while, we stopped looking at the catalogue.

We moved within the mirrors, silently counted Stravinsky, worked against our bodies. We hadn't turned on the lights. The front-desk was whining again about wasted electricity and Company debts. Still, it was familiar to be dancing in the sad grey window light, like being in Simon's apartment, our bodies harmonized together in another silent movement. We were inside the music, gliding, turning, flowing amid the shadows and the notes. Then there was an explosion of light and Magda's triumphant voice: "We've finally found your hideaway." We were frozen in mid-movement, just going into a lift. Magda turned off the tape and strode briskly across the floor. She was wearing silver-edged pumps. Valerie, a veteran principal, posed casually in the doorway, sweatered arms folded across her chest. A fuchsia-red scarf dangled from her neck. Waggling a finely manicured finger at Simon, Magda promised, "We'll watch with generous eyes." She smiled. "Whatever *Simon* says." Settling herself into the director's chair at the front of the room, she arranged herself gracefully, then extended a braceleted arm to Valerie.

Simon's eyes were like two muddish marbles. He went over to the recorder and ran back the tape, then motioned me to join him in the far left corner, where we would start the *pas*. "It's for real, babe," he whispered. As he took hold of my damp wrist and pressed his thumb into it, I glanced over at Valerie, who was now leaning across the piano, flipping through Simon's choreography notes. "Why is *she* here?" Simon ran his tongue over his teeth. "Interested, I guess." I waited nervously through the last few counts of taped silence, then swallowed air and offered my body to the music.

Simon promenaded me about in two tight circles, then his hands slipped down to my hips and guided me into a snake-like movement. I wrapped my body around his legs, focused my eyes on his, resisted his upward pull before surrendering myself to our synchronized torsos. Sinking to his knees, he extended his arms above him, then grasped me by the thighs and slowly, outside the music, pulled me down. I was still on point and had to take the full weight in my feet, curling through each vertebra before extending one leg behind me in an *arabesque*. It was going well, better than in any of our rehearsals. Somehow, we'd found a way to move simultaneously with and against each other. When we finished, with Simon on one knee and me folding slowly backwards into his enveloping arm, I had that cold certain feeling that, finally, we had made this *pas* our own.

When I looked up, I could see Simon in the mirror, and behind him Magda and Valerie locked in a quiet conference. Simon's arm was still embracing me, but he was staring at them. Finally, their conference broke up and they began moving towards us. Fluorescent bright lines wiggled in front of my eyes, formed a spectral nimbus around their approaching bodies. Then their shadows fell across us. Magda jutted a proud powdered chin at Simon. "What *long* hours you've put in." Simon turned and tilted his head to the side, away from her shadow, and squinted into the wet light. "Do you like it?" Magda shifted her eyes towards Valerie, who held out her hand to Simon and hoisted him up. "Opening isn't quite right," she said thoughtfully. "I'd like to begin it with a big lift, something more . . ." She paused, flickered her black-rimmed eyes over me, offered a thin concentrated smile. ". . . more sophisticated." Marking the floor in heeled boots, she turned slowly and fluttered her arms in the air. "Beginning to feel it," she said. She did a little of the snake movement, but I could see she didn't really feel it. "With a little cut and patch, we'll make it work," she said. "Sure," Simon said, "I'm flexible." He walked after her. "I've got a rehearsal," I said quietly. Magda glanced at her wristwatch, smiled demurely. "Of course, dear, the demands of a soloist." Simon said nothing, wouldn't even look at me. As I grabbed my dance bag and ran from the room, I heard Valerie say, "Now there's a temperamental one."

I bumped along the crowded corridor with a lowered head. I didn't want anyone to see my tears. The hall faces were unfamiliar, mostly students from the school, waiting in their usual black leotards for the classrooms to open. A few lower-level teachers clustered in the smoke-filled lounge, sipped from diet cola cans, exchanged professional gossip. I wandered in a frantic zig-zag among the students and teachers, occasionally stumbling into someone, starting to apologize, then breaking down and wandering off again. No one took much notice anyway. If they saw me coming, they stepped out of the way; otherwise, they just brushed past me. Finally, I ran down the hall to the foot of the staircase, hoping, I suppose, that I'd find Simon coming down to tell me he'd made everything good again. Instead, a purple dance bag followed by a cursing Lincoln bumped down the marble steps and landed at my feet. I threw myself into his arms.

"Hey, bunhead," Lincoln comforted me, resting the warm palm of his hand on my back. Humming under his breath like running water, he rubbed my shoulder blades. "Gave it to someone else," I cried against his chest. And then, between sobs: "Simon said . . . it was my part . . . our *pas de deux*." Lincoln pulled me down to the steps, crouched in front of me, pushed the bangs out of my eyes. "They don't play fair, honey." I wrapped my arms around myself and tried to stop the shaking. Lincoln's hand spider-crawled along the step. "He's Magda's boy." I lifted my head. "What do you mean?" My voice sounded rusty and hollow, like an old gas can. Lincoln's eyes darted up to the wall clock, then he took my hand and patted it. "We're gonna have us a heart-to-heart. Get things straight. But I gotta fly right now." He placed his hands gently on my shoulders. "You got somewhere to go? Someone to talk to?" I shook my head. "Then you stay right here." He shouldered his dance bag, then draped his rehearsal towel around my back. "Hang on to this. Watch 'til the little hand hits six. I'll be back from rehearsal in one hour."

But I couldn't wait. The hands on the clock moved so slowly, dancers nervously pattered up and down the steps, the studio walls breathed in and out, my stomach jumped crazily. When the big hand jerked for the twentieth time, I bolted from the step and ran off to the dressing room. My locker was just beneath a cheap print of a generic landscape. It didn't look like any place I'd ever been or wanted to go. The picture was slipping out of its cracked casing. I unlocked the door, threw in

Lincoln's mascara-teared towel, began rummaging through the clutter of leotards, shoes, ribbons, bandages, and half-empty peanut-butter jars. When I pulled out my street clothes and slammed the door, the landscape wobbled on the wall, then fell on the floor in front of me.

"Simon says, 'Hey, babe,'" I cried, kicking the broken picture. "Sure, daddy, whatever you want." I knew I had to get out of there, but where to go? I quickly pulled my jeans over my hips, slipped my head under a heavy fringed sweater, jammed my feet into ankle boots. Where to go? Dragging my dance bag across the floor and around a corner, I collapsed over the bathroom basin. When I finally looked up into the mirror, I was peering angrily at myself with slitted eyes. "Fucking-A, fucking-B, fucking-C." Tears and eyeliner were sweating down my cheeks. I turned on the faucet and watched the rusty water swirl mindlessly down the drain. "What does Natalie ever say? Nothing! Nothing! Nothing!" I slapped some water on my hot skin, then looked at my reflection. I wanted to break the small sharp face glaring back.

The pay-phone gleamed in the mirror next to a tampon machine. I checked the wall clock but it was too late to call Henry. He'd just be starting one of his Adult-Ballet classes. I couldn't go to him anyway. I'd temporarily broken the connection, run away from his illness. There was too much explaining to do. So where the hell could I go? I wandered into one of the toilet stalls. The walls were written over, and over again, with graffiti. They never painted in here. Desperate mocking messages from past and present overlapped and intertwined. Sentence fragments, parts of clauses, bits of rhyme appeared, disappeared, reappeared in a constantly changing syntax of dance terms and swear words. I looked in my bag for a lipstick or eyeliner. I wanted to make my mark in this Company history, even if what I put down would be broken into floating parts of speech as I wrote it. And that was when I thought of Fran's painting, the musical one with the shifting fragmentary rhythms of repressed notes that had first brought us together.

I couldn't call her, she didn't have a phone. We usually met on the Wharf. She'd warned me not to go to her place alone. But it was dark out; she should be back by now. I couldn't wait. I'd have to risk it. Where else could I go?

I rose on tiptoe, peered through the door-hatch into the dark shadows, then tentatively called out. "Fran?" There was no answer, but I could hear movement in the room. I raised my voice. "Is Fran here?" Armand's voice floated back. "Yeah. In the back." I grabbed at the doorknob, shook it, felt the door give. Slumped at a table next to an open window, Armand was stringing his guitar by candlelight. He didn't look up. I ran across the front of the house, past the death masks and the beaded curtains. "Fran?" I yelled, pushing through the green door. Her room was streaked with the murky light of early evening, and my voice touched nothing. I whipped around, searching the room, but found only my unfinished portrait on the easel and Armand's obscure dark face framed in the doorway. "Where is she?" I cried. He shrugged his shoulders, thrust out his hands. "I don't know. Just goes away." I moved back behind the easel, seeking protection. "Hey, little frog." I held on to the edge of Fran's stool. "What?" He hadn't moved from the doorway. "Come on," he said softly. "Armand not hurt you." I shook my head. "Why'd you say she was here?" His face was folded in sinister pockets, and yet he made no move to enter the room, as though standing behind an invisible boundary. Holding out his hand to me, he whispered, "Armand's your friend."

Toby squeezed through the doorway, crawled low on his belly to where I stood, then sat up looking at me with worried eyes. I stroked his head. Speaking in measured increments, Armand slipped his hands up and down the sides of the door. "You can wait in my room." I shook my head again. "No. I want to stay here." He sighed, shifted his gnome's body, stepped back. "You come with Armand to the front room." A tired whimper escaped from Toby's throat. "No," I said. Armand took another step back. "Why you afraid, little frog?" He turned sideways, peered indifferently down the hall. "I make you a cup of tea, is all. We talk." I knelt down and wrapped my arms around Toby's head. He licked my chin. "I can't," I said. Armand backed up, crouched down, clapped his hands. "*Maintenant*, Toby!" Tail curled around his good back leg, Toby reluctantly hobbled to the door. Armand extended his hand again. "Come on," he coaxed. I held back, uncertain, then stepped out from behind the easel and started to move toward him. Just before the doorway, I hesitated. Armand reached across the threshold. Where else did I have to go? I gave him my hand, and he gently pulled me through the door and down the dark hallway.

"A grey grey day," Armand was saying, as he handed me a yellow mug of tea. I sat on the edge of a ripped brown couch, unraveling one of the loose cushion threads. He squatted in front of me, speaking in a low voice that I had to strain to hear. "But I got plans," he was saying. "Big ones." I glanced at the dusty sound equipment, the stack of unsold cassettes, the worn grey hat dangling from a nail in the wall. He was talking to me through tight lips. "Need help." I stared down into the steaming mug, then poked my finger at the teabag. "Citizenship," he said darkly. He pinched his eyes. "Marry. Divorce. No sweat. I pay." Sure, I thought, in quarters. Still, it was my first proposal. "What about Fran?" Armand grimaced and turned his head away. "Bah! Too old."

I kept poking the teabag, waiting for the liquid to cool. Armand flashed his eyes from me to the closet. A stained bare mattress protruded through a half-opened door. "People sleep there," he said somberly. I pressed myself into the corner of the sofa, looked over my shoulder at the front door, then returned my eyes to him. "No," I said. Armand leaned towards me. "I make you feel better." I put the mug in a crack between the couch cushions and spread open my fingers in front of my face.

70

"I can't feel anything anymore," I sighed. Armand took my hands in his. "Sad little frog." He slid my hands up around his neck, then softly cradled my face. I *was* sad, and tired, too sad and tired to resist anymore. At least someone wanted me for something.

And then Fran was circling the living room, glaring first at Armand, then at me. "What the hell's going on here?" She was sniffing the air suspiciously, like an animal. "I told you to leave her alone." Her hands were on her hips, her shabby wool coat flaring around her. Slowly, Armand straightened up, shrugged his shoulders, picked up his half-strung guitar. Fran continued to glare at him as he disappeared into the shadows. Then she turned back to me. "I told you not to come here alone. He didn't . . . ?" I shook my head. Then she noticed the mug between the cushions. "You didn't drink any of that, did you?" I shook my head again. Then, finally, she removed her hands from her hips. I ran over to her and wrapped my arms around her solid body. "They took it away from me," I sobbed, "it was mine." She pressed me close to her, as though trying to squeeze out the pain. "Yeh," she said, "they do that." And then she held me and rocked me until the crying stopped and only the pain was left. Later, when she drove the boys to the Lake for their gig, she brought me along. I rode up front with Toby.


A streak of silver light glitters in the fog like a piece of tinsel, white-blue steam rises from the Lake, birds whisper on the damp soft bridge. Fran's head is just a muddy clump of hair; my own body feels gritty and frozen. Our lips barely move, our voices are wet and arthritic. The night monsters have disappeared; only the three of us remain. We climb wordlessly through the bracken, until we can see the dull glint of the green van. The boys are nowhere around. They probably hitched back into the city hours ago. "Looks like they missed their ride," Fran says. She looks at me. We both smile.

*71*

But, as we near the van, she scowls at her watch. "I'm late. You'll have to come with me." I climb gratefully inside, wrap myself in Toby's dog blanket, collapse immediately into a numbing half-doze. As we bounce along the quiet streets, I rise and fall out of consciousness, my dreams mixing with the tattered fragments of the previous day. We'll hit a bump, I'll sit up suddenly, peer out the bug-splattered window, see only the passing grey city buildings or a blinking neon sign, then drop back down again into an interior landscape of fog, graffiti, teabags, and mirrors. After a while, I can feel the van start a gradual ascent. I give myself over to the sensation of the upward movement, to the irregular coughs and spurts of Fran's shifting, as if I'm a smoke ring swirling in a cross breeze, propelled haphazardly toward some other place. I pull the blanket up around me, breathe in Toby's musty hound odor, and let my head roll forward.

A damp paw pierces my arm and I sit up quickly. We're surrounded by waist-high manicured shrubbery, rows of boxed elders, newly planted acacias, open-faced white-shuttered houses. Fran slows at a four-way intersection, then rounds the corner, her body thrust forward, hands gripping the steering wheel. "Where are we?" I ask. She squints into the rear-view mirror, reaches up, yanks a clot of mud from her hair. "Hub of the universe," she says. We sweep around another corner and crawl along a line of two-story curtained boxes. The curved driveways are randomly cluttered with station wagons, tricyles, basketball hoops, large draped picture windows. A fleshy robed woman carrying a newspaper, blond hair wrapped in curlers, darts into a house. "One of the natives," Fran mutters.

Then she pulls into a driveway and parks. Toby starts whining at the window, his tail thumping eagerly against my floating body. "Easy, old boy," Fran says, as he leaps over me and scrambles out through her door. I slide out my side and follow Fran around to the back of the house. She holds open a white wooden gate for Toby and me, then follows a flagstone path through a small rock garden bordering a green lawn. The lawn is divided in thirds by a swing set and a barbecue pit. Toby has already started digging in the soil beneath the picket fence, and emerges now with a wet brittle bone hanging from his mouth. His ears lie flat on his skull. Fran lifts up a rubber Welcome mat, puts a key in the lock of a redwood Dutch door, pushes it open. Flicking on a lightswitch, she puts a finger up to her lips, then pulls me into the house. "Get the milk and eggs," she says.

I turn slowly about the kitchen: a shiny black microwave, a row of potholders embroidered with flowers and geese, a grey-capped blender, a stack of plastic placemats with scalloped edges, a half-empty glass of chocolate milk. I run my hands along the smooth Formica counters until I find the cool handle of the humming olive-green refrigerator. The milk is on the top shelf. I can't find the eggs at first. Finally, I locate them on the inside of the door, nestled snugly in plastic form-fitting containers. Fran is ransacking the cupboards: two plates, two coffee mugs, two bowls rimmed with cartoon figures; a cereal box with a toothy fairy and a carnival of colorful shapes; two forks and two spoons, two blue paper napkins. I slump over the stove and watch the milky white of the eggs turn brown, then wedge a rubber spatula under them. "Don't burn them," Fran warns me. I slip the eggs onto the cartoon plates. "I'm really confused," I say quietly. "Join the family," she says, pushing open a swinging door that leads to the rest of the house.

A skinny boy of about ten pops his head through the opening. "Mom," he says, "Brian's picking his nose and eating it." His mobile brown eyes dart about the room, land briefly on me. Screwing up his face, he crosses his eyes, then sticks out his tongue. Fran pours a glass of milk, takes a sip, sets it down on the table in front of me. "Is that so?" she says flatly. "Yep. And he's got dog breath, too." Fran shuffles across the floor, points to the plate of eggs, then rattles the cereal box. The accused Brian, younger than the first boy, suddenly appears, scrambles into a seat, sends a racecar flying over the table. It hits my milk

*73*

glass and bounces off the table. "You're dead," the boy says. He wears thick Coke-bottle glasses that rest low on his freckled nose. "Brian!" Fran admonishes. "Eat your breakfast." She raises an eyebrow at me, as if to say, "You're on your own," then disappears through the swinging door.

Brian slurps at his cereal bowl, looks at me as though he's examining a bug, makes a few other indistinguishable noises that sound like car engines, then stabs at his eggs with stubby fingers. "Yuck," he complains. The other boy forks an egg into his mouth, swooshes it around, then lets the yolk ooze through his teeth and down his chin. Pressing on his fork as if he's going to flip it, he crosses his eyes at me again. "Double yuck, dogbreath," he says. Fran returns with a red-faced man stuffed in a dark three-piece suit, carrying a briefcase. He seems to be having a hard time breathing: either his vest is too tight around his stomach or his tie is cutting into his throat. He glances at me with only polite curiosity, ruffles the oldest boy's head, grabs one of the coffee mugs, stuffs a newspaper under his arm, and marches out the back door. "You do carpool tomorrow," Fran shouts at his retreating back. Then she turns to me. "My husband," she says dryly. "The Silent Majority."

We run carpool in a brown and white station wagon with a luggage rack and a leather seat that faces backwards. Fran will pull up in front of another blank-faced house, hammer the horn once or twice, then rap her fingers on the steering wheel. The kids will fly down the driveway, toting schoolbooks, lunch boxes, baseball mitts, jars of captured insects, loose papers, gnawed pencils. An occasional mother will appear in the doorway, shade her eyes, wave to Fran, call a warning to one of the restless boys. The boys ignore everything but each other. Fran is simply the driver, I am the unnoticed passenger riding shotgun. Among themselves they spit and swear, trade punches and gouges, boast of fights and games and ancient tortures inflicted upon friend and foe. When they all finally tumble out of the car and run in a pack onto the school playground, Fran sighs and lights a cigarette. "Boys will be boys," she says, exhaling deeply.

Shards of broken morning-yellow light are slipping through gaps in the schoolyard's chain-link fence. The fractured pattern flickers through my window until we turn the corner, then I close my eyes and fall asleep in the undisturbed suburban daylight.

A plastic zippered curtain surrounded Batman's head so that he wouldn't get any germs. Robin and I crouched on stools in the sweltering dark bedroom, holding hands, telling stories. His eyes would open briefly, a stringy smile might appear, then he'd hold up a papery hand to the plastic. We didn't know if he could see or feel us, but we would go up to the plastic tent and press our hands against his. Their father shuffled through the room, just a thin shadow moving stealthily from one end of town to the other. "A bad man," Robin said. "Eats live dogs." She slitted her eyes. "Gots himself fourteen wives." I didn't really believe her, but I understood what she meant. I'd only seen him twice. His arms seemed too loose, like a puppet's, and stiff black hairs matted his scarred chest. He never wore a shirt. We waited through that whole long summer for Batman to breathe proper, but his lungs only got weaker. One day he just disappeared. I ran through their house calling for him, flinging the doors open, looking crazily inside cupboards. I don't know what I was thinking. I finally climbed into his empty bed and sobbed until I felt like throwing up. Granny pulled me out by the feet, fed me frybread and milk cubes, washed my face with a cold rag. "'Bout give me a heart attack," she muttered. "Thought the boy'd come back the wrong color." Her knotted hands worked evenly over my hot skin. "Don't belong in this place." I threw my arms around her thick solid body and held on. "Lord, help us all," she said.

# Act Two

The theater is an act of collaboration.
              –Agnes de Mille, *To A Young Dancer*

I reach out and steady myself with the heavy velvet of the curtain, inhale, exhale. My white dress is tightly gathered at the bodice, flows and swirls out from my torso, becomes transparent in the dusty footlights. It is illusive, like a gossamer. I cannot feel my body. Rising on point, I grind the tips of my shoes into the rosin box, while Billy the Kid gallops across the stage in frenzied circles, leaps over hollow rocks, dashes behind wooden cacti. Soon he will pose against the desert backdrop, raise his arms to usher in the dimming of the lights, fall asleep to the practiced swellings of Copland's score. Greasepaint sweats behind his black felt mask and down his cheeks, as if he's crying. He removes his cowboy hat but doesn't reveal his identity. Metal treelights sprout in the wings, wash the stage in amber shadows. I am the Dream Girl, I am the real phantom.

## Act Two

The waiting is almost over, my time is coming, my entrance. It is cold; my body feels fragmented, made of tiny, separate pieces of ice. I unravel the black wool leg-warmers from my neck, concentrate on warming my muscles. I stretch forward so that my chest rests lightly along the length of my legs, then roll up through my spine. The communal urgency of live performance envelops me. For a brief moment I am connected—by heavy cords and thin wires, amber treelights and velvet curtains, bright Western costumes and classically orchestrated folk music, by the indolent gruntings of stagehands and propboys, the nervous chatter of seamstresses and technicians, the sad whispers of the *corps* girls gathering for the caravan finale—with the transient cluttered intimacy of the American theater. I am the Dream Girl, I am the soloist.

I run my hand across my stomach, then abruptly pull it away. I can't let my mind wander to what will happen after I've danced the dream segment, taken my bow, clocked out for the day. Right now, I have a Saturday matinee to get through. The Kid walks five counts to center stage, swivels on his heels, offers his exhausted arms to the audience. He wears only a mask, dance belt, boots. I listen and watch for my cue, stab my feet into the stage floor in slow exact *bourrées*, try to link the incessant phrasing of the music with the dreamy movements of my limbs.

As I float across the stage, the Kid sits up, shades his half-concealed face. He imagines a wispy vague outline but never really sees me. I skim the floor, arms softly gesturing, reach out to my dreaming unseeing partner. My hands and fingers drift and curl about my body, open into the space around me, but he's unaware of my *real* presence, even as he shifts his body, stares through me with crusty masked eyes. Moving backward into the fading light, as though some other force is pulling me away, I kiss the length of the floor with my ghostly feet. At the edge of the stage, I pose for a moment, then, reluctantly, return to my partner and offer myself to him. Lifting me by the waist, he rocks and swings me back and forth, waltzes me slowly and sensually. I keep my eyes lowered. He does not look at me. I am the soloist, I am the real phantom, I am the Dream Girl.

Rhythm changes, stage lights brighten. Pushing me away from him, the Kid drops to the ground and curls back into his embryonic sleep. I am abandoned, must now quietly, without protest, leave the scene. As the cloaked caravan dancers travel across the stage to sorrowful music, I waver, then fade into the wings. I have danced the Dream Girl fourteen performances without a break. I am ten weeks' pregnant.


Over the phone twelve days before, a quiet female voice said to look for a white oblong building next to a demolished theater. "Entrance is on the side." The county women's clinic, unmarked and windowless, was in the Mission District, almost hidden behind a row of transplanted withering palms. Transients squatted in the gutted ruins of the hollowed-out movie house next door. They smashed green bottles on the broken sidewalks and pushed stolen grocery carts back and forth in front of the clinic. The carts were filled with newspapers, chicken bones, torn cushions, and laceless old shoes; their wheels spun crazily on the cracked pavement. I walked past the entrance door several times. I wanted to just float up into the sky, a balloon escaping from a child's hand, floating freely above the city. But I knew I couldn't stay outside forever, circling around myself, holding back this moment. Something was lurking inside me.

The door opened into a large sallow room of waiting women. Most of them slouched in plastic orange chairs, stared at the green tile floor, rested hands on protruding flowered bellies; others dug restlessly through handbags, rattled change purses, sipped from Dixie cups, clutched labeled bottles of urine. The room smelled bitter, like earwax or sour milk. Bulletin boards and posters blazed the walls. I stood just inside the door, unable to move. I wanted to apologize. Beneath a sunburst wall clock sat a receptionist wearing a corduroy smock. She glanced up at me and pointed to a clipboard on her desk ledge. I nodded. I'd come too far; now I lacked the courage to leave. Besides, there was another form to fill in.

I drifted toward the receptionist's desk through a labyrinth of children's building blocks, dispirited voices, diaper bags, dusty green hanging vines. Attached to the clipboard were a two-page medical form and a pencil dangling from a string. I leaned against the desk ledge and started to fill out the form. Suddenly, a bottle appeared on the clipboard. I looked up. The receptionist was pointing to the restroom. I waited there for my turn behind a black girl with a large low stomach. She wore a blue sweater held together with safety pins and dirty pink thread. She looked about thirteen.

After I returned my damp bottle and forms to the reception-ist, I found an empty chair in the corner next to a rusty floor heater. The orange plastic was sticky and the fluorescent ceiling lights kept blinking on and off. The woman to my right was ripping pages out of a magazine, crumpling them into balls, dropping them on the floor. The stringy turbaned woman on my left reached into her child's mouth, pulled out a tiny plastic doll's hand. The kid's face wrinkled up like a dried avocado, then she started crying. "Everything goes in that mouth," her mother snapped. The black girl in the blue sweater sat across from me. She was about Robin's age, the last time I saw her. That was after Granny died, the day Robin and her mother left to go to live with her aunt in Detroit. We were waiting for the bus in front of the feed-and-grain store. She was carrying a cardboard suitcase with a rope tied around it. "Gonna get me a baby," she said, "and go on welfare. My cousin's 14 and gots two already." She was thin and small, less developed than even I was. When the bus came, we hugged each other and promised to write. I sent her three letters; she never answered.

"Natalie Barnes." I followed a pink-jacketed nurse around a corner, then sank into a padded metal armchair. She took my blood pressure with cold hands, skimmed my forms, chewed on her flat lips. "Sixteen," she said. I wrapped my ankles around the chair legs, slipped my hands under my thighs to warm them. "Be seventeen soon." She leaned forward on her elbows, as though about to say something, then turned her face away. "Date of last period?" I calculated in my head, but couldn't really remember. I looked down at my knees, thought of Simon's shadowy apartment, Henry's craggy face. "Sometime in December." She made a note on the form. "Birth control method?" One of my hands had fallen asleep. I didn't say anything. She put a large check mark on the top of the page, then circled it. Her voice was weary. "It's 1981. Don't they teach you kids *anything*?" Behind her head was a poster. Two shadow figures were walking away from the camera down a rainy dark street. The man's fingers were crossed behind the woman's back. "Maybe I'm just late," I said. The nurse pressed her lips together, sighed. "Maybe so. We'll let the doctor decide."

"Do you know how this happened?" The counselor's fat chin dangled low from her blotched face. The doctor had decided not even to run a test. She could feel the expanded womb; it was the size of a small grapefruit. So the nurse had led me to the counselor, whose circumflexed eyebrows jutted skeptically above a pair of horn-rimmed glasses. "No," I said. "Well, yes, of course, but . . . no, not really." A plastic flesh-colored uterus was propped on her desk. The counselor slipped a pencil up and down the hollow canals of the model. "Well? Do you or don't you, Natalie?" It was a makeshift office: condom boxes, yellow patient files, synthetic body parts, a tacked-up child's drawing of an angry clown, the counselor's double chin. "Made a mistake," I finally said. Her eyebrows darted up even higher. "Yes . . . well, are you going to tell your parents?" I shook my head, started to tear up. "Why not?" I wiped at my nose, tried to find my voice. "Not here." The counselor sighed, put down the pencil, handed me a tissue. "There are options," she said. "Carrying to full term, adoption, government programs." I quickly shook my head. "Right." She pressed on. "So, okay. Doctors, prices, instructions." She pushed a mimeographed yellow sheet across the desk. "You've got to come to a decision soon, you understand? *It* doesn't just go away."

The list was long and complicated, the names blurred together. Silverman, Kinder, Chung, Bass, Langoni, Evers. "Which one?" I finally whispered. She twisted the pencil in her hand and shrugged her shoulders. "Not supposed to recommend. Figure roughly $500 for the whole thing, start to finish." No tears came out, but I started shaking again. "If it were me," she offered softly, "I'd go to Chung. Nice family practice." She knotted her forehead and squeezed her eyes together. "Evers, however, is very efficient. In and out on lunch break. A lot of women swear by him." I folded the paper in half and stuffed it into my dance bag. "I really don't know what I'm going to do," I said quietly. She placed both hands on the plastic uterus. "Natalie, you can't let this thing drag on." I lowered my head. "I know." She caressed the model. "Is there a steady boy involved?" There was a glass cabinet full of books next to the patient files. I got up from my chair and, turning my back to her, stared into it. "Yes," I lied. "Will he be supportive?" I reached out and touched the glass frame, tried to focus on the book titles, but they were long and unfamiliar. "No," I said.

A little later, when I was leaving the counselor's office, I stopped at the door and turned to look back. Her face remained thick and closed, like a glob of sealing wax. "You can always call me." Her voice was remote, already buried in the next file. I didn't believe her.

I wore all black to Company class the next morning. But I didn't want to dance: cotton-stuffed head, thick stomach, tingling breasts. Beneath my sweater and plastic pants I was swelling up, like a grain of rice. Simon was on the other side of the room, behind a mound of dance bags, thermos bottles, and stacked rehearsal chairs. His back was pressed hard against the mirrored wall. He was tapping out the counts with the heel of his foot, his extended leg rising and falling mechanically, like an oil rig. He didn't look at me.

Curled around my bones in tight stitches, my flesh felt raw and torn—a blistered bunhead, sore beyond my sixteen years. What if it *was* his? I wanted it to be, because he had hurt me, and yet I didn't want it to be—because he had hurt me. They'd told me it was only the size of a small grapefruit, but I felt as if a monstrous thing had been planted deep in the shadows of my body. It clung to me, fed off me, threatened to consume me. In this way, at least, it *was* Simon's. It couldn't be Henry's; he wouldn't do this to me. This is the way you think, or try to think, when you're sixteen and pregnant.

I turned away from Simon and placed my weight on the wall *barre*. I wanted to lose myself in pure unthinking physical routine. I began a series of *entrechats*, beating my thighs together, moving my feet like a pair of scissors. Despite the fear and nausea, I repeated the step twenty-four times, willing my legs to slice through the air, a furious desperate movement deliberately counterpointing Simon's impervious face and mechanical tapping.

After class, I slipped along the corridor wall, a few bodies behind him. A low murmur of joking, complaining, gossiping voices enveloped him. The sound meandered nonchalantly, obliviously, down the hallway. It was all so casual and heedless. I reached into his group and grabbed his arm. "I want to talk to you." Flashing cool eyes at me, he shrugged off my hand and kept walking. "Simon!" I called to his back. A blur of moving torsos seemed to carry him away. He glanced over his shoulder. "Not now, babe." I ran after him. "It can't wait." But he walked on, faster now, more purposeful.

I caught up with him again near the soda machines, across from the men's dressing room. He had outdistanced the others, was by himself. "Simon!" Reeling around, he glared at me. "What?" I took a few steps toward him, then stopped. "I have to know why." He shrugged. "Why what?" I fiddled with the strap on my dance bag, took another step into him. "You know . . ." I couldn't say it. Words suddenly seemed like such sad vehicles for expressing what I felt. I started to cry, softly, quietly. It all seemed so stupid, so hopeless. Simon ran his fingers through his hair. "Gotta run, kid. Another time, okay?" He reached out, pinched the side of my cheek, and strutted past me into the dressing room. Finally, I found my voice. "No, it's not," I sputtered. But he was gone.

I leaned against the cool humming metal of the soda machine, looked up and down the now empty hallway, kept muttering "It's not okay, it's not okay." I'm still not sure why I did what I did next. Perhaps it was the soda machine. There was an old dented one outside my father's garage. It was just a large rectangular box with some refrigeration coils, a motor, and a lid. The soda bottles were inside, their necks clamped between rows of cold metal. Sometimes, after school, when my mother was on the swing shift and I didn't have ballet class and my father was sober enough to work, he'd tell me to come over to the garage and wait for him to close up. While he clanked and swore beneath some farmer's Chevy pick-up, I'd pull my dress down around my ankles and sit on top of the soda machine. As its vibration resonated with my body, I'd begin to drift inside its steady mechanical beat, try to harmonize with the music of the machine, with the feel of its sound. But then his greasy hand would be gripping my arm, jerking me out of the dance of my imagination, steering me down the street toward our empty house. I didn't make the connection then. I couldn't have, at least not consciously. But somehow I knew I just couldn't lean against that soda machine in that empty hallway and wait for him any longer. Goddam it, it wasn't okay, never had been.

So I walked across the corridor and pushed open the dressing-room door. The stalls and urinals were on one side, an empty shower room on the other. I marched past them through an archway into the locker room. An island of tan lockers divided it in half. There was no one in the right side. Simon was over on the far left, sprawled across a sofa. He was alone, a dance towel wrapped around his neck.

Jumping to his feet, he yelled at me. "Hey!" His voice echoed off the lockers. I kept moving towards him. "Why'd you do this to me?" He circled behind the sofa. "Don't belong here, babe." I stopped, midway between the sofa and the archway. He was staring at me, angry, exasperated. I felt I was losing momentum. "It hurts," I murmured. Simon shrugged, opened one of the lockers, started pulling his clothes out. "It's just the way things are." He wouldn't look at me.

Framed photographs of old-time Company dancers randomly filled the spaces between sets of lockers. There wasn't much else there—a couple of wooden benches, a long mirror above a counter, a few Company posters, some scattered shoes. I felt as if I'd swallowed dust. "It doesn't just go away," I said to Simon's ridged back. "Oh, come on, kid," he rasped, still searching through his locker, "it's no big deal."

"No, I guess not. Just the size of a small grapefruit."

He turned around and looked over at me. He was holding one white sock in his hand. "What are you talking about?"

"I'm pregnant."

The sock fell out of his hand, landed in a tight little clump under the bench in front of his locker. "You don't look it."

"Yeah, well, I am," I said quietly. I reached into my bag and pulled out a pink receipt from the clinic. I held it out to him. "Want to see my report card?"

He waved it away. "You can fucking forget it," he snapped. "Not my problem." He caged the room, eyed the archway, moved around the sofa again. He hadn't zippered his jeans. "Where the fuck's my sock?" he muttered. I pointed under the bench. He leaned over, bent down, then bunched up the sock in his hand and flung it across the room. "Damn it! Okay, look, what do you want from me?"

Something had collapsed in his face, he looked worn-out and scared. I knew I had him, I wasn't going to let go. His eyes focused wildly on my face. "What are you going to do?" I didn't say anything. The whole room smelled of toilet bowl cleaner, salty and damp and metallic. Patchy white spots had appeared on his bare chest, like a quick-spreading fungus.

"It's ours," I said finally.

"Yeah, I know." He pointed to the pink paper I was still holding. "You got an A."

"No," I said. "The *pas*."

Simon shook his curls. "What the hell's that matter now?"

"Why'd you ask me? Why'd you take it away?"

"Can't expect someone like Valerie to put in all that time," he said bitterly. He turned away and walked to the far end of the room, stopping in front of the counter mirror.

I spoke to his reflection. "So I was just cheap labor?"

He rubbed at the white spots, as if he could erase them with his fingertips. "C'mon, kid. It was good for what it was."

I recoiled from his image, which suddenly looked huge and hairy. "I've got a name, you know!"

Simon held up his hands in front of him, spread his fingers. "Okay, Nat. Take it easy."

But now it was all coming out. "What about Magda?" I yelled at him.

His eyebrows met in a pointed inverted V. "What about her?" he said indifferently.

But I could tell I'd gotten to something. I wiped at my face with the back of my hand. "All these secrets make me sick."

Simon's face looked flat and shallow. I wanted to hit him. "C'mon, Nat. That old bag of bones?" He was trying for a laugh, but his voice was deflated.

I turned away from him and leaned against one of the lockers. "God," I said.

Simon came up behind me, but didn't touch. "Hey," he murmured. "Magda doesn't mean anything to me."

I wheeled around. "Who does?"

For a moment, he looked hurt. Then the little muscles in his jaw began twitching and his eyes got hard again. "Grow up, Natalie." He pulled out his wallet. "You want money?" I didn't say anything. "Take it! You earned it." He threw a couple of fifties at me. They fluttered in the air, drifted to the dirty floor.

I stared at the bills, then at him. His eyes were like two nuggets of dried mud. When I finally spoke, my voice was surly and low, yet the words came out slowly and precisely, one after the other, like the second hand on a schoolroom clock. "Natalie says, go fuck yourself." Then I turned and ran out of the room.

Blocking the doorway was Himmel, awkwardly trapped in the open space between the urinals and the shower room. He didn't look happy to see me, though he didn't seem very surprised. Perhaps he'd been in one of the stalls. Tired flaps of skin shadowed his face. "Uh, Miss Barnes," he started. I didn't know what he'd heard. I was sweating and my legs burned. "This isn't a good idea," he said. "You, uh, ... you don't belong here, you see." One of his hands crept up his chest, then tugged unconsciously at his scarved neck. There wasn't much I could say, I'd already said too much. I stared past him to the bathroom stalls. Himmel brought a finger up to his lips, slowly shook his balding head. "My suggestion? *Go.*" I nodded. He stepped forward and pushed the dressing-room door open. I slipped through the narrow gap between his body and the door frame.

"So you finally called," my mother was saying, her sleepy Midwestern twang drifting into my ear long distance. "Folks been asking questions." I called her the night after I spoke to Simon. I just wanted to hear her voice. And hearing it, I remembered. How we'd walk the cold hard alleyways every spring, dig through garbage and nettles for all the things people didn't want: cracked icecube trays, a cigar box full of bubble-gum cards, a frayed rubber mat, last year's telephone book, a set of red plastic jump-rope handles, a pair of cheap reading glasses, yellowed dress-patterns from Singers. She'd pull out something like one of those blue Milk-of-Magnesia bottles, hold it up to the April light, wonder aloud how, if we washed it and scraped off the label, it would hold a knot of early daisies. I'd be pushing aside moldy wet vegetables and ragged tin cans, trying to retrieve some other kid's UNICEF coloring book or limbless doll or punctured ball. One year, I found a miniature metal Christmas tree. Its branches still gleamed with tinsel. "You were always secretive," she whispered into the phone.

I'd sit on the front porch steps, not thinking about anything, just listening to the rain, smelling the damp things rise all about me. And she'd come to the door, tell me to stop daydreaming; it was getting time to hoe the vegetable garden, hunt for cooking greens, sell the little baskets of cherries in town. Or I'd watch her beating the bedspread on the clothesline, her freckled arms turning pink in the sun as she waved the yellow jackets away. And I'd wonder why we didn't just leave him, go off somewhere by ourselves, a quiet place, green and new in the morning sun, with purple flowers and climbing vines and butterflies and wide lazy meadows full of grasshoppers. But this was not the kind of dreaming she meant. We never could talk about that. "Are you still there?" she asked me. "Yes, Mommy." But now there's something growing inside me.

"Uncle Eugene sold one of his paintings for $35, frame and all." She was going to reel me into that other place: cloistered fragments, old news, tatters of a life that couldn't mean the same to her anymore, wouldn't mean the same, because *he* was gone. "Now he's a *real* artist," she sighed. "Next thing he'll be on a talk show." And there it was. Another memory weaving its way through me. How old was I the first time it happened? Maybe six or seven. I woke up with a sharp needling low in my ears. I found my father in his boxer shorts propped in front of the TV. "It hurts," I whispered, cupping my hands over the draining ears. He wouldn't turn away from Johnny Carson, who was wearing a turban and holding envelopes up to his forehead. "Go back to bed." I don't know if he was drinking that night, I almost think he wasn't. I pressed my mouth against the receiver. "What else, Mommy?"

"Aunt Effie's legs is acting up. Gave her a box of Epsom salts." She was good at that kind of thing. I'd gone into the kitchen, gotten the flashlight, then dialed the nursing home. Secretly called her away from the swingshift. "Mommy, my ears are breaking open." She'd told me to put some cotton in them, get dressed, not to bother my father. When she got home, she dropped two pink children's aspirin in a glass of orange juice, held it to my mouth, made me drink. She'd brought me a bag of marshmallows, but it hurt too much to eat. Then she called a cab, wrapped a hotwater bottle in one of my father's oil-stained T-shirts. She held me in her arms on the front porch while we waited, rocked me back and forth. He never even came outside to see us off.

"Charlene got married. Sudden-like. A nice boy from church." I knew she was talking to me in code. It didn't really matter about Charlene. "Always said we oughta keep an eye on her, getting her hair permed and all." What was the message? That I should come home, return to that other darkness, a void filled only by his shadow? Or maybe she knew the worst thing possible had already happened. But that was unlikely. She couldn't know. "Did everything for her mother. Don't reckon how Opal'll get along without her." It had been a long bus ride to Indy. I'd clung to her warm arms, pressed between her body and the worn leather bulge of her nightbag. Painful hot rivers seeped from each ear. "It hurts so much," I cried, while she rubbed my head, hummed a few Patsy Cline ballads, told me a story about Raggedy Ann going to a party. As the bus bumped along the dark winter roads, I buried myself in her. "Mommy's here, my little dream girl," she kept saying, her faraway voice slipping down the tunnels of my cotton-stuffed ears. Her hands smelled of talcum powder and rubbing alcohol. Something was scraping the inside of my head. "Mommy's here, my little dream girl."

I wound my fingers around the telephone cord, stared out the window. The neon sign across the street purred and blinked. One of its lighted nipples had burnt out. I couldn't think about Charlene, though I was secretly and momentarily glad for her. Maybe she wouldn't have to pray so much. I remembered the hospital lights, so bright and large, like flying saucers: a mask fitting over my face, a rush of air too strong to breathe through for long, white cloth draped around my head. The doctor told me to count to sixteen, but I'd forgotten how and my voice sounded strange. Afterwards, I threw up in a yellow kidney-shaped pan. She told me they'd put tubes in my ears, like drinking straws. When I grew up, I'd get a new pair, because the old ones would've turned to pearls. I never forgot that. Later, after the fourth or fifth surgery, I imagined that my ears were two small pink secret oysters.

"People next door moved away." She rattled the receiver and her voice quavered, the words falling from her mouth, each sounding the same. Why'd you leave me? Why'd you leave me? Why'd you leave me? "Left a sick cat behind." I was nine. I'd run away with a suitcase full of coat-hangers and no place really to go. He'd been drinking straight through for three weeks, coming into my room late at night. One morning I'd gone in the opposite direction, against the railroad tracks, away from both of them. Holding a skillet of cold bacon grease in her hands, Granny came to the kitchen doorway. She took a hard look at my suitcase and safety-pinned coat, then told me I had to go home. "I can't," I said stubbornly. But Granny pushed me out the door, the flats of her hands nudging me down the steps and back across that field. "You gots legs," she said firmly.

"Spring's coming early. We got daisies already." Why'd you ever leave? Stay close to me. How'd this happen? I left her hanging, while I searched for Fran's words, something she'd said while she was painting me. Sure. Never get the roles right. I wanted to tell my mother this, but it would've taken too much explaining. "That's nice," I said. I suppose I should've understood then what I'd known long before I was even born, when she was leaning against one of the junkers down at the garage, swaying and holding her protruding stomach, provoking herself with the myth of the maternal glow. I should've known too how neither Simon nor Henry would've thought to protect me. That really, I was on my own, suspended in some other time, between rising and falling, between all the roles I wasn't prepared to play. "How can you live in that wet city?" Her voice was accusing.

"I like the rain," I finally said. I could see her pulling the old red quilt around her bones against the shafts of cold night air, eyeing the whistling wood door. Outside my window, some men were hitting garbage cans with baseball bats. Glass shattered against the side of the building. There was a long silence. I'd started to fade. "You get some sleep," she whispered. I cupped the phone against my ear, rocked from side to side. Everything hurt. I wasn't ready to let go. But I was learning how. "You too, Mommy." Afterwards, I crossed hands over my stomach and waited for some sign of life. I stayed by the window until the neon lights stopped flashing.


Dr. Chung's waiting room was a garden of delights: lush potted plants with long tapered leaves, small framed pictures of daffodils and curly-haired children and spotted dogs, little glass jars of gumdrops, jelly beans, and sourballs. A rainbow of magazines about birthing and mothering arced across a slick oak table. On the right side of the room three very pregnant women flipped casually through the magazines. Their pumpkin-ripe stomachs rose and fell in sympathetic unison. I was on the wrong side of the room, out of sympathy and into self-pity.

I hadn't been able to sleep or think or dance. I'd get up in the middle of the night, wander over to the knee-high refrigerator, open it, peer in. There was never much there, maybe a withered head of lettuce, an open can of diet soda, some watery cottage cheese. But I kept getting up and looking, as if something would miraculously appear.

Sitting next to me was a slim freckled woman. She wore a business suit and tennis sneakers. A pair of low-heeled pumps peeked out of her bag. She wasn't reading either. Like me, she just stared across the room, waited silently for her turn. The three pregnant women also weren't talking, but somehow their silence was different—patient and abiding, as though nothing could ever shatter their belief in what was moving inside them, in the realities of birthing and mothering and magazines. It was holy quiet in there, only deep breathing and page turning, as if the preacher had just announced the hymn. The freckled businesswoman and I were in the heretics' pew, on the wrong side of OB/GYN, lost souls incapable of giving ourselves over to the secret of life. So we folded our hands in our laps, crossed and recrossed our legs, tried not to look at the daffodils and the children and the dogs. I never did talk to her, except when they called my name and I knocked her bag over when I got up. Even then, I just retrieved her purse and excused myself.

Rolling his stool away from the bottom edge of the examining table, Dr. Chung spoke to his blue-speckled floor tiles. "Miss Barnes," his voice was professional, but melodious, like a gospel singer's, "did you get counseling at that clinic?" My bare legs dangled vulnerably over the table. "Yes." Chung placed his hands on his knees, stared glumly at his shoes. "Decided on abortion?" I swung my feet back and forth, eyed the bottles of cotton balls and packages of moist pads on the polished counter behind him. "Yes." The wallpaper had teddy bears all over it. A white-starched nurse stood guard at the closed door. I avoided looking at her. Chung's voice resumed its resonant sing-song; his eyes, encased in black-framed glasses, darted along the tile floor. "Absolutely certain?" A bulletin board hid some of the teddy bears. It was covered with birth announcements, thank-you notes, baby photos. "Yes."

Chung made a quarter-turn on his stool and finally looked up at me. He had round shoulders and slippery eyes. "Local anesthetic," he said. "Need someone to pick you up afterwards." My legs were cold and mottled. "You can manage that?"

I had drifted away, hadn't really been listening. "What?"

"Can you manage that, Miss Barnes? Someone must be here to take you home."

I nodded, then glanced at the nurse. She was balanced on one leg, her shoulder against the wall. She quickly averted her eyes. Chung reached over and took my file from the counter. "Any questions?" he said briskly. Sure. Would it hurt? Was it a baby? Would I burn in hell? How'd this happen? "No."

Chung opened my file. "Well, then, it's easy enough." He seemed to be speaking to himself. "Not too far along." He was talking about the surgical procedure but I couldn't listen to his words, only to their sounds colliding in mid-air with my own fears. "A D&C is relatively uncomplicated. Some discomfort." He paused. Discomfort? What did that mean? Now he was flipping through the pages of my file, squinting at my handwriting. "What kind of dancer?" he said, his tone full of judgment. "Ballet." He looked up briefly. "Oh." His voice trailed off as he swiveled again on his stool. "Wife likes to go."

Now he removed a small green ledger from the drawer of a desk next to the counter, turned the pages slowly. He slipped a pen from his pocket, uncapped it, bent over the ledger. "Friday evening or Saturday afternoon?"

"I can't."

He rotated the stool and appraised me carefully. "Miss Barnes, those are the only times I do them."

How *did* this happen? "What time on Saturday?"

He turned sideways, studied the ledger. "Four's open."

"I've got a matinee."

"Five's the latest. Can you make *that?*"

"I guess so."

He handed me a white appointment card out of the back pocket of the ledger. "Payment same day."

"I know."

Chung closed the ledger, then slipped it back into the desk drawer. "That's set then." He stood. "You'll see yourself out?" I nodded. When I went back through the waiting room, the slim freckled businesswoman had disappeared. Only the expectant mothers remained.


Fran was sitting along the wiggling Aquatic Park shoreline, her old tattered coat spread over the ground. She was just staring out at the dark grey water, her arms wrapped around her knees. Dots of black circled the sky, occasionally dove down, skimmed the foam, drifted off again. Some turbaned men with beards and bongo drums occupied the bleachers behind us. They were passing joints. I sank into the damp sand next to her. "Whatcha doing?"

"Waiting." She didn't look at me.

I pushed the toe of my boot into the sand. "For what?"

"Light to change." She was very still, focused on the roiling water.

"I've got a ticket for you." I rested a white envelope on the frayed collar of her coat. "Saturday matinee."

A wry smile. "So you finally learned them."

"Yeh," I said. I'm the Dream Girl."

"That figures." She shook her head. "No chiaroscuro," she muttered.

"What's that?"

"The harmony of light and dark. Grey sky's washing out everything." She stretched out her legs, leaned back on her elbows, looked at me sideways. Her eyes narrowed. "You don't look too good, Dream Girl."

I watched the birds swoop down, skim the indifferent surface of the Bay. "Water's turning," I said.

"Too late. Light'll be gone soon." Fran reached out and picked up the ticket. "So," she said, "what else is new?"

"I'm pregnant."

The drummers packed up, now strolled past us, slapping their buttocks, leering with stoned eyes. "Oh, Natalie." Fran's voice was exasperated, tinny, unfamiliar. "How'd that happen?"

It was getting darker. The wet air was seeping under my clothes. We met eyes momentarily. "Stupid question, right?" she said. I tried to smile. The narrow stretch of beach was fading indiscriminately into the water. "Need someone to pick me up afterwards," I said quietly.

Fran took a handful of sand and threw it to the side. "After what?"

"I'm not keeping it."

She grunted, sat up straight. "*It* is a human life."

The skybirds overhead were flying in a dizzying synchronized circle. I hadn't expected her to say this. "Fran, I'm not done growing up myself."

She was pulling her socks over her white ankles, gathering up her sketchbook and pencils. "Should've thought about that sooner."

"Why are you so angry?" She started to get up. "It's not happening to you."

She scooted around, faced me. Her eyes were hollow. "I'm not much of a Catholic anymore, but I don't believe in killing babies."

"It's not a baby." The drummers had settled down a few feet away from us. Their calloused brown hands rapped out a staccato 2/4 beat around abrupt and angry rests. "Just a floating seed. That's all."

"That's not all." She stood up. "Look, I've got two kids. They may be monsters, but they're mine. You understand?"

She handed me the ticket. "You have to believe in something, Natalie." Then she began walking away.

I didn't bother to stand, it wasn't any use. "Thought you were my friend," I called to her retreating back. The drummers had broken into a mournful chant.

Fran whipped around. "I am." One hand held her coat together at the neck. "But I can't have anything to do with *this*."

She turned away from me and hiked along the disappearing shoreline. I watched her for a while, as the drummers' chant drifted in the easy wind. Then I jumped up and ran after her. I caught her just where the beach tapers off. "Here." I thrust the ticket into her hand. "I still want you to come." Fran bunched over inside her coat, crammed the ticket into her pocket. I bolted around in front of her, blocking her way up the concrete steps. "Do you think it's always wrong?"

Her eyes were clear and burning. She stared at me for a long time, then closed them. "Don't know," she said.

I took her hand and placed it on my stomach. "It hurts, Fran."

She wrapped her arm around me, pulled me into her. "So stupid," she said bitterly. "Damn him."

"Simon?"

She leaned back. "Who else?" I lowered my head. She pushed me away from her. "Jesus, Natalie. You don't know, do you?" Then she brushed past me and climbed the steps.

The streetlights had come on. Just as she was about to walk into the shadow of a warehouse, she paused and looked back at me. "Do what you have to," she said. Then she turned away again and I lost her in the darkness.

Henry took a long time answering the bell. His old brick apartment building was only a few blocks east of his studio. The street breathed quietly: lanky redwoods, green-berried hedges, a nodding row of white-capped street lamps. He'd lived here for thirty-four years, up a dark wooden staircase at the far end of the corridor. I'd had to look up his address in the phone book, then search for his faded name among the little mailbox rectangles in the entrance foyer. The bell's sound was hesitant and scratchy, a voice unaccustomed to speech. I had to ring it several times.

His frayed robe was tied dramatically to the side. Over his shoulder I could see a bookcase, an armchair, a glinting floor lamp with a swivel arm. Otherwise the room was dim and shadowy, an undefined space to which I'd never been invited. "I want to stay the night."

He rubbed at his temples, as though trying to wake up, then reached out and caressed my arm. "Of course, old heart." But he sounded tired and uncertain.

"I'm sorry I didn't call."

Taking my dance bag, he held the door back for me. "Is everything all right?"

"Sure," I said. "Just missed you." I hadn't seen him in a week, since the opening night of *Billy the Kid*. He put my bag down on a low scarred cabinet inside the door, then shuffled to the center of the room and just stood there by the floor lamp, as if awaiting instructions. I tried to make things easier. "Well, here I am!" I threw out my arms and struck a mock pose, as though I were popping out of a cake.

Henry smiled. "So you are, old heart." He reached out and took one of my extended hands. "I should have invited you, I know. I'm not sure why I didn't." He paused, searched for an explanation. "Old bachelors have their ways, I suppose. I'm sorry."

"I'm here now," I said softly. "That's what matters." I leaned into him and nuzzled his cheek. The wall behind him was almost entirely covered by a set of heavy drapes. "Can we let some light in?"

"Light?" He was puzzled for a moment. "Oh, yes, of course. You would want that, wouldn't you?"

I pulled back the cord. Late afternoon streamed into the large room, filled it with yolk-yellow bands. To my left I could now see an archway leading into the dining room. "Do I get a tour?"

Henry fiddled with his robe, then held out his arm. "There isn't much to it, I'm afraid."

We moved silently through the dark rooms. He was wrong. He'd filled the space with the things he loved: history and theater books, old paintings of mystics and harlequins, stacks of records, dance memorabilia, odd vases, an occasional carved piece of furniture wedged between cluttered dusty tables or broken-down chairs. His bedroom was at the end of a hallway, across from his study. A pair of heavily stamped traveling trunks served as night tables. On one of them was a framed photograph of the two of us, taken that day on the Wharf. I went over and picked it up. "Remember that day?" I said. I stared at the picture. I could just make out the Human Jukebox in the background. "You were right."

"About what?"

"When you said that happiness has nothing to do with art."

Henry sat down on the edge of the mattress. The bed was unmade. "What's the matter, old heart?"

"Nothing." His hands were trembling. "Really, Henry. I'm just tired, that's all. A matinee and evening yesterday." I put the photograph back on the trunk. Next to it was a cluster of medicine bottles. "What's all this?"

He raised his thick eyebrows. "Keeps me going."

A double dresser was centered across from the bed. On top of it were some loose coins, the bronze money clip his mother had given him a thousand years ago, a small porcelain statue of a ballerina on point. "What's wrong with you?" I asked.

"Rusty bones. Don't worry yourself."

I went over to him and hugged him. My chin rested on his head. "But I do, you sweet man."

"You mustn't," he murmured and wrapped his arms around my waist.

Something stirred in my stomach. I was hungry again. "Is there anything to eat?"

He slid his hands to my sides, patted me professionally from ribs to hips. "How's your weight?"

I pushed away from him and drew in my breath. "I'm doing fine," I said sharply.

Henry washed his pale eyes over me, crinkled his face skeptically. "If you say so." He stood up and began taking off his robe. "There's leftovers in the refrigerator. I'll change."

Black-and-white photographs hung on each side of the kitchen doorway. Henry's oft-told tales had made them recognizable, even familiar. One was a faded head shot of his mother's rehearsed bright face, her vaudeville eyes caked with charcoal liner. She was the luminous romantic figure of his youth, an exotic tropical wind from the Orpheum circuit, unpredictably blowing in and out of the frozen village in Michigan where he'd lived with his Aunt Judith, his father's sister. Sometimes his mother was between engagements, would stay longer. These were his keenest memories. Her trunks would come with her on the train; they were stuffed with colorful flowing scarves, dancing shoes, silk hose, bound scripts. She'd kiss his face, leave lipstick marks on his wrists. "My darling boy," she'd say over and over. Then they'd roll up the old fringed rug in Aunt Judith's front parlor, push the sofa and chairs against the wall next to the piano, and she'd teach him how to dance. He'd spent most of his childhood waiting for these visits, for his chance to partner her. The other was a glossy action shot of his father tap-dancing in striped pants, his long body leaning forward at an almost impossible angle. He'd died on tour in the influenza epidemic of 1919. Henry, who was seven then, retained only fragmentary memories of large soft hands, happy hazel eyes, a deep voice offering a fat pink peppermint candy, his mother and his aunt in long black dresses, black gloves, and black veils, a fruitcake on the mantelpiece, flower petals on the rug.

## Act Two

The tuna casserole was on the second shelf in a Corning-Ware pot. I took a fork from the dish rack and sat at the kitchen table. I was hungrier than I'd ever been, but I ate slowly, guiltily. Henry came in, poured two glasses of red wine, sat in the other chair. He watched me carefully. "Why don't you warm it up, old heart? Get a plate, be civil."

"I'm happy this way," I said. But I wasn't: the noodles were cold and soggy, the tuna dry and crusty. It wouldn't stay down long.

"I've been clipping reviews." He sipped his wine. "They liked you." He recited from memory. "'An unusual combination of the ethereal and the pensive.' 'A wistful illusion of youth and innocence.' It's a good part for you."

I dipped my finger into the wine, let it drip on my arm. I wasn't feeling any of those things. "It's cold in here," I said.

"Hadn't noticed." He got up and switched on the radiator. The casserole was turning inside me. He came back in and brought me a paper napkin. "Any other news?"

The radiator was rattling, the wallpaper peeling, the linoleum curling. Everything here was coming apart, breaking down, but gradually, almost predictably. It already felt familiar, comfortable. "Talked to my mother."

"Oh?" Henry sipped from his wine. "And . . . ?"

"Changes. Uncle Eugene sold a painting. Charlene's getting married." A wave of nausea. "Spring's coming early." Beads of sweat everywhere. "Everything's the same, I guess. Isn't it hot in here?" A spinning sensation. "I'm sorry," I managed to say, "I just don't feel right."

I ran down the hallway, slammed the bathroom door, turned on a faucet. The running water silenced Henry's concerned voice. "Natalie?" I wouldn't answer at first, I needed to be alone. "Natalie?" I leaned my face against the edge of the bathtub. "Old heart?"

"I'll be okay," I finally said. He backed away, a reluctant thump against the wood floor. I spread my hands over my hot

99

face. Of course, I wasn't going to be okay. That was just it. I'd never be okay again. It was like being wrapped in gauze, layer after layer, thicker and tighter, suffocating slowly. I'd been feeling this way for a long time, farther back than I remembered.

When I came out of the bathroom, Henry was in the living room. He sat in his reading chair, eyes closed, hands folded in his lap. I went to him, curled up on the floor, rested my head on his knees. He'd pulled the drapes against the encroaching night. "You feeling better, old heart?"

"Yes." He smoothed back my hair with one of his hands, a rhythmic warm motion, almost like rocking.

"You should have warmed it up." His fingers massaged my neck. I closed my eyes, felt the pleasant pain of hot shivers dart up the back of my head. "Now, tell me," he asked, "why did you come here today?"

"Missed you." I'd planned to stay over, perhaps talk to him in the morning.

"That's very nice, old heart," he said, "but don't kid a kidder."

I lifted my head and looked up at him. I loved the little lines at the corners of his eyes. They looked like sunrays. "I'm pregnant."

He closed his eyes. When he opened them, he was staring past me. Then he smiled and said dreamily, almost to himself, "Imagine that."

I hadn't expected this either. "Henry?" I said, trying to break the spell.

He spoke slowly, as though unraveling something fine and waxen, like thread or floss. "You'll come live here with me . . . Yes, that's the best way. Then, . . . then I'll teach you the business . . . and, well, naturally, some time will pass. We'll make the study into a nursery—."

"Henry," I said firmly. "I don't want it."

Henry's eyes finally focused on me, but even then, I don't think he could really see me. "Of course you do. It's mine. It's ours."

I scooted away from him and wrapped my arms around my body. I was cold again. There was something insistent and primitive pointing his face: the flared nostrils, the upraised eyebrows, the sudden strength in his knotted body. I couldn't stop the shivering. He leaned forward. "Things will look different five or ten years down the road," he said. "They always do."

I shook my head. "I'm going to dance."

"At best you'll last to thirty. *If* you don't get injured. Then what?"

"So let me have that." I didn't want to ask his permission, I didn't think I had to. "At least I'll know."

"It's better this way." His tone was tolerant but resolute, like the counselor's. "Set for life. The school, this apartment, some investments, . . . our child." He reached out and pried my hands away from my knees. "It's a miracle."

I leaned back until our linked arms were stretched tautly, like a footbridge. The old voice, the one I'd listened to so long alone, was rumbling to the surface. I couldn't keep it still. "You've got it all figured out, haven't you?"

"Some of it, yes." Now his tone was vague, flat, defensive.

I dropped my half of the bridge, let go of his hands. "I'm not going to have it."

His arms remained suspended in the air for a moment, then he brought his hands to his head and pushed his fingers through his silvery hair. "You get to be my age—." He stopped, gathered himself. When he spoke again, his voice was steady, earnest, confessional. "Look, I've had my days. Some were better than others. I had my chances, my opportunities, you understand? But, you see, I didn't waste money on anything— on anyone. I lived . . . ," he searched for the word, and when he found it, was chastened by it, " . . . carefully." The lines around his eyes were ragged and deep, like cracks in dry earth.

I went up behind him, hugged his shoulders. "I don't have much," he murmured, "but it's all yours." I didn't say anything.

He turned into me and pressed his ear against my stomach, as if listening. "Between us," he said softly, "something precious."

I stroked the back of his head, a mechanical numbing motion. My stomach was quiet. "Yes, sweet man," I soothed, "between us."

I'd tried to tell him the truth, or at least most of it. But he didn't want it. So now I held him and told him what he wanted to hear. Between us. It might not even be his. I knew I had to get rid of it. There was something already dead inside me—a kind of belief long ago murdered by another masked man. Or maybe it was never there, was just another myth. Perhaps everyone's childhood is, or can be, a horror, a dark space of shadows and gaps: mirrors that sprout monsters' eyes and send you running to the nearest adult, only to hear what you know to be true is just another lie; strange cracks in the ceiling above your bed that threaten to open up their jagged mouths and swallow you; the yellow dandelions that blow timidly in the wind, as you run toward the dropping sun, trying to catch it in your hands and, just once, hold the day. How many times did I back away from that shadowy shape, the cold steel belt, that humid finger pressed against my lips. And even then, when the backing away did no good, I held onto myself, because there *was* something there. Don't say a word, Natalie. Be a good girl.

So I held Henry, let him think what he had to, let him dream aloud of some impossible future where he'd hold his child, tell it stories no one would ever hear. Because, old heart that I was, I'd seen something his young heart would, mercifully, never know: a vast hard-pebbled empty shore, where infant after infant washed up into the deaf wild. And I thought of that day when he'd brought me the mirror. He'd wanted to watch, wanted to see the difference: my age against his, the horror of history juxtaposed in our reflected flesh, our bodies, our vessels. Now, through him—or maybe it was Simon—I was marooned again on the wild shore of childhood, naked and screaming, unprotected and unheard. And so I rocked him against me, against us, against the dark, his ears straining to get inside the music. And I let him believe in that terrible beautiful dream.

Beneath the chipped chandelier masked men in ten-gallon hats and cowboy boots sat at dirty wooden tables sipping pink ladies. Behind them, three hairy men in stuffed bikinis strutted across a small stage. They flipped chartreuse boas over their shoulders, waved peacock fans. "Those are the Bimbos," Lincoln said. Now they were squatting at the edge of the stage, hissing, baring their teeth, waggling their tongues through thick red lips. The cowboys moaned, waved their legs, grabbed their crotches. Then a tall fiftyish man slunk across the stage in a sequined blue evening gown. Plastic flowers streamed from his wild blond wig. The man cupped his breasts, then held out his arms like a torch singer. He had long black fingernails. The cowboys started whistling and clapping. "And *that's* Golda," Lincoln said.

Golda Goldstein and the Bimbos—the down-market drag act Lincoln followed all over town. He'd been on his way to see them again when I caught up with him outside the theater. It was two days after I'd visited Henry. "I need to talk," I'd said. "Can we go somewhere?" Lincoln had draped his arm around my shoulders. "Where I'm going, you can say anything." The bar wasn't that far from the theater, but I still don't know how we got there: we cut through parking lots, snaked down alleyways, even climbed garbage cans to get over a chain-link fence. Lincoln did it all with a kind of conspiratorial exuberance, as if we were spies being followed. We'd lurk in dark loading zones, run in zig-zag patterns across open spaces, double back to cover our trail. Before we'd climbed the fence, he'd thrown our dance bags over first and told me if we got separated to swallow the microfilm and meet him again in exactly one year in the Trailways bus station in Binghamton,

New York. "Why Binghamton?" I'd whispered. He'd put his hands on my shoulders. "The less you know the better," he'd answered solemnly, and then *jetéd* on to a garbage can.

Lincoln had introduced me to the bouncer, a huge sweating man in a mini-skirt and tank top who used to play pro football, as his older sister from Oakland who favored his father's side of the family. But I'd gotten carded anyway, and so now we sat on the barstools sipping ginger ales as the cowboys hooted obscenities at Golda and the Bimbos. Golda was bumping and grinding to Tammy Wynette's "Stand By Your Man," mouthing the lyrics. The cowboys joined in the chorus: "Stand by your man / Give him two arms to cling to / And something warm to come to." Golda had his arms around the Bimbos, all three were swaying with the rhythm. I felt oddly connected to them. I knew what it was like to be trapped in the wrong body. Lincoln was rocking and singing along with them. When they finished, he got off his stool and whistled.

When he sat back down, he took a long sip from his ginger ale. "Lousy, aren't they?" he said.

"Yes," I said, and started to cry.

"Oh no, bunhead," he said, putting his arms around me. "It's all right. They're *supposed* to be lousy." I buried my head in the crook of his shoulder and cried harder. "Shit," he said, as if in wonderment, "they're better than I thought."

"It's not them," I sputtered. "It's me." I pulled back from him. "I'm pregnant."

Golda was stripping to a tape of "You are Woman, I am Man," but, instead of sliding the gown down around his ankles, he was trying to hike it up over his head. He kept tugging and grunting and jumping, as if he were wrestling with a glittering blue bear. "No joke?" Lincoln said.

"No joke."

"Holy shit," he said softly. "How'd this happen?"

My face was burning, as though I'd just scraped it against the pavement. "Why does everyone ask that question?"

He put his hand on my knee. "'Cause it's so frigging stupid, girl." I let my head fall forward so I wouldn't have to look at him. "'Cause you're supposed to know better. 'Cause it didn't ever have to happen."

I curled my shoulders, pulled into myself. It was a little lump with claws. "I want it to unhappen, Linc."

He put his hand on my chin and raised my head until I was looking right at him. "Of course you do," he said. Then he reached under the bar for his dance bag, pulled a few wrinkled twenties out of a zippered pouch. "It's not much. You got any more?" I shook my head. "Talk to Magda yet?"

Apprentices and soloists had to see her for advances. She didn't often give them and she always wanted an explanation. "How can I go to *her*?" I said.

"Look, bunhead, unless we sell that microfilm to the Russkys, you've got no choice."

Golda was down to a leopard-skin leotard. He was gyrating his hips from side to side. When he turned around, I could see that he even had a long black tail. The permanent curl at the tip kept bouncing off the floor. "Will you go with me?" I asked.

Lincoln's eyes popped wide open. "To Magda?"

"No. The doctor. Saturday, after the matinee. I need someone to take me home."

"I've got a call at 6:30," he said quickly. "We're doing that fucking abstract quartet again. I'm a parabola or something."

"Won't take long. You'll make it."

Lincoln gulped down the rest of his ginger ale. "Jesus, woman stuff." He was muttering, his lips quivering. "My momma had all hers at home, eleven of us." Now his voice lost all its tone. "I watched the last four." He stared at me. "You dig?"

I nodded. Then I put the wrinkled twenties in my dance bag and got off the stool. Golda had only a pair of pink panties on. In one hand he held a black bra, in the other his blond wig. His eyeliner had sweated down his face. He looked like he'd been crying. The cowboys were clapping, yelling, waving their hats. Lincoln didn't look up at me as I started to go. He just stared at the place where I'd been. "See you in Binghamton," I said, leaning over and whispering in his ear. At the door the bouncer was showing his Super-Bowl ring to a couple of squealing tenderfeet. I still don't know how I found my way home.

By Friday afternoon I'd gone to almost everyone I knew, and some I didn't. Even Payroll had shaken me off, a desperate humiliation I was willing to suffer because there wasn't any other. "Sorry, Miss, we aren't authorized." I already knew this. I'd been trying to find Magda for days. She was everywhere— and nowhere: the School, the theater, the Company offices, teaching, choreographing, scheduling, fundraising, managing. She'd sweep into classrooms, studios, board meetings, receptions; correct a *port de bras*, hear a complaint, set a *pas de deux*, charm a patron, promote an apprentice; and then rush out again amid a swirl of scarves and bracelets and cigarette smoke. I couldn't catch up with her. I'd hear a rumor, dash over to the theater, lurk by a staircase, wander through the School, post the front desk. But I was always in the wrong place at the wrong time. Finally, I decided to camp out in front of her studio dressing room. Let her come to me. And, finally, in the gathering darkness of late Friday afternoon, she did.

I had fallen asleep with my head on my dance bag across the threshold of her door. The jangle of her voice and keys startled me awake. I was looking up into an arched pair of penciled eyebrows. "Homesteading?" she said.

"I must talk to you. It can't wait." I scrambled to my feet.

"It never can," she sighed, then unlocked the door and held it open for me. I scooted in as she toed it shut with the back of her foot.

She eased onto a shawl-draped divan, crossed her legs, and pointed to a grey contoured chair across from her. I sat down and covered my stomach with my dance bag. Her incandescent eyes danced nervously up and down my body. I looked away, tried to compose myself. The room was more cramped than I'd expected. The wall I was staring at was completely hidden by a row of beige and black character shoes beneath a portable clothes rack weighted with dance skirts, scarves, that evening's theater-going clothes, a sleek black coat. "I thought it couldn't wait, Natalie."

Her voice startled me again. "I'm sorry, I, I . . ." The words were stuck. I'd been waiting so long I couldn't say them. I hadn't really thought I'd have the chance.

"Some sort of little problem, dear?" she prompted.

"I'm late," I blurted, " . . . on my rent."

"Yes?" She didn't believe me, but was urging me on. She'd played this game many times before.

I was still sorting through the partial lies and truths. "My father died, it was very expensive."

Her eyes were glittering and hard. "That was several months ago, wasn't it?"

I was shaking. "Indiana's far away."

Now she was mocking me. "Yes, I seem to recall . . . farmland, isn't it? Corn?"

She was enjoying this. I looked away from her again. Old Company posters covered most of another wall: a young Magda dominated much of the artwork. There were also a few green-framed photographs. In one picture, a morose Himmel stood in a line-up of other now famous dancers, choreographers, directors. "And soybeans," I said, almost defiantly.

She stared at me for a moment. "Yes, soybeans. Well, how did you manage it?"

I was confused. "Manage it?"

"The airfare, dear. To Indiana. To your father's funeral."

"Oh." I swallowed nervously. "I borrowed it."

"Ah." She leaned back, shifted gracefully on the divan. She seemed to be waiting for me to say something, but I wasn't sure what. So I waited for her. It was what she wanted anyway.

"You know, I was Bay City's original Dream Girl." Her voice was low and syrupy. "It's a lovely role for a young soloist." She laughed, a small stage laugh, then rested her hand on the side of her cheek. "That was a long time ago. Before you were even conceived." She gave herself over to an exaggerated shrug, splayed her other hand against her ribbed chest. "Mr. Himmel, of course, danced Billy."

At the first sound of his name, I wrapped my fingers tightly around the leather straps of my bag. "That's very romantic," I said.

"Yes, well, I suppose." She settled back on the divan, drew her feet up behind her. She looked like a cat. "Tell me," she whispered, taking a cigarette from a crushed-blue case, "this *source*, surely it isn't completely depleted."

"Depleted?" I was having a hard time keeping up with her verbal turns. "Oh. Well, yes, no . . . I didn't ask him."

"*Him*?" She lit the cigarette, blew a ring up to the ceiling. "What a shame." She tipped the ash in a ceramic ashtray on the three-legged table next to her. "Funds are short, dear." Her voice was sharp, like fractured glass. I stared down at my dance bag. "Not a good time at all." The zipper had broken, was held together by a link of paper clips and one large safety-pin. "Besides, Natalie, what happens next month?" I glanced up at her. "Surely you can see there's more problems down the road." She paused, sighed, pushed one of her bracelets back up her sculpted arm.

I stared at her. What was I supposed to do now? Magda lit another cigarette, then wedged it into the ashtray next to the other one, which was still burning. "I need $460," I finally said. "By tomorrow." The smoke curled about her head, wispy and bitter. "In cash." She was silent but I could tell that she was thinking, that something in her small hard heart was making room for me. "I'll pay you back. Somehow." I leaned forward, pushed my ribcage over my dance bag. "I really need the money."

"But, my dear," she whispered through the smoke, "that's such an exact figure. Do you owe the Mafia?"

I sat up straight. So I'd been wrong again. Maybe she didn't have a heart. "Of course not."

"Well, thank goodness. We wouldn't want them breaking your legs." She leaned back, scanned the walls with clever eyes. "Is Vincent a good partner?"

The name was unfamiliar. What was she up to now? "Who?"

"Ah, right, you wouldn't know him." She waved her hands, rocked her small head from side to side. "Last year's Billy."

"Oh," I said. My throat felt tight and sore.

"Messy business." She stubbed out both cigarettes, then pushed the ashtray to the center of the table. "Had to let him go."

I didn't know what to say. "Why's that?"

"Ah, well, how to put it." Her face broke into an abrupt painted smile. "Let's just say, he was not an adequate partner." She stretched out her hands, inspected her long chrome-red nails. "Now, *our* Mr. Himmel . . . ," her voice trailed off, then picked up again, as if a wind were propelling her words, "was a *fine* partner."

"Yes," I said. "I'm sure he was." Neither of us believed this. Himmel had never been a great dancer, had quickly dropped from a Principal in the Company to a teacher in the school.

"What was that number?" Magda fiddled with still another cigarette.

I pushed my back against the soft cushions of the chair. "$460. But even $400 would help."

"And you need this by tomorrow?" I nodded. My scalp was tingling. "How peculiar. You have a matinee tomorrow, don't you, dear?" Again I nodded. "How very peculiar." I stared at her, tried to figure out her motives, what she knew, what she didn't. But it was no use. "And now you've lowered the sum." She shook her head, posed a finger against one of her cheeks. "Really, dear, you ought not to underbid yourself."

I stared at my bag again, quickly subtracted Lincoln's money and the remaining cash from my last paycheck. Nothing balanced.

"The Girl may be only a dream, Natalie, but she must be an authentic illusion. Do you understand?"

I shook my head. Nothing balanced, nothing computed.

"Those little *bourrées* at the end," she sang out slowly, "need to be more insistent." She eased off the divan and showed me the steps, her small feet moving quickly backward across the floor.

"Yes, I guess so." I couldn't get up the energy to interpret what she was saying. So I just watched, as if she were marking a new combination. There was something compelling about her slim controlled body dancing to the internal counts of memory. As if the message, whatever it was, were in the movement, and there only. She twirled around, lifted a pointed foot, dropped her head.

"Oh my dear," she breathed, flopping languidly across the divan. "Make the most of whatever they give you . . . it's not often very much." I kept myself still, tried to hold on to her little performance, to that fleeting image of someone I could glimpse now only over the dark chasm of the past. "Natalie, dear," she whispered, "why don't you ask Simon for a loan?"

"Don't want anything from him," I said flatly. I had to maintain control, I couldn't let her see me cry.

But Magda was persistent. She'd had a lot of experience breaking people down. "No?" Her tone was innocuous, almost speculative. "Not generous, not forthcoming?" She pressed a finger against her lips, as if urging me to secrecy, then dropped her hand. "It takes them a long time . . . if ever they do." She tugged at the hem of her skirt, until it covered her calves. "Well, I quite agree with you, dear." She crossed her legs, put both hands around her knee, and leaned back. "Don't believe it's ever wise to ask *them* for anything." Her chin was raised, her eyes staring off into the airspace above our heads.

Suddenly, she lowered her head and squinted at me. She held out a jingling braceleted arm. "Come here, Natalie." I reluctantly put down my dance bag and joined her on the divan. "You know," she said, "I told Simon to watch out for you." A flowery dressing gown hung from a hook on the closed door. My mother had one like it, except hers had come from a thrift shop and the lace around the collar was torn and yellowed. "This girl will work hard, I said. In turn, I was adamant on this account, she will help you."

"But he didn't."

She squeezed my arm. "Natalie, he's just a boy. For fun. Nothing serious. You helped him with his little *pas*, he taught you how to partner. That's the way the theater works, dear."

I stared at her hand on my arm. It was odd: her feet were tiny but her hands were large, long and bony and expressive. "I guess so," I said. "I did learn a lot about partnering."

"Yes, I should think you did." She faced me, took my hands in her own, then turned them over and studied my palms. "Dream Girls shouldn't have secrets from one another, should they, Natalie?"

"I don't know. I guess not."

"Perhaps we can arrange something. A little personal transaction. Between us. Between . . . *friends*."

I didn't know if I wanted this. But at least it was something concrete. "I'll pay you back."

"Of course you will."

So it had come to this. One Dream Girl to another. It would have to do. "I'm having an abortion tomorrow."

Magda let go of my hands, reached for one of the half-smoked cigarettes. "Well, yes," she said. Her tone was calloused. "We certainly know how that happened."

Suddenly, we both started laughing. It was as if I'd never laughed before, as if the feeling and the sound were something entirely new. I laughed until my shoulders and ribs ached and then I laughed some more. It felt so good. Magda's laughter was more controlled but her eyes sparkled and her hands fluttered. It was, I felt even then, a special moment for each of us, perhaps because, for once, we were both in on the joke. "Now, you take care of it, Natalie," she said, pulling her purse from under the divan and fishing out her checkbook, "put it behind you and get on with your life." She handed me the check. "It's the best we can do."

I looked around at the room again. Somehow, she'd made it. She was running scared, like all of us, but she'd made it. She'd escaped the Isadora-Duncan chiffon wrappings and the feathered *Swan-Lake* piety. Once she'd adorned the posters; now she ordered them. Whenever she got tired of being a wife, she took a lover or divorced Himmel or both. She had a dressing gown on the back of the door and a cocktail dress on the clothes rack. It wasn't neat, it hadn't been easy, sometimes it wasn't very nice. But she'd gotten on with it, made the best of it. "Thank you," I said. "This means a lot to me."

She was putting her checkbook back in her purse. When she looked up at me her jaw was set and her eyes hard and furtive again. "You may go," she said, and I did.

I'm a bundled floating cloud of nettles and briars. A tumbleweed, bounding aimlessly across the Painted Desert. I've never noticed the wooden coyote's head at the top of my staircase before. I reach out and touch a soft wooly doorknob. It yawns, licks my hand. Suddenly, I'm rooted in the center of my flat, gnarled and thirsty, a thousand-year-old cactus burning slowly in the scalding sunlight. Fran urges me to rest, her voice cools my skin. So I stretch out on the bed, drift and undulate in a kind of limbless twirling incomprehension. I'm vaguely aware of Lincoln's smooth dark happy voice. "Bunhead lives in a first-class dump." My arms are boneless, dripping wax. The radiator spits fire, rattles a congratulations. I'm drugged, I'm celebratory, I'm the Dream Girl. I'm no longer pregnant.

I lie on a foamy mattress, begin to connect events. After the amber stagelights, the audience, the veiled red curtains, Fran comes to the door of my dressing room. Her hair is pulled into a straggly knot, two crystal leaves dangle from her earlobes, an orange smear blots her lips, a strange black sack hangs unevenly above her knees. She's got wings made of glass. Somehow she's patched herself together for the occasion, escaped the suburban monsters, beamed down and rematerialized on my small planet. "You were good," she says. "Can I carry your dance bag home?" She reaches out, strokes the side of my face. "I'm not going straight home," I say. She smiles. "I know."

I roll over on the bed, lift my arms, let them waft down through the haze. I want to hug her but I can't, not yet, not until it's all over. Then there's Lincoln. He lopes up the corridor, tugs at the fake white beard hanging from his matinee face, eyes Fran warily. "Who's this?" she says. Bits of cotton are still stuck to Linc's skin. He juts out his lips, throws an arm around me. "Bunhead's little brother." Fran's lost her wings, the program's sweating in her hands. "Dancers," she says. "Don't you ever get the right roles?" I'm pulling hairpins from my scalp, whispering to Linc that it's all right, Fran's guarding the door. "Go on," I say to him. "She'll take care of me." Linc's shaking his head. "Already done told them I hurt my *maximus humerus*. Gotta go with you now." He's stealing the show, letting Fran know who's who. She gives him her critical eyes. "Don't need you." He puffs himself up, does his macho thing. "Hell you don't!" They look at me. I'm pulling on my coat, telling them we gotta hurry, it's rush hour, everybody comes.

My body is wrapped in a frothy tongue, safe and warm, imponderous, riding the downy waves. I'm still wearing pancake and fake lashes, my toes are bleeding beneath the Band-Aids. I've forgotten to clock out backstage. We're bumping through the traffic, hitting every red light. Linc praises the invisible world, sings gospel tunes, makes up words as he goes along. Fran keeps her eyes on the road, clamps her lips together, tells him he's got it all wrong, the only thing worth believing in are meter-maids and minimum wage. He's beginning to like her: she's so sound he can hear an echo. That's the gas tank, she says, we're running low. We double park off Union Square, sprint the last block to Chung's office. They each have one of my arms, I'm sweating mascara, shivering, giggling. The cash from Magda's check is sealed in an envelope, pinned inside my coat. I'm hidden in an oyster shell, a small pearl gleaming and hard. Hey, I think, there's seaweed in my bed.

Chung's nurse gives us the fisheye, discreetly signals me to join her behind her clipboard. Linc throws himself into a chair on the wrong side of the room, drapes his legs over the magazine-covered coffee table. Fran sits down across from him. "How come we never met," he wants to know. "Different worlds," she says, "infinitely expanding universe." The waiting room is shadowy, only a table lamp is burning. "Ain't that the truth," he says, opening up one of the magazines. I drift away, behind the nurse's clipboard, down a long dark corridor. I know I'll return different.

My toes itch but I can't reach them. "Chinese food and a gallon of Gallo," Linc is saying, "we all in the ghet-to now." He puts a greasy bag and a large bottle on the bed. Fran is smoothing back my hair, my forehead is damp and spongy. I take her hand and hold onto it, begin to feel a throb low in my sore stomach. I'm bleeding deep inside. "Scraped me out," I say. "Only took four minutes." Linc is opening the bottle. "Got some painkiller right here." Fran pulls up the sheet, tucks it under my chin. "Sleep," she whispers. She's right, I need to sleep or drift or something. "Felt like forever," I say.

There's no teddy-bear wallpaper in the abortion room. Just a big machine with flashing monster eyes and tubes hanging from the sides, an examining table with stirrups, a counter and basin. A woman is crying behind one of the other doors down the corridor. The nurse switches on a radio. Swelling strings, mellow horns, a 4/4 beat. It's an easy-listening station. I'm lying on the table in a hospital gown, staring into a flying-saucer lamp. The nurse holds my hand, says to think about pretty things, like bluebells and parades.

"Return to the living, bunhead. We got fried rice, egg rolls, wonton soup . . . " They've shot me up with a local, but all it does is make me weak. That's what they want: no sudden moves. Just like a vacuum cleaner with teeth. "Chow mein, greasy egg-fu-yong, moo shu pork . . . " Fat bands of black cover a bald spot on the top of Chung's head. I'd like to laugh, point this out, but it hurts so damn much. "Peking duck, Mongolian beef, Lake Tung-tin shrimp . . ." A soft whirring motor vibrates the room, my body. I'm cramping up, pulling inward, sinking. I want to scream. Instead, I inhale, exhale, say 'Fucking-A' over and over. I count backward to a thousand, I walk on glass, I eat thorns. Suddenly, it ends. Chung stands over me. He's wearing a green surgery mask. "Such soft skin," he says, rubbing his hand over my stomach. "Try the spare-ribs." But maybe I dream this, I don't know.

Linc sprawls on one side of the bed, pushes a stained white carton toward my curled fingers. "If you eat some of this, you get to open all the x-rated fortune cookies." I'm propped against the pillows, sliding the chopsticks up and down, dropping black mushrooms and peas all over the sheet. Fran's hanging out the window, yelling at the garbage pickers. When she pulls back from the window, Linc says, "Momma, you got some mouth on you." She walks over to him, grabs his head, gives it a Dutch rub. "Got it from scolding little boys," she says. "I'll be good, Momma," he hollers, "I'll be good." "Hell you will," she says. It's raining rice. I lose them both to the night.

Days and weeks pass, it seems, until someone comes back to this cold empty room where I'm shackled in metal straps, bleeding and raw, drifting in and out. I can't see the face . . . he's masked . . . removes something like clamps or forceps, drops a bloody strip of liver into a small pan . . . slowly moves the long way around the room . . . passes the pan right by my face. You like it, don't you? Wanna watch? Wanna see what a good girl you really are? I open my mouth to scream, but a tiny six-year-old voice comes out. "Take it away." I'm rising out of the electric chair, arms rigid and angry, clawing at the tethers. You did this to me. Go away. But everything is dark and still. I've seen my trophy and I don't want it.

Fran sits cross-legged at the helm of our boat, drinks straight from the bottle, makes complaining noises with each gulp. The curtains are pulled back. Across the street the porno theater's neon nipples are blinking furiously. I'm mesmerized, they're out of rhythm. "Gonna bomb that place," I say. Fran looks out the window, bobs her head. "You'll miss the show. They got a classic tonight." Linc slurps from a plastic container, then reaches for the wine bottle. "What's playing?" Fran walks over to the bed, readjusts the chopsticks in my hand. "*Natalie Does San Francisco*," she says. The three of us laugh, easy, connected, drifting together above the night and the mean streets. I'm coming back. Not so changed, after all. I take the wine bottle from Lincoln, let the terrible wine trickle down my throat. "Ain't America grand," I say. I've never been fuller or happier. I am the Dream Girl.

# Act Three, Scene One

The true artist will develop a sense of rhythm
complex and subtle, not just the mechanical reflex
to a downbeat, but a sense of shape and dynamism
in musical phrase and dynamism in gesture, and
an inner pulse that lies beneath all these and that
is the true life-beat.

–Agnes de Mille, *To A Young Dancer*

An intersection of tubes, wires, and bags extends
outward from Henry's body, terminates in the silent wiggling
lines of a monitoring machine. I can't read their scrolled
meanings. Small strokes have shaken and cracked him, like a
series of tremors along a faultline. Something seems to have
given way inside: he looks like an old boot folded in on itself.
I rub his good hand. The other is tied down, limp, paralyzed. He
tells me it's happened before, once while he was teaching class,
but he never thought much about it, just a slight numbing of his
body, a streak of pain running from his shoulder to his ribs, an

under-the-weather sort of glum. "How are *you* feeling, old heart?"

I squeeze his fingers, reach for one of the books stacked under the night table next to his bed. After two days in Intensive Care, he's been tucked away in a semi-private room. There's an old man with wild tufts of white hair propped up in the other bed. A major earthquake has struck him: he doesn't move his body at all, just sleeps, or stares at a nail in the bare wall beyond the foot of his bed. His outlook wasn't always so barren; his wife removed the Norman Rockwell print. Usually, she sits primly on a chair next to the bed, clutches a small black handbag with a gold clasp. When she comes into the room, she takes off her white gloves and folds them neatly in the purse. She puts them on again to go eat in the hospital cafeteria. When she leaves, I pull the shades down; she draws them up again when she comes back. "Me?" I say almost buoyantly. I open the book, hoping Henry will forget.

But this is one of the few things he hangs on to, a lifeline as the earth collapses beneath him. "Both of you," he says, peering at me with hollow pale eyes. I've seen those eyes before, along the railroad tracks in Indiana. Some farmer shot a hunting dog by mistake. I heard the rifle crack, then the howling squeal, then saw him fall. I got to him before the farmer did. He was an old hound dog, black and grey, with floppy ears, a mangy coat, and a heaving belly spurting blood. He looked up at me with astonished yellow eyes rapidly emptying out, as if to say, "What's happening, where am I going?" I wanted to bend down and stroke his head, tell him it would be all right, but I was scared to touch him.

"Fine . . . everything's good." My face is cooled by the lie, I'm relieved he can't see the truth. The room is veiled, protective. The lady next door has put on her gloves, gone for coffee. I don't know how to tell Henry there's only one of me. I don't think I should.

"When I'm stronger," he begins, "we'll get things in order." He glances up at the ceiling, closes his eyes, wets his lips. He's having a hard time forming the words, as if something dry and round is stuck in his throat. He sinks back into himself; speaking exhausts him. I begin reading Russian history aloud, but I can't pronounce the names. After a while, I simplify things, call everyone Stravinsky or Pavlova. Henry flutters his hand briefly, doesn't want me to struggle through the past. "Next time . . . bring poetry."

He drifts off. I shove the book back under the table, stare at the monitor. The room smells plastic and cold, like carnations kept too long in refrigeration. "I'm doing a new ballet," I say.

"What's that?" He perks up a little, though one half of his mouth droops to the side.

"You know, modern style." I smooth his hair. "Just lighting, bodies, and counts." I take his hand again. "Music's by John Cage." His hand is thin and soft, as though there are no bones left. "I don't know if you'd like it."

"You're dancing, old heart?" He speaks from some other place, travels the long solitary distance between his spasms and a concern for me. His eyes are shut again.

"I'm okay, Henry." My voice is definite. What I really want to say is, "Let's give up this charade. We both should know I'm not going to have a baby." But I won't say this. I'm committed to playing my role in a fantasy he needs to believe in.

A nurse barges into the room, carrying a medicine tray. Her name tag has come unpinned, hangs from a white collar. She's already thinking up a reason for me to go, I can see it in her eyes. "Mr. Pershing, you should be sleeping." Her tone is grainy, tired, pushing at extremes. Her shift is almost over, she just wants to get out of here.

I stand, haul my dance bag up to my shoulder, bend down, kiss Henry on his icy cheek. "Tomorrow," I whisper. "Poetry." His eyes flicker for a moment, a small flash of recognition passes across his face. The nurse is stooped over her tray, squinting at the pill cups.

He offers me the uninjured side of his face, rubs his good hand over my stomach. "The locks on the studio," he worries.

He drops his hand back onto the bedside, kneads the sheet between his fingers. "And the mail."

As I've done each day since Henry's been ill, I assure him I'm taking care of things. But I'm barely coping. I'm on express all the way, flying between rehearsals, performances, the hospital. Henry doesn't know this, but Lincoln's been going out to the studio every day, making the phone calls, gathering the mail, clipping the shrubs. Linc's got the time, they've been giving him some small parts and lightened his apprentice schedule a little. He's not sure what this means.

The nurse cups Henry by the neck, helps him swallow his pills. One of them is large and orange. He has trouble getting it down; the end of the pill is sticking out of his mouth. "Mr. Pershing," the nurse admonishes, "we can do better than that." He tries again, it disappears. "Now, that's a good boy," she says. I blow him a kiss from the doorway but he doesn't see me. He's pleased that he's taken the nurse's correction so well and he's straining to smile. The right side of his face rises but the paralyzed left side droops. The smile line looks like a sliding board.


Henry was hospitalized opening night of the new run, ten days after I'd had the abortion. At first, I was dancing in several pieces, nothing major, mostly technical parts. Then one of the principals got injured and I was called to replace her in the new ballet. I finally had a picture in the program, my own dressing room, a fifty-dollar raise. I didn't even have to perform every night. These were, as Linc said, "small rewards for being a stupid bunhead." The second night, during intermission, a bouquet of strange tropical flowers was delivered to my dressing room. There wasn't any note, and the messenger boy didn't speak English. The flowers were ugly, odd, and wild, like something from another planet. They had bruised-blue stamens and leathery yellow-speckled spikes. I didn't like them.

## Act Three, Scene One

At first, I suspected Simon, but this seemed unlikely. He was too busy changing partners, he didn't want to have anything to do with me. And he knew I had no interest in him. Henry was in critical condition and Linc was broke. There wasn't anyone else. I had a dimestore fishing-gear box that I used as a make-up case; I'd covered it with varnish and then pasted on cut-ups of dance words and pictures. I hid the flowers behind this. The third night, I slipped on stage, broke rhythm, lost my composure. I'd been with Henry most of the afternoon, I wasn't thinking. A bundle of livid discolored flowers with rectangular terminal ears appeared at my dressing-room door. This time a cramped note accompanied the flowers. I couldn't read the writing, it looked like Latin. I threw out the first gift of alien flowers, arranged the new impostors in a vase. I stuck the card in the siding of my mirror.

I wasn't exactly prepared for the new Cage piece. On stage I tried to adapt my classical training to the modern movements, but I spent most of my time searching for lost counts, wandering through the other dancers' complicated designs, improvising during those long gaps in memory. Off stage I obsessed. All of the solid soloists and principals who were at least familiar with this ballet were on tour in Brussels; there really wasn't anyone around to coach me in the role or explain the meaning of the steps and the timing. Besides, if someone like that had been available, they wouldn't have given me the part in the first place. A new soloist almost never got the chance to carry a ballet on her own.

The twelve other dancers in the piece made up the ensemble. They couldn't help me, they had their own problems. Even the choreographer was long gone, already in New York with a different company. I was also pushing myself against something larger and even more consuming than this, but I didn't know what it was. All I knew then was that everything seemed to be changing and that I wasn't who I thought I was, or perhaps, that I hadn't thought much about who I was and, now that I was thinking about it, I realized I was out of practice. Anyway, after curtain the third night, Magda swept backstage, trilled out her disappointment in us, and scheduled extra rehearsals. This was a Company. We were dancers. She was determined to set things right.

The rehearsal room was closed and sweating, relieved only by the smudged wall-length mirrors and two dingy windows. Slim shafts of late-afternoon March light fell across the scuffed floor. The portable *barres* were pushed against the back wall, draped with soggy practice-clothes and towels. The ensemble sat along the sides, drinking from thermoses, whispering diet secrets, knitting leg warmers, spooning runny heaps of yogurt into their mouths—and watching me. Rising on point, I shot across the room in vibrating short steps, counted to myself, then collapsed flat on my stomach and rolled up through my body. Magda clapped her hands: the music stopped, and I froze.

"No, no, *no*, Natalie!" Her sharply defined face jerked up and down. She was pacing the floor at the front of the room. Behind her was a benched wooden audience of board members and Company supporters. They were observing the rehearsal, and she was playing to them as well as directing us. "Phrasing," she lectured, glancing sternly at me and then complicitly at them, "is the essence of modern music." As the perched patrons nodded their heads, I got up and marked through the movement again. No doubt thrilled to have captivated them—obviously, I hadn't mastered this concept—Magda clenched her hand in a tight ball, then opened her fingers, as though releasing something. "You see," she intoned, as if imparting the secret of life, "it's in the counts, the silences, those little moments that separate conception from execution." She squeezed her eyes shut, sighed profoundly, paraded before the audience. "We must learn," she said, spreading her long fingers and holding them out in front of her, "we must learn to dance the gaps *between* the notes." I tried not to take any of this too personally.

In any event, Magda didn't sustain this reverie very long. Suddenly, the notes became fingers again and the gaps were closed abruptly by a loud handclap directed at the drummer, cymbalist, and pianist, who were slumped together in the corner muttering away because this was non-union piecework and it was starting to get dark. They reluctantly stopped talking and leaned back to their instruments. "Second movement from the top," she announced, eyes flashing. The audience sighed, the drummer swore, the ensemble groaned. I limped across to the tensely postured dancers on the right side of the room and began rehearsing the counts internally. "That drummer's stoned," one of the *corps* girls whispered. I ignored her. I knew they were blaming me for unpaid overtime, bleeding muscles, another lost afternoon. They'd be looking for some way of getting even. I stared at my feet, two disobedient creatures with willful arches throbbing beneath the dirty satin. I wasn't sure how I was supposed to behave, what kind of attitude to take. But I knew I couldn't trust the ensemble. To hell with them, I'd count it my own way.

I thrust my arms out like stiff wings, as if to rise on the howling wind of the nightmare music. The two women in front of me jammed their feet into the floor, preparing for flight. In four counts I was pushing through the rhythm—a ritualistic medley of drumbeats and cymbals, odd ringing scrapes that jarred me first in one direction, then in another. I couldn't count it, my body wouldn't respond. I felt as though I were dancing between the metal concave plates themselves. Once again, Magda clapped her hands. As the musical wind died down, she swept to the center of the room, her philosophical fingers already shaped into notes and gaps. Suddenly, she looked past us to the audience—and froze mid-movement, like a cat caught in the middle of an open field. Her hands closing into tight fists, she spoke just to us, quietly and rapidly, without intonation—

"Girls, you aren't with the music"—then crept unobtrusively back to the piano.

As we walked over to our starting places, we could all see the brittle lean body of Mr. Pristie, the composer, slipping in among the restless knotted audience. Pristie's brooding presence made everyone uncomfortable, even Magda. We all knew the story: a descendant of old San Francisco wealth and connection, he'd once produced a strange brilliant score that had briefly given Bay City an avant-garde reputation. That was almost ten years ago. Pristie had offered the Company nothing since, although he was rumored to be working on something that would turn music and dance upside-down or inside-out, and that would probably unsettle our comfortable story-ballet audience even more than his first one had. People said he worked in mysterious and miserly ways. Apparently, he composed through the dancers themselves, somehow extracted the music note by strange note right from their bodies. In any event, all this really made no difference. His name alone mattered. Attached a century ago to a jumped mining claim and then a stolen railroad, it prompted now a not-altogether different kind of fear and respect among the archangels who supported the Bay City Ballet. Magda tolerated him because she had to.

"Five minutes," she said tonelessly. The musicians stayed behind their instruments, as if on guard. The audience remained quiet, attentive. A couple of the girls standing behind me tittered nervously. Pristie's tongue shot between his bloodless lips and curled back against his front teeth. I walked off to the side, wrapped some leg warmers around my spasming back. Magda *chasséd* around the piano, flipped through choreography notes, sipped from her coffee mug, muttered to the drummers. Every so often she'd take a cool sharp view of Pristie, who was fumbling with the buttons of his wool cardigan. Finally, she rapped softly on the piano hood and hiked up her eyebrows for the pianist to begin again.

## Act Three, Scene One

It was the ensemble's turn now. Momentarily free of Cage's music, I leaned against one of the *barres*, concentrated on breathing, tried to focus on the other dancers. Their movements too seemed unrhythmical, over-rehearsed, uninspired. Magda paced the small strip in front of the piano, counting under her breath. My entrance was coming up again. Inevitably, I glanced once more at Pristie: tight lips, tapping foot, a dismissive tuck around his sooty eyes. He certainly didn't doubt anything. He lived and walked alone, carried a pile of yellowing composition papers, never smiled. I counted up to thirty-two, watched Pristie roll the buttons back and forth under his fingers, cursed my rhythm, then plunged my body into the ballet.

But I still couldn't count it. I threw myself around the room, accidently touched fingers with a passing *corps* girl, bumped into a bundle of legs, somehow managed to successfully execute a controlled jazz turn on point, then promptly lost the music again. The notes were running across the floor, like mice. I couldn't keep up with them. The room was spinning around me. Two of the male dancers, faces rankled with exhaustion, dragged their back legs behind them, scraping blistered arches against the floor. I wound up in front of Pristie, almost in his lap. His eyes were weightless carbon particles; his lips held back the judgment. But I knew the verdict just the same. I was just a silly bunhead, but he was the thing itself, the measure of privilege, the gap between the notes from which the music and the counts mysteriously emerged. Another count slipped under me. I backed up miserably and came to a stop.

"That's fine," Magda said weakly. We both knew it wasn't. It was a mess. But Magda was determined to shine now that Pristie was here. "Natalie," she mewed, "why don't you double up that last movement, add a bit of your dashing style."

"Right," I mumbled to myself. I'd watched Pristie come and go for months. He'd slip through the glass doors of the musty old school building, give a cursory nod to the front desk, climb the marble staircase. His head would be bent, his shoulders curved, his footsteps heavy and even as he rose to the top. He wasn't going to be impressed, or fooled, by a bit of dashing style. In fact, nothing impressed him, nothing moved him, except the soundless echo of his own strange interior music. Not much to build on there. So to hell with him too. I'd find *some* way to count it.

The music picked up again. Magda was tapping her hand against her chest, mouthing the rhythm. One of the girls fell out of line but continued to dance alone in the center of the room. She rolled her hips seductively with the drums, extended her trembling fingers, as though reaching out to the audience. Again, Magda rattled her hands. "We won't have any of *that*," she chastised. The desperate girl slunk back into line but sneaked a flirtatious smile at Pristie. He, of course, ignored her. Even so, the room was damp and throttled with tension, every member of the ensemble competing now for a glance, a smile, a nod. The guys were strutting differently, the girls removed rehearsal clothes and reapplied lipstick. The rehearsal was spinning on its own axis, beyond Magda, beyond Cage, beyond the dance. "With the music, *again*." Magda's voice was wooden and plodding, like a stuck piano key.

Once more we moved with the discords, immersed our bodies in the antimusical measures. Magda was beating the counts mechanically now, one arm rising and falling irregularly, like a tollbooth gate. Feeling as though my knees were on backwards, I ground my teeth together, thrust out my ribcage, pushed my resistant body forward. At precisely that moment, Pristie rose from the bench and crept over the row of lazy legs blocking his path. He whispered something to Magda, who, startled by the sound of his voice, forgot to drop her arm. The music howled on but the counts just floated away again, drifting aimlessly in the air above Magda's head, then plummeting down in a confused heap at the stoned drummer's sneakered feet. As Pristie disappeared behind the door, Magda clasped her hands together and glided to the center of the floor.

Act Three, Scene One

"Well," she sighed, "we know where the gaps are. Now let's see if we can find the notes." The audience stirred, as though surprised and delighted to have been delivered unharmed from the dead.

"I have an admirer," I say, placing yesterday's wilting Yucca plant on the night table. "Sends me flowers every performance." Slats of light filter through the hospital window, fall warmly across the bed. The neighbor lady's keeping vigil. Henry's been cranked up for an hour, somewhere between sitting and reclining. A catheter bag hangs over one side of the bed.

"That's something, old heart." He really does seem pleased. "You're getting a following."

"Any requests?"

Henry looks at me sideways, runs his eyes over my body. "Baby's breath." He offers me his sliding-board smile. "Old World perennial, aren't they?"

I'm getting used to living with partial truths. "I'll have to ask," I say. "Maybe they're out of season."

"Oh, you needn't worry, everything grows in this climate." He coughs a little, looks over at his neighbor. The man is still staring at the wall, but a row of sunlight has fallen across his face and he squints ever so slightly. Maybe this is why his wife always opens the shades. I pick up Wordsworth and begin to read aloud, "For I have learned / To look on nature, not as in the hour / Of thoughtless youth; but hearing oftentimes / The still, sad music of humanity…"

A few days later, I took Magda the extra fifty dollars from my paycheck. She was just on her way out of her dressing room, swooshing down the hallway in a perfumed blur of creamy immaculate clothes. She looked semi-approachable, so I went

127

right up to her and tried to hand her the cash. "Ah, but Natalie, you needn't be so hasty," she demurred. She pressed a finger to her lips and stared at me thoughtfully. Her eyes glittered, like two hard-set amethysts. Then she quickly scanned my body. "You've been looking. . . in form. Even if you can't count it."

I decided I wouldn't let her get to me. "Thanks. Actually, I'm doing just fine."

Magda inched up one of her eyebrows, pulled her shoulders into a perfectly straight line. "You know, dear, fifty dollars here and there is so, well, so *desultory* a way of repaying a debt."

I shifted my dance bag from my shoulder to the floor, stared into her stony face. "It's all I have right now."

She suddenly reached out, gripped my chin, jerked my head up toward the ceiling light. "Hmm," she rhapsodized. I didn't trust this at all but her grip was strong. "Hmm, hmmm, *hmmmm*." She dropped my face. I could still feel her fingers on my skin. Now her tone was casual, as if she were speaking more to herself than to me. "Though, of course, Jared might wish to utilize only an arm or a leg, or even just an elbow." She sighed, patted the sides of her neck. "An *artist*, you know. Quite unpredictable."

"I've done some posing before."

"*Really?*" Her mouth drew in at the sides, as though repressing laughter. "Well, my dear. Call Jared. Tell him Magda sent you." She glanced at her studded wristwatch, made a clucking sound low in her throat. "Ah, before I forget, Mr. Pristie was asking about you." She pronounced his name with a noticeable wince.

"Oh?" I was still trying to get my mind around the Jared business. "Why's that?"

Magda stepped into me, rested her cool fingers on my wrist. "Seems he's *quite* taken with you." Her nervous eyes cased the hallway, belied a calculated yawn. "Most disagreeable person, really."

"I guess so," I said, pulling my hand away from hers.

"Stay clear of him, dear," she whispered. She crossed her hands on her chest and shuddered. "Cold as a slate. Everything in order." Her voice broke rhythm. "I imagine," she began, " . . . well, never mind . . ." She pointed her powdered chin east, preparing for take-off. "Explore the more lucrative enterprise, Natalie."

"But who is he?"

"*Pristie?*" Her upper lip was almost touching her nose, as though catching whiff of some terrible odor.

"No," I assured her. "Jared."

Looking relieved, she reassumed her tight composure. "Photographer, my dear. For the Company."

"Where do I find him?"

"Oh, here and there." She was now talking over her shoulder, making quick butterfly steps down the hall. "Front desk will direct you his way."

So I went to poor arthritic Harry, who was balanced, as usual, on a wobbly stool beside the Master Ledger at the front desk. He was fussing over electricity and enrollment and overlapped rehearsal time, one hand wrapped around the perpetually ringing telephone. "Don't know it," he said, when I bothered him for Jared's number. I leaned over the desk and spread my hand across the ledger. "Of course, you do," I insisted. He gave me his eel eyes and shimmied on the stool. "I'm busy now. Columns don't balance. Can't be bothered." I glanced at the ledger: he used aquamarine ink for assets, shocking pink for debits. All the figures were beautifully formed. "Those are pretty numbers, Harry, very pretty numbers." He leaned back on his stool. "Do you think so? I use them every Spring. It's my seasonal adjustment." He smiled at his little joke; his teeth had huge gaps in them. I smiled back. "Really, Harry," I said, shades of Magda wafting through my tone, "it's a *small* favor." He shrugged, then flipped through a spinning index-card holder. Wetting one of his fingertips, he squinted over his reading glasses and primly counted off the numbers. I copied them down with his pink pen. "See, Harry," I said, "more pretty numbers." He waved me off. "Yes, yes, now go away, go away. I'm busy. Columns don't balance. I'm not your service, you know." It was an unimportant victory, but I was beginning to learn how to get what I wanted.

I slipped out of my black unitard and wrapped myself in a yellow cloth robe, then propped open the door to my dressing room. All of us did this, not so much to welcome the stream of voyeuristic strangers, but because we couldn't bear to be cut off from each other, alone behind a closed door with a million sensations buzzing through our bodies. The impersonal chatter of the backstage audience would drift down the hallway, temporarily connect with this unglamorous, more authentic part of ourselves, and create the necessary distance between the ballet and self-identity. Stripped of our costumes, make-up, choreographed movements, we weren't very exciting. In fact, most of us looked like garbage heaps, slouched down in chairs, sprawled across sofas, mindlessly fixated on some chore we wanted to do that night when we got home. We bled, we sweated, we swore. What we wanted were jars of cold cream, names of *sushi* bars and hamburger dives, the lyrics from a popular song, a hot bath and a glass of beer. Amidst all this were the people who just had to come tell you how well you'd danced, just had to have their programs signed, just wanted to take a look, make sure you were real.

I sat in the fold-out chair, began to cut the ribbons from my tights. I'd sewn myself into my shoes and now they were useless—too soft to make it through the Sunday matinee. Bringing my legs up to my chest, I hugged my knees and contracted into a tired but comfortable huddle. I stared into the mirror, dabbed at the eyeliner tracks, wiped my lips off on the sleeve of my robe. I was almost seventeen. I counted the years slowly and automatically, a ritual I now practiced after each performance, as though I couldn't quite believe where I was or how long I'd been moving this way. It calmed me to count. This was, in a way, my own private music.

Of course, I still couldn't find a comfortable place in Cage's music, but Magda's relentless rehearsing had at least taught me the movements. I'd even received a reasonable review, which I'd carefully cut out, photocopied, sent home to my mother. I was saving the original to read to Henry. Gradually, the tingling dull feeling in my limbs was being replaced by a spongy relaxed energy; my blotched skin was fading back to its usual pale color; the echoing voices that pursued me as I danced, directing me through each movement and count, were receding. Finally, there was silence inside me, a feeling of communion with the bright room, the hard chair, the soft hem of my robe.

Mr. Pristie seemed to step out of the mirror. I was so relaxed I hardly reacted. He was carrying a gnarled thorny orange growth with bleeding leaves. It had to be the strangest plant I'd ever seen. And it was apparently all mine. He placed the thing carefully next to the sink, then pulled out an extra chair from under the counter and sat down. He wore a buttoned overcoat and leather gloves. I didn't bother standing, I figured it was going to be his show. Besides, I was rather enjoying this.

Pristie leaned forward from the waist and handed me a small business card. His face was neatly pleated, like a white pillow-case dangling from a clothespin. I took the card, turned it over, recognized the cramped handwriting. "Thank you, for the plants," I said. "They're very . . . odd." I don't know why I said this. I guess because it felt good to tell the truth.

Pinching his lips together, he straightened back, then tugged at the edges of his gloves. "I grow them." His sooty eyes curled, as though they knew a dirty secret.

"Well, they're unusual."

"You think so?" He was watching me carefully. "I'll show you the others Saturday."

I tucked my robe under me. "Huh?" I was really feeling perverse.

He cupped his hands, as if catching water, then flattened his palms together. "Will seven be appropriate?" His voice was exact and measured, as if unaccustomed to speech.

"Mr. Pristie," I said, "I appreciate your gifts." I paused, tried to think out what I wanted to say, though I wasn't at all certain what I should do. "And it's an awfully nice invitation," I continued. "But I can't. I've already got plans."

He rose from the seat, motioned for me to join him. I didn't want to, but I did. "Monday," he said. "Your evening off." He was very precise.

I leaned against the counter, folded my arms. "What's this about?"

"Music," he clipped. He wasn't smiling. He wasn't even looking at me. "You're the music."

"Oh." So he liked my weird counts. I felt kind of sorry for him. "Well, I'm certainly not Cage's."

Suddenly, his tongue darted out and flicked his upper lip. Then he began wrapping his eyes around my neck in quick dizzying circles. This was even stranger. I wanted to laugh but didn't. Then, more oddly yet, he smiled. It was brief and awkward, certainly not very warm, but I suppose it had to count as a genuine attempt. I gave him my best smile in return and hoped he would go away.

He walked stiffly to the open door, rotated his head, again stared at me with his distant eyes. "Address is on the card." I stared right back at him. "Seven *is* appropriate." The whole thing seemed ridiculous. "Telephone me if you aren't coming."

"Sure," I said. "I'll try to make it." This lie didn't even convince me. I shrugged, placed the card on the counter. He was still standing there, as though waiting for me to say something more. "Maybe," I offered, "you ought to find someone else." But Pristie had heard all he wanted to hear. As he backed out of the room, he kept his eyes focused on some invisible point floating above my head, as if I were no longer there—or anywhere. It was too much. I reached up and grabbed the air, then took a few steps toward him and held out my closed fist to him. I figured two could play this game. He stared at my extended hand, as though he expected that somehow I really had rolled the world up into a ball. It was only after I slowly uncurled my hand, spread my fingers, and showed him what wasn't there, that he finally turned and went silently away.

"Magda said you might need a dancer." Jared's secretary had just pointed me through a set of swinging glass doors and into a small bright studio. There wasn't much in it but a white backdrop and a snake-like tangle of wires, cords, and tripods. A small man in tight jeans crouched over a black leather bag, riffling through camera lenses.

"Okay, honey, just take off your clothes and lie down in front of the drop. I'll be with you in a sec." He didn't even look up.

Over the phone his secretary had sounded indifferent and rushed, but Magda's name had secured an appointment for the next morning. I'd forgotten to ask what I should bring, so I'd taken my Program head shot, several changes of coordinated practice-clothes, and the Dream-Girl costume, which Carabee had reluctantly loaned out only after I'd signed a document nearly promising to disembowel myself on stage if I lost or ruined it. In any event, I hadn't expected this, or, if I had, not so abruptly. So I just stood still and waited.

After a minute or two, Jared glanced over his shoulder. His straight black hair was pulled across the top of his head and wetted down. It looked like he was wearing a wig. "You gonna change or what?" His voice was harsh, impatient.

I leaned against a fold-out chair, wrapped my fingers nervously around my dance bag. "I'm with the Company," I said, as if correcting a misapprehension.

THE BODY OF DANCERS

THE BODY OF DANCERS

"Yeh, I know. Magda sent you." He took a lens out of the bag and began screwing it into one of the cameras hanging around his neck. I was still leaning there staring at him when he slowly straightened up and turned around. "Look," he said, placing his palms on his small hips, "you gonna do this or not?"

"What are we doing?"

"Jesus," he said under his breath, shaking his head. "I'm shooting, you're posing."

"I know, but—"

"—but, you're a *dancer*, with the *Company*." He was mocking me now. "And you've never been paid to display your body."

"Well, yes, but—"

"—but you were wearing your snowsuit and rubber booties." He blew in through his mouth. "Come on, honey, this is a job. You take your clothes off, I shoot some of your body parts, the secretary hands you a check, you go home and watch *Sesame Street*."

"Body parts?"

"Shit." He threw a hand in the air. "Didn't Magda tell you what I'm doing here?"

"Sort of. Not really."

He balanced on his heels, looked up at the ceiling. "Oh great. Okay, look, I'm putting together an exhibit, a serious gallery show, called 'Body Parts.' Thousands of photographs of individual body parts. Knees, elbows, shoulders, thighs, feet, ears, you know, the whole *shmeer*, naughty bits too. Then I put them back together again," he smiled, a little tight smile, "but *my* way."

"What for?"

He took several steps towards me, lowered his voice. I saw for the first time that he had a wispy little mustache, a gently arcing thin black line belying the jagged curves of his upper lip. "Art, honey."

"That's art?" The whole thing seemed morbid and dull, not very enlightening.

"Bet your ass. Dismember. Remember. What else does the artist do?"

"I . . . I don't know. I thought it had something to do with ideas, history, responsibility."

He laughed. "Yeh, sure. Look, honey, I'm losing time and you're losing money here. Let's get to it, okay?"

As I removed my clothes, I thought of those double-jointed pink inflated dolls, the kind that are boxed in cellophane and crowd the department-store aisles around Christmas time. When you pull a cord their plaintive mouths move in jerks, crying "Mama, Mama." When I was down to my underwear and bra, I wrapped my arms around my torso and edged over to the drop. Why did I go this far? I guess partly because I wanted to believe Magda. She'd said Jared was an artist. I think, too, I just did what was expected. I'd learned to numb out, like a real professional, leaving my feelings behind, as if they weren't an authentic part of me. But nothing felt real, least of all Jared. He patrolled the perimeter of the white matting, appraising my body with expressionless eyes. "Okay, okay, I'll take what I can get. Now turn around, honey, give me your back."

I faced the bare white wall, tried to imagine myself in some other place and just drifted, only vaguely aware of the camera's pitiless snaps. "Holy Shit, great back!" Yes, I'd been told this before. It was my best feature as a dancer, my own odd center of balance. "You ballet dancers sure got definition. Put your hands over your head, honey. Oh, wow, fabulous lumbars. Don't move. Just flex." I held up my arms, stared blankly at the backdrop. All I had to do was get through this, be a good girl, pay off Magda. It was all the same to her. "Turn to the left, honey. Need a side view of those ribs. Yeh, that's it, good." The camera clicked and whirred, clicked and whirred. I really wasn't anywhere. I just followed Jared's instructions mechanically, as if this were happening to someone else. "Okay, now lie down. Stretch out on your side. Big stretch, honey, *stretch* those ribs for me."

I lowered myself to the floor, rested my head on my wrist, pointed my toes to lengthen the rib line. With my free arm I covered my chest. Jared walked over and straddled me, spread his hands in front of him, squinted his eyes. "Honey, you're going to be the star of my rib collage." Great. All the dieting was finally going to pay off. He started shooting again, moving the camera closer and closer to my body. "Flex it, flex it!" he kept saying.

We went on this way for about an hour. He also liked my calves and upper arms. "Charlies and pecs," he called them. "Love your charlies and pecs. You ballet dancers got great charlies and pecs." After a while it got real hot under the lights and I started to sweat. He liked that too, liked it so much he started doing super close-ups of drops and rivulets. "Goddam," he kept saying, switching his cameras, twirling his dials, scrambling around next to me on the mat, "goddam." I just closed my eyes and tried to pretend I wasn't there. It didn't help much.

Finally, he was finished. As I slipped into my jeans and stuffed my head through the opening in my sweater, he was counting the rolls of film strewn all over the mat. "—21, 22, 23. Twenty-three. That's a good haul." He flashed that tight little smile again, the upward curves of his lips pressing against the unyielding little mustache. "Even if you wouldn't go all the way."

"Do I get paid now?" I asked.

"Yeh, sure. See the secretary."

"I've got something to say."

"Yeh, I knew you would. Go ahead, honey. Give me your words of wisdom. Tell me to fuck off. I don't care. I got your parts."

I picked up my dance bag. "When I walk out this door I'll still be a dancer."

"Oh, wow, that really hurts. What's the kicker? What will I be, huh, what will I be? Come on, honey, give it up. I've heard it all. I'm immune."

"You said it." And then I walked out through the swinging doors, picked up my check, and went home. Oh sure, there were other things I wanted to say, if I had thought of them, if they would have made any difference. But I hadn't, and they wouldn't have. What it really came down to was a business transaction. Jared had his twenty-three rolls of film and my body parts; I had his money and my silence. That's the way those things usually work out. At least Carabee could rest easy: the Dream-Girl costume was still safe in my dance bag.

Depicted on the soft pink and blue baby blanket are pastel building blocks, rattles, round smiling infants. "It's very sweet," I say. But I feel rotten. Henry's given money to the neighbor lady, asked her to buy something in the hospital gift shop for his expectant granddaughter. Now she sits in the corner eying me severely, twisting the leather handle of her purse. She's forgotten to remove her white gloves. "Here, feel how soft it is," I whisper, slipping the satin edges of the blanket under Henry's veiny fingers. The excitement has tired him. Most of the shape is gone from his face, as though even his bones have collapsed.

Lunch is unsuccessful. Puréed diet, nothing solid, everything boiled and strained. The green-cubed Jell-O is rubbery. He doesn't like the food, spits it out behind the nurse's relentless back, pushes it under his pillow, hides it in his good hand. At least there's one less tube running from his body. Says he wants a bottle of apricot brandy, don't sell it downstairs, has the craving. Sneaking a piece of chocolate between his lips, I tell him I'll see what I can do. Most of it ends up on his chin. I wipe it off with my hand. "One of us has got to be civil," I say. This makes him laugh.

We don't talk much. We're both waiting for something to change. Or we play tug-of-war with his night-dreams, pull at the broken images, search through seventy years of living for some immediate meaning. I ignore the obvious, but Henry's too smart for this. He doesn't understand my reluctance to make plans, my silence, my restraint. He's counting on me to see him through this, wherever it goes. "I drew up a will," he finally says, after one of the nurses has swept away the tray, "a few days before this happened." His tone is speculative, as though he believes there's some connection between the two things. Perhaps there is, but I don't like to think so.

"Oh." I touch his hand, press my fingers against his.

He turns his head, rests one side of his cheek on the pillow, slides a crooked smile my direction. "Everything's in your name."

My heart swells up, not because I want these things but because it seems so final, so permanent, so real. He can't die, he's all I have. This is one of the voices that rolls around inside me, the one that gets tangled up with God and my parents and all those other points of disconnection. The other voice is a hard-wired torch that burns right through the walls. You've always known this. Something dying there when you met him. You have to accept it. "My sweet man," I say, closing my eyes so he can't see me cry. "It wasn't necessary." He doesn't respond. I tilt my head, listen to his quiet breathing. He's already faded out, returned to his sleeping dreams. I watch him for a few minutes, then release his hand. I've just realized how tightly I've been holding on.

# Act Three, Scene Two

The dancer becomes the plastic material of the art impulse, the physical brain through which someone else thinks. It is almost as intimate and exquisite a function as love-making.

–Agnes de Mille, *To A Young Dancer*

I contemplate Pristie's unreal estate from behind a black iron gate on the deep edge of the Richmond District. The house, a formless indistinct mass wrapped in the day's dying shadows, is set back, orphaned from everyone and everything. It seems to mock its own existence, like Pristie, like San Francisco. It's after seven; I'm late, a fluctuating body suspended between my time and his. Now that I'm here, I'm not so sure I want to be. I don't know why I've come. I try the barred gate, it won't budge; I press the sweating bell, I wait. The gate swings open on its own, slowly, silently. Once inside the bars,

# THE BODY OF DANCERS

I walk against the last light of sunset. The driveway curls through misty green flatland, then veers suddenly and sharply to the top of a steep cliff. I teeter on the edge of the world, held back only by the tragic drum-beat of the Pacific breaking against the continental shelf and the inexorable rhythmic progress of the gnarled twilight. It's as though I'm the only witness to this joining of day and night, my private equinox. I could never have dreamed this moment, this place, because they shouldn't exist, not for me, not here. Perhaps this is why I've accepted Pristie's invitation.

As the horizon disappears, I step back from the edge and follow the question-mark curve of the driveway around to a lighted brass doorknob, the only solid evidence that a house, a dwelling, fills this nocturnal space. There is no bell, no knocker. The doorknob is spherical and huge, the size of a bowling ball. I turn it with both hands, but even so, nothing happens. I twist around, look back the way I have come. The driveway, the cliff, the sea, sky, and grounds are gone. There is only the darkness. A hand touches my shoulder. I pivot and jump back. It's Pristie. He's standing in the doorway, his hands together in front of his chest as if ready to play 'here is the church, here is the steeple.' He's combed his reddish hair back flat, slicked it down with gel. "You are late," he says. "I knew you would be."

I can't say I haven't been warned. Magda winces at the mention of his name, whispers her admonitions. Lincoln claims he makes no reflection in mirrors, sleeps in a coffin lined with black velvet. Fran thinks he's freaky evil, one of those hyper-sonic types only San Francisco breeds. I haven't even told Henry about him. Just inside the doorway, above an electric candle, is an austere oil painting of a bearded man in a double-breasted suit, a bow tie, and a high upturned collar. Like Pristie, he has slicked back reddish hair and a massive forehead. His beard is magnificent, red, yellow, brown, spilling down over his mouth and chin and neck like a waterfall. He is turned slightly to his left and his eyes, deep set and black, stare off past us. He stands perfectly erect, his shoulders balanced exactly over his legs. There is nothing else in the painting, no background, no foreground, just this enormous human presence completely filling the frame. "My grandfather," Pristie says, standing off to the side of it, "the robber baron."

The portrait is almost mesmerizing. I follow its expectant gaze out of the frame, into the dark shadows of the entrance foyer. "Did he build this house?"

"Once upon a time. But I tore it down. Primitive splendor. Nevertheless, his spirit presides." He touches my elbow. "Come. I'll show you the greenhouse." He leads me down a dark narrow corridor, then another, and still another. There are no other pictures, no decoration or ornamentation of any kind in this solemn labyrinth. Just the same dark textured wallpaper everywhere and, at regular intervals, a small electric candle perched on the end of an iron bracket. Finally, Pristie stops under one of the candles and pushes against the wall. Cold artificial light and warm humid air rush through the unseen door.

The greenhouse is a seething orderly glass-roofed kingdom of peat spades and hand rakes, seedboxes and hoses, neatly stacked bags of dirt and fertilizer—and row after row of weird growths. There are green wiry things sprouting multi-colored tentacles, fat bulbous plants bristling thorns, exotic lush creepers studded with breathing eyes. Pristie shifts sideways, a hermit crab scuttling across silent seas. "Do you like them?" he whispers.

There's a strain to his voice, a kind of urgency pushing out the words. I think he wants me to feel uncomfortable. So I point to a scrawny oozing stalk, the ugliest thing I can find. "That's really something," I say.

Pristie's eyes follow my arm, then drop off at the edge of my extended finger. He studies the plant's brown leaves intently. "It's a hybrid. Took me seven years to grow it. I've named it *Vigilantia Abjecta*." He looks at me, anticipates my incomprehension. "Watchfulness debased," he translates. He runs his hand over a neighbor tendril—a thing with roundish mock-orange umbrellas and disk-like fruit. "This one," he says fondly, "is *Gloria Irrita*. 'Futile Ambition.' My plants teach me humility, you see. The true artist must learn debasement, don't you agree?" I ignore him, wander down the row of plants. But Pristie's tenacious. He scuttles past me to a worktable, offers me a small white pot. There's nothing in it but soil. I sniff at the pot, shrug, return it to him. He's making circles with his eyes again, staring at my neck. His hands are cupped around the empty pot.

"A new crossbreed?" I ask. I'm beginning to wonder if maybe Lincoln's right.

"No," he whispers again, balancing the pot between two wooden crates of soil on the long white table, "just more of the same."

"Oh."

Pristie's face colors, as though disappointed. He's now shown me his plants, taken me into this other shell, revealed something about himself. What else is left? I don't think I've behaved badly, not really. I borrow Henry's words. "Guess most things grow in this climate."

He stands perfectly straight, his head tilted slightly to the left, stares past me. "But not everything lives," he intones, his cold voice creeping like one of the plants. Then he glances over at me. "Come," he says, formally and solicitously, as if I have just landed in the space shuttle, "you must be hungry."

I always looked for what wasn't there, learned early to temper my faith in the Second Coming and the 'Blessed Is Our Home' embroidery hanging on the kitchen wall. My mother was like one of Pristie's plants: a beautifully weird hybrid sprouting unexpectedly among the regimented rows of corn. Even her "nervous spells" slipped by almost unnoticed, just one more oddity in an isolated family of women whose motherline had died early from consumption and farmlife and childbirth. My father could not live peacefully inside this corseted desperate world of women. He festered like an ulcer, ran solo between booze and broken-down cars and god-knows what else in those dark nights, as though if he kept moving he might wander into a different dimension, a parallel universe unfettered with memory. He'd come home with torn pockets and whiskey breath, outraged and vindictive, at war still with himself and the unchanging world and all its motherlines. His mother was a social-climbing Baptist from Tennessee, God-fearing and hard-working. She gave him an enema every day until he was twelve. Then, two months before his high-school graduation, he hitched a ride to Indiana. He never saw her again, but every once in a while he'd get drunk and call her and hang up when he heard her voice. Then she died, then he married my mother, then I was born. But it was no excuse. It never is.

Why do I think of this now? Perhaps because it is only now I realize that, even after I refused to return to the canning shed and even when I put a lock on the door of the utility room where I slept, he didn't really believe in my resistance. It wasn't until he saw how I clung to the dance, how I gave my body so fully and willingly to the ballet, that he knew he had lost me. He left me alone then, but he was always watching me, as if I still owed him something and he was just waiting for his chance to collect the debt.

Around this time, Mrs. Pike, who'd never had a student of any real talent, somehow secured me a scholarship for a weekend dance workshop in Indianapolis. It cost a lot of money and I wouldn't have been able to go otherwise. It was her way of encouraging me. Major dance figures from New York City would be teaching technique classes, offering individual conferences with the most promising young dancers, and, possibly, talent-scouting for their school. I'd also get to attend a real full-length production of *Giselle*. I'd never seen a live professional ballet.

It was a big deal in our small community. The local paper even ran a photo of Mrs. Pike and me: her clunky repressed body buttoned to the neck, standing guard over my leotard-clad adolescent frame posed in an awkward and not-so-promising ballet attitude. The other girls were simultaneously envious and excited: maybe I was, after all, going to be a ballerina. Of course, I know now how small a thing it really was, how little difference it made. Dance careers don't suddenly blossom in weekend workshops; they too are beautifully weird cross-breeds, incredibly delicate exotic growths developed slowly and painfully over long years of obsessive care. Yet, even had we known, I don't think either Mrs. Pike or I would have cared.

"It's the going that matters," she told me. Mrs. Pike harbored few romantic illusions. Though the town granted her artistic sensibility a certain amount of their skeptical esteem, they knew, and she knew, that she wasn't much different from the people who sent their daughters to her. In another world or time, she'd have been a farmer's wife rising dutifully before the sun. None of us really knew how she'd come to this life in this place: insubstantial rumors trailed after her, like the powdery residue that lightning bugs leave behind. She ignored them, kept to herself, inscribed a tight little circle. Every Sunday she went to church. Once a month she visited her husband's grave. Each year she led us through a recital in the high-school auditorium. Because, like so many of the women in town, she didn't know how to drive, she walked everywhere. Although a common sight, her straight back propelling her forcefully along the dusty streets, her hatted head tilting to the same side as her hearing aid, she moved indifferently among us. No one hailed her in the streets, not even her students. I don't know why. Perhaps because she always wore ankle boots, even in the summer heat.

## Act Three, Scene Two

The upcoming workshop was an event, something we both had to work toward. After the regular class each day, Mrs. Pike would take me through an extra routine. She wanted me to shine in Indianapolis, to see that there was a road out of town—and how hard I'd have to work before I got on it. Beyond this, I don't think she thought much. The ballet for her was a practical matter and she had little idea what to do with me. "All limbs, no coordination," she'd say. "Where *did* you come from?" But this wasn't a real question, and I knew it. I would check the old dance books out of the library, prowl through them for advanced movements I thought I could manage, try to imagine what they were supposed to look like. Then Mrs. Pike would rearrange my body according to her own beliefs. Eventually, of course, I had to unlearn most of this stuff, but it was all I had at the time and I clung to it passionately.

My father, of course, disapproved. At first he'd viewed my dancing as an embarrassment, something designed to thwart his control. As I'd begun dancing out of his reach, he'd grown even more uncomfortable. "Whore's work," he'd say, "selling your body." Sometimes, he'd come up to the studio and loiter outside the door. He knew enough not to come inside. Mrs. Pike always seemed to sense when he was there. She'd suddenly stop mid-movement, tilt her head toward the stairs, then clamber down with one hand curled around the bannister. I don't think she ever said anything to him, but her presence at the door would be enough. When she returned, she'd gaze at me for a few interminable seconds with her knotted eyes and tug primly at her dance skirt. She didn't have to say anything to me either.

The day the article in the newspaper came out, I stayed late at the studio, talking with Mrs. Pike about the trip. There were still several weeks before The Event, as she called it, and she wanted to plan our itinerary down to the minute. This time my father surprised her, opened the door and called my name before she knew it. The quiet talk between us fell off flat.

Neither of us said anything, just listened as his flushed foot-steps began closing in. Abruptly, Mrs. Pike rose from her chair, clonked over to the top of the staircase. "Go on," she said firmly down the stairs. "Get out of here. No men allowed." This wasn't strictly true. She usually let the fathers stand in the stairwell during the cold winter months. He must have known this, but he obeyed her. She walked back over and stared at me, then began to put away the records. I reluctantly tucked my ballet slippers into my dance bag. "Thank you, Mrs. Pike," I said before I left, "for everything." But her back was to me and I don't think she heard me. Perhaps she'd already turned off her hearing aid.

Outside he was pacing the street, smoking a filterless Camel, muttering to himself. "Goddam dancing school," he said, one hand gripping my shoulder, leading me homeward. "Filling your head with fancy notions." I wasn't scared of him anymore, not really, but I hated him. And he knew this. I held my silence, put one foot diligently in front of the other. "Ain't going. That's what I say."

I peered into the descending dusk ahead, counted the dim lampposts lining the street. "What do you mean?"

"Not going to Indy. Haven't earned the right."

"Yes, I have," I protested. "Mrs. Pike says I'm a real hard worker."

"Maybe so," he said, his voice hard and low, "but you aren't a good girl." His grip tightened on my shoulder. "*Are* you?"

I didn't say anything, just pulled deeper into myself, franti-cally tried to find some reasoning that would change things. But it was always the same, a twilight secret that I lived with, a time I inhabited where I had no voice. We turned the corner, cut across a dry gully, slipped into a strip of land between someone's back yard and a chain-link fence. The weeds were half my height and broken bottles covered the hard ground. "Please," I finally said, "let me go."

"Nothing doing." His voice was determined and sober. We'd now covered the distance, come close to home. "Have to earn it, Natalie, have to be a good girl."

I could see our house just ahead. "I won't!" I cried, running out from under his hand and toward the front door, praying to God or someone to hear and believe me, running away from him though I couldn't really, sobbing over and over, "I won't, I won't." When I got to the house, I locked myself in the utility room. The light switch was on the outside wall. I'd turned it on, but when he came in he turned it off again. I was afraid to open the door, so I lay there all evening in the darkness. I don't know when, or if, I fell asleep.

Pristie bows over his white plate at one end of the long dining table, arranges his measured peas so they won't touch the sliver of poached salmon or the boiled onion. A monogramed cloth napkin is tucked neatly into the neck of his black cardigan. A vase of very ordinary white roses sits in the center of the table. I move the food around on my plate, dutifully try to swallow a pea. There are thirteen remaining; I've eaten six. He has served them to me himself, counting them out one by one. "Nineteen," he said, "a prime number. Just the right amount." The memory of this causes me to smile, then choke, then reach for the wine glass. Pristie's still looking at me over the flowers. His face hasn't changed. "Do you have any pepper?" I ask. I figure something's got to help the food go down.

"Yes." His voice is hesitant. "But it's not good for you."

"Really?" I spoon another pea into my mouth, let it sit there a while. "I put it on everything."

"You shouldn't." Pristie rings a bell for his servant, a tall spongy fellow wearing blue jeans who has yet to say a word to me. "Pepper is crushed from the immature berries of a pungent plant," Pristie announces. "Even if finely ground, it is intestinally erosive." Now the servant enters the room carrying

*147*

another wine bottle, though we've hardly touched the first. He looks at me with filmy unexpectant eyes, as though blind.

"I'd like some pepper, please." I try to sound cheerful.

"There isn't any." The servant is anywhere between my age and a hundred. He's got acne on his neck and white hairs growing out of his ears. He walks to Pristie's end of the table, takes his plate, returns, stacks it on top of mine, then backs out through a swinging oak door. I'm really hungry but I don't say anything. In an uncharacteristic move, Pristie slides a dish of vanilla pudding toward me. But it ricochets off the vase of roses and wobbles over to the edge of the table. I jump up and retrieve it just before it falls, a packrat scrounging for food. But I can't eat it. I see Henry's closed eyes, the bowl of Jell-O going untouched, the chunks of hidden food in his bed—all evidence that he's losing spirit. I drink the wine instead.

At night, while my mother was working, he'd try the door to the utility room. But I kept it locked. "Go away," I'd say, "just go away." I'd brought in an old table-lamp from the living room, so I could do my math homework. I'd spread the papers out around me, but I could never get the numbers right. It was hard for me to concentrate—the figures were so exact, there was only one right answer. And he was outside, twisting the knob, retreating, returning, trying again. I felt queasy and trapped, as though I were on one of those terrible rides at a carnival, turning upside-down inside a steel-barred box. Finally, I opened the door. I don't know why; I just wanted him to stop.

"What you doing?" he said, peering suspiciously over my shoulder.

"School stuff."

"Been thinking 'bout our talk?" His voice was flat and tinny, as though he were struggling with something inside him. Whatever it was, I didn't want to see it.

I averted my eyes. "No," I lied.

He took a step toward me, reached out his hand. "Sure you have."

"I have to do my homework, Daddy." My tone was firm and threatening, an attempt to match his. He didn't say anything, he didn't have to. It was in his unwavering eyes, the way they pinned me down, made me feel exposed. I now understand that kind of passive abuse, it takes place all the time. Just walking down the street, the way a man looks at you, or, going into a grocery, the remarks they make under their breath. There's no unviolated place, no way to escape, no sanctuary free from those hard knowing defiant male eyes that appraise and seize your body, turn it into something you barely recognize, then, with a blink, reject or dismiss or destroy what was never theirs anyway. As he slowly withdrew his extended hand, I slammed the door in his face.


Pristie leads me from the dining room, back into the labyrinth of dark hallways and electric candles. This time we are going to the music room, on the other side of the house. Or so he says. We could be anywhere—or nowhere. There are no distinctions in this place, every passageway, every turn, is exactly the same. Pristie says nothing, moves along at a steady even pace. Could he be counting the steps, the turns? What will happen to us if he loses the count? "Miss Barnes!"—his voice is far behind me. I stop and look back. He is standing at the other end of the hall, three electric candles away. He pushes the wall in front of him, walks through it. I run back down the corridor, afraid the opening will disappear again before I get there.

The music room is still and white. Crisp stacks of white composition paper lay undisturbed on the white marble mantelpiece over the white-brick fireplace. There are no logs in it, no signs of a fire ever having been lit. A white concert grand is in the exact center of the white tile floor; a white bench is positioned precisely beneath the middle of the keyboard, on which the colors of the major and minor keys have been reversed. In the midst of all the whiteness, this gash of darkness is sudden and vertiginous, a black hole in space-time beckoning a fall. Fortunately, this is when I become aware of the parrots. They are perched about the room like magnificent statues. Their chests rise and fall in quiet beats beneath unblinking black eyes and the slight ruffling of blue and yellow and green feathers. The pale long claws of each bird wrap around a wooden white stand. Why haven't I noticed them before? Pristie notes my interest. "There are eleven of them."

I stare at the colorful shapes, the notched curled beaks, the restless eyes. "Do they talk?"

"No," he says disdainfully, as if the question is unthinkable. "Now come." He turns sharply, like a soldier. "I'd like you to hear something." He directs me to a white molded plastic chair, then settles himself carefully in the middle of the piano bench and leans into the nocturnal keyboard. His fingers strike a chord, then another, but the notes are sluggish and disconnected. He speaks to me over his shoulder. "When moving against the music, as you do, I hear a very different thing. A semi-tone. Do you understand?" I do not. I shake my head. As his white limp hands flutter on the keys, mocking the notes, the parrots are breathing all around me. "Always a half-step between the notes," he says. "In music, this is a semi-tone. An imperfect interval between major and minor, mediant and dominant. A constantly shifting gap between the notes that is always, in the traditional sense, wrong." His hands stop moving. "This is where you dance, Natalie, in the semi-tonic scale. It is why you are *never* with the music."

"I know," I admit, "I can't count it. They've always told me that."

"Ignore them. They know nothing. You *can* count it, but not in their so-called 'natural' scale. You always find—intuitively, remarkably—the irregular patterns of silence inside the music.

They do not understand what you are doing." He pauses and turns sideways, so that he's almost facing me. "But I do."

I'm not sure what to think or say about this. Perhaps he's right. Is this good or bad? Am I an unnatural musical genius on the verge of great discoveries or a freak of nature imprisoned in the inverted keyboard of Pristie's semi-tonic solitude? Just as probably, he's wrong, a loony blocked composer playing mind games with a teenager. I look around the room: it is cool, white, unblinking, silent.

Pristie turns to the piano again, stares at his hands, then lowers them slowly to the keys. The haunting notes of Chopin invoke swiftness and flight. "Familiar?" His voice rises sardonically just above the music. I nod. Now his fingers thunder across the keys: a brisk and gay tarantella, an expressive waltz, a frenzied cadenza. "This is what *they* like, isn't it?" His voice is rushed, anxious, plaintive. He is taking me through an entire repertoire of familiar ballet music. "Offenbach, Strauss, Tchaikovsky," he counts. "Or is it Vivaldi? Yes, of course, that's what they want." He plays on, changing tempi and composers abruptly, obsessively, as if this is exquisite torture and he must be punished. Suddenly, he stops. "This is not," he whispers, "what *we* want." He knuckles a chord, shoots off into a cacophony of reckless clashing sounds. "*This* is our music. Imperfect perfection. Unnatural sounds and unexpected silences." Then he stops again, and, without looking at me, in a toneless growl issuing from someplace deep inside him that shouldn't be there, he finally gets to the point of it all. "Come, Natalie, let me see you move. Let me work against you."

I continued resisting my father's will, as though somehow his power would miraculously change on its own, comply to my desires, become the inverse of what it never was, never could be. I think it was in opposition to him, as much as anything else, that I decided I was going to be a ballet dancer. And, once I'd felt this through, I actually considered telling someone about what he was doing to me. There seemed to be an open channel between Mrs. Pike and me, some kind of opportunity for unloading the terror and shame all twisted up inside. But how to do it? What was I going to say? So I'd stand before the bathroom mirror and rehearse the whispered words, like trying on a costume and seeing yourself transformed. "He's forced me to do things." I'd watch my face for the change, then repeat the same words or a vague variation on them. "He's hurting me."

Maybe he overheard me during one of those bathroom sessions. Probably not. He just seemed to see into me, know my thoughts. It was yet another violation. Anyway, he barged into the bathroom one day, slammed the door, pushed me down to the toilet, held me still by flattening his hand on the back of my head. As if he wanted me to pray. But what for? Maybe for him. "You gonna do it?" he snapped. I stared into the rusty toilet bowl, held my breath. I wasn't going to, ever again. "Want Mrs. Pike knowing what a bad girl you really are?" God, no. But why was I bad? He pressed down harder until my head was almost in the toilet. I closed my eyes. Why couldn't I be good? "Wanna disgust her, do you?" I tried to resist his force, strained away from the water. "No, Daddy." He removed his hand. But I remained on my knees, hovered over the toilet. I knew he'd probably hit me if I stood. "You do filth." After he left, I threw up. Whatever voice I'd tried to reach was now gone. He'd found it and taken it, like everything else—except the dance.

During the next two weeks my father and I lived behind invisible boundaries inside the house. The old Zenith in the front room kept him company; I stayed mostly in the kitchen and utility room, even when my mother was home. I didn't often have reason to be in his territory and he'd withdrawn from mine. After a while, I even began to relax a little. We didn't exactly have a peace treaty—it was more like an armed truce—but it was as if, after years of his plundering raids, I had finally built a fortress and he didn't have the patience or the resources for siege warfare. But, as always with him, it was a false sense of security. I never did realize just how desperate an enemy he was. I'd left a flank unprotected and he was just waiting for the right moment to strike.

When I came out of the studio the night before Mrs. Pike and I were to leave for Indy, he was leaning against the brick wall. I smelled whiskey before I even saw him. His ragged face was bobbing up and down, as though he had a secret. I started to walk on past him. I was being willful about the trip: I had my mother's permission; I was going without his blessings; there really wasn't much he could do. But he stopped me with his words. "Little bird," he whispered. It was what he called me only when he was abusing me. He'd say it over and over under his breath, like a secret litany. "Little bird," he repeated, low and plaintive. "Don't fly the nest."

I turned around, squinted into the porch light outside the studio. "I'm going, Daddy."

He pushed off the wall with the back of his foot. "Then Mrs. Pike and me got some talking to do," he rasped. He swiveled and reached for the door. "Reckon 'bout time she knows just what kind of a dancer you are."

I ran toward him, tried to block the entrance. "What are you going to say?" But he'd already opened the door, was shouldering his way inside. I slipped in after him.

The downstairs area was small and empty, just a waiting cubicle with a couple of chairs in it. He lurched through it to the bottom of the staircase, looked up, started to climb. His balance was off because of his drinking but his grip was strong on the bannister. "Hey, Mrs. Pike? You there?"

I shadowed behind him, whispered desperately. "Don't tell her . . . *please.*"

He crept up another two steps. "Mrs. Pike? Oh, Mrs. Pike!"

I scrambled around in front of him, dropped my dance bag, pressed my hands against his chest. "No!" I pleaded. "Don't do this to me!"

For a moment he paused, as though the fact I'd touched him was in itself a small victory. But it wasn't enough. He knocked me out of the way, rose another step. "Mrs. Pike!" His voice came from low inside his stomach, filled the stairwell.

"Daddy!" I lay my hand on his tight arm. "I'll do what you want."

Suddenly, he clamped his free hand around my wrist, turned, yanked me back down the stairs. "Goddam right," he hissed, kicking my fallen dance bag to the bottom. When we went back out the door of the studio, I was crying the kind of tears no one's ever supposed to see. I guess Mrs. Pike had turned off her hearing aid, because she never did come to the top of the stairs.

I'm swaying next to the piano, listening to the thudding heartbeat of the metronome. Pristie's impatient hands hit the ebony keys with frenzied precision. He's offering me an unnatural composition, something which will make me a star, as though art survives only in the resistance, over the edges of music, buried inside the dark gaps. He wants me to dance around the abyss, but the music makes me feel as if I've got things crawling across me. Maybe I'm not ready to perform the necessary rites and cross over into his liminal world. "You must circumvent the actual movements," he whispers, "be wittier than the music." His skin is drawn white, pinched like a dead man's.

"Like so?" I stubbornly improvise a few steps.

Pristie looks at me sideways with his sooty eyes. A knot of perspiration has gathered in the crevice between his nose and his upper lip. His neck is mottled. "Forget your training. Show me something new."

The carpet has sprouted tentacles and sucks at my feet. "I can't feel this music, it's not working."

"Good," he hums, as though dropping into a trance. I try out one of Linc's parabola movements, something I've never done. It feels strange, unfamiliar, as though my body is a broken circle. Pristie's breathing is shortening, his fingers are skipping keys. I can't sustain this for very long, it doesn't feel right. I hear a comfortable note, mentally run after it, return to swaying inside the music. Suddenly, he slams his hands down on the darkling keyboard. "Not what I want at all!" He bows over the piano, presses his bloodless wrists to his eyes. "You must empty your mind. We've exhausted ideas. We're at the end of history."

"How can there be a music of exhaustion, a dance of emptiness?" I'm not entirely sure what he means; I'm suspicious of the ideas. It's the exact opposite of what Henry said at the Wharf.

"How can there *not* be," he says bitterly, "it is all we have left." He lowers his hands to the piano. The room is beginning to feel small, tightly sealed, like a living tomb. "Listen to it! This is the true music of the spheres. Chaos and eternal night!" His fingers strike the inverted keys: a thunderous cackle of unholy chords rises and falls.

I'm starting to sweat, get sick in my legs, feel a hard and determined thing rising from the sewers inside me. I know I'll never catch it if it escapes. I just don't understand what he's talking about. "Is this your composition?" Pristie's barely breathing inside his crab's armor. "I mean, is it between the notes?"

"There are no notes." Pristie taps on a key. "No counts." The piano whines flatly beneath his drumming hand, a fused inflection of gesture and tone. "No relationship." There is something unbridgeable between myself and his words. "There is nothing but difference . . . that makes no difference."

I can't bear to look at him anymore. One of the parrots cocks her head, cements her sad eyes on my own, hops to the side. They cannot fly; he has clipped their wings. As though he knows what I'm thinking, Pristie says, "Miss Barnes, they are only birds." Yes, yes, of course. Just like his music is only what it's not.

"You lack gratitude," Pristie suddenly whispers. I hear but I don't. I keep wondering why I'm really here, what I've possibly got to gain from this experience. No doubt Pristie has tremendous power. He can create a ballet for me, something entirely my own, perhaps make me famous. But at what price? He needs my body to resist his nonmusic, to mark the difference that makes no difference. If I cross that bridge and dance to the end of history, where will I be?

"I'm grateful, Mr. Pristie, really I am, but . . ."

Pristie ignores my hesitation. "Of course you are, Miss Barnes, of course you are. And I shall be grateful to you too." His hands return to the keys, fondling them roughly, pushing them down, easing them up, forcing them, as if against their will, to produce sounds that are not sounds. I take a step forward, close my eyes, begin not-feeling my way into the nonmusic. I pause next to the piano, roll my head mechanically off-rhythm. It's hard work not to count. Pristie's arms are angularly contorted, his fingers are knife blades. "Yes," he hums, "exactly so." I circle the piano, crawl over myself, my shoulders whipping from side to side, my legs rising and falling, my torso writhing beneath his shrieking fingers. "Yes," he's saying over and over, groaning now, turning inside-out right before my eyes. It is happening and not-happening. I am plunging down into that secret place of irregular silences, where the light and dark strips of broken sunlight are, where the day is night and the night goes on forever. I am there and not-there, splitting off, myself and not-myself. I am coming inside his music. It is coming inside me. "Against me," he moans, "keep going . . ."

And then I see them: the birds. They are not moving, they are just staring at me with their unblinking eyes. And I see what they are looking at. And I am ashamed. Not so much for myself, because, after all, I am only the uncomprehending dancer and so very young, but for him, because he is the adult and should never have debased his sacred vigilance. Under the cover of chaos and eternal night, he has come inside *my* music and transformed the natural relationship between us into an imperfect interval. I cease moving and turn to gaze at him. It feels as though blood is pouring from my eyes. He seems very far away, very small. His hands stop mid-air, wintry branches in a dead landscape. I am alone, all alone.

Silently, purposefully, sadly, I gather up my things—my purse, my coat, my wool scarf—and, without looking back again, for I have lingered in this place of darkness and abjection too long already, I leave. He says nothing; there is nothing to say. And I discover that the way out is less mysterious, less labyrinthine, than the way in: I keep turning right until I find the old man's portrait, and then, walking away from his gaze, I go through the door and out into the night that can and will become day. From this perspective I can see the lights of the city. With my back to the westernmost edge of the continent, I turn inland, toward home, toward the lambent glow in the dark sky.

I made the most of that weekend workshop in Indy. I danced for myself, inside the music, beyond the rage. I think, in some sense, I've never danced that way again. It was wild, frenzied, painful, probably psychotic. Mrs. Pike just sat on the sidelines with ten other dance instructors, one hand tugging at her neck, chewing on her smalltown lips. Afterwards, when the guest teacher complimented my talent, Mrs. Pike could only nod her head, as though she'd loaned me her voice and there wasn't anything left. The effort had made her sick. God bless her for her ignorance. All the same I washed away what my father had done that last night in the canning shed. Though my body was bruised and torn inside its skin, my will to defeat him carried me through things, earned me the right to go. When I took my place at *barre*, surrounded by all those other girls, I knew I'd found a home. I'd learned the required quiet endurance, what it takes to be a dancer. The worse part of abuse, beyond the physical pain or the humiliation, is that it goes on so long.

# Act Three, Scene Three

Endeavor always to become more and more sensitive, more and more aware, quicker in response, and then—but only then—be loyal to yourself. Stand fast. Never mind what they say in the dressing room or in the dance columns. You must yourself know. When you do, you will have stopped being a student and become an artist.
　　　　　　　　–Agnes de Mille, *To A Young Dancer*

'm watching Henry sleep; I don't want to disturb him; I need time to think. The doctor has come and gone. Outside, in the corridor, he has finally told me. "Metastasized carcinoma of the liver." Poetic words for something so terrible. "Inoperable tumor. Three months at best." I can't get my mind around this day, this night. I keep pulling at the past for an answer, as though if I look hard enough I will find a neatly ordered pattern. But whatever has passed between Henry and me—this transit across the irregular contours of the ballet, history, our love—is ineffable and inscrutable. I'll never really see it for what it is. Now Henry's going home to die. It's what he wants.

I don't know what I want. It seems that things just happen to me. This morning Magda told me I'm going on a six-week China tour with the Company next month. She said this tour will make my career. I'll work closely with all the Principals, perhaps become one myself. A rare opportunity. I cannot disappoint her. She has seen something in me, she has chosen me. There will be no turning back, not really. She believes only in the self. It is a relentless pursuit: no room for sentiment, for love, for death. She will not understand if I turn down this trip. She will lose faith in me. My career will be over before it has barely begun. So, when Henry awakens, I will tell him I'm going to China. I'll never get another chance like this, it's what I must do.

Or I will tell him what he needs to hear. I will go home with you and nurse you. I will stay with you until the end, comfort you, love you. I will hold your hand, feed you, change your sheets. And because the lie that is swelling inside me is growing now inside you, I will even continue to carry your baby. And I will bury you. Because otherwise I cannot live with myself, not now, not ever. Not if the only way I can dance is over your dead body. Of course, I won't actually say these things. He wouldn't let me. He'd tell me to go, if he knew. He'd tell me to go, and he might even mean it. And then I would go, because he had told me to. And we'd write or call every day, and he'd warn me to be careful, I was living for two now, or three, and I'd promise him I'd be home soon to take care of him, and then one night I'd call and there'd be no answer and I'd realize that, finally, I was no longer pregnant and Henry was dead and I was a dancer and I'd never be anything else but a dancer, and that it didn't matter what he had said, I was always going to be dancing over his dead body and our child's, and that, knowing this, I should have been there to hold his hand and sponge his forehead and see him, this gentle sweet man who loved me, into his grave.

Henry goes home tomorrow. Will I go with him? True, things just keep happening to me. But not this time. This time I must make something happen. And I will have to live with this decision for the rest of my life. It's going to be a long night.

"Flash flood, bunhead, flash flood!" Lincoln was calling me from Henry's studio. His hysterical voice squealed through the receiver. "Man the lifeboats! Women and faggots first!"

I was at the front desk, wrapped in the telephone cord, caught between an irritated Carabee and a frustrated Harry. Magda had just told me about China. I hadn't yet learned Henry was going home.

"I am *not* over budget," Carabee was barking at Harry. Poking her measuring stick over the top of the desk, she nudged his Master Ledger. "Been counting every thread, every button, every scrap of documented fabric! I'm right on the line." Harry lifted the telephone cord away from his chest with his finger-tips, fluttered eel eyes at me. "It's right here," he said, pointing to a row of shocking pink figures. Carabee wagged her fuzzy head. "You keep changing the color, Harry."

I pressed the receiver against my mouth. "Don't panic, Linc. The roof leaks a little."

"A little!?"

"Okay, maybe a little more than a little. The pails are in the women's restroom."

"Great," Linc said ironically. I held the receiver away and rolled my eyes at Harry, but he was showing Carabee the boysenberry-blue debits from last month. "Can't get to it." Linc's voice was jumping all over, as if he were climbing something. "Hallway looks like the Mississippi."

"Oh, come on, Linc."

"Not a penny over," Carabee muttered. "It's right there in the tangerine column." She jerked on the phone cord. "Isn't it?" I glanced at the indecipherable rows of figures and choked out a nod.

"Come on nothing," Linc bellowed. "We got a situation here."

I loosened the phone cord but I couldn't get out of it. "Look, Linc, I don't really have time for this." Fran was due to pick me up any minute. We were supposed to be going up to Napa Valley for a showing of the only femininst painters she took seriously. Then she was going to drop me off at the hospital on the way back. And the China trip was buzzing in my head.

"Listen up, bunhead, you *make* time. I'm drowning here." Now Carabee sprawled over the desk ledge and started flipping through the pages of Harry's book. He tried to grab the ledger away from her, but she swatted him with the ruler and he got wrapped up in the cord with me.

"You have to get off the phone," Harry pleaded. Carabee had come around to his side, was uncapping his markers, shaking them up and down. He was fighting the cord while trying to grab them back from her hands. The motion was twisting me in circles. "I tell you, Mrs. Carabee," he whined, "you've gone too far."

"Geez, Linc," I giggled, unable to resist the obvious pun. "I'm all tied up here. Guess you'd better call 911."

"Like hell. Waiting room's a lake. Can't get to the telephone. Ah, shit."

"Linc?" There was no response. Maybe there was something to this. "Linc?! Where'd you go?"

"Friggin' bug with two hundred legs. I'm on a ladder."

"Lincoln Freeman, you come down off that ladder and get those pails from the ladies' room!"

Carabee suddenly poked her head around Harry's protesting body. "Is that Mr. Freeman? You tell him I found a rip in his parabola costume. Right in the crotch."

"It's a tidal wave, I tell you," Linc cried.

I looked at the wall clock, figured Fran had to be outside by now. "Okay, just tread water and hold on. I'm coming out."

Carabee had pushed Harry from his stool and was studying the ledger. "There, there it is! Raspberry says I'm under budget a dollar-sixty-four."

"My word against yours," Harry insisted. "It's shocking pink this month, not raspberry. Can't you see the difference?"

"Hurry!" Even Linc's voice sounded wet. "I'm going under for the third time."

I hung up the phone and slipped out of the cord just as Carabee slammed Harry's book against the floor. She was clutching his shocking pink marker in one hand, the measuring stick in the other. "I am *not* over-budget," she said firmly.

I'm half-listening to the cold March rain drum against the draped hospital windows. The neighbor man died last week, his bed is empty. Norman Rockwell is back in place. But where am I? Magda's whispery voice and hard eyes keep coming back, doubling over me, like an overlapping circle from which I cannot escape. Last time I was in her dressing room I borrowed money; this time I pay off my debt. "Ah, good," she says in a conspiratorial whisper. She looks at me, as though to really say, "Yes, you've earned this money—dancing, posing, living on the edge. But we needn't point our finger at it." So I babble, fill the silence, tell her defiantly that I've seen Pristie. She doesn't take this news well—puckers her face, flutters her eyelashes, sighs with displeasure. "But, Natalie, dear, I advised you against this." She did; I should have listened. She makes a 'tsking' sound inside her mouth, her own form of death rattle. "Really, you are so so *so* stubborn."

Then, draping one of her lovely strong arms over the divan, she breaks into a vivid description of the China tour: raked stages and balletomanes; haunting street operas and exotic costumes; colorful brocaded silks and delicate rice-paper fans; market-window entrails gleaming like strands of shining beads. A whole universe pours forth from Magda's imagination. My senses are overloaded. "Double your normal salary." Her voice is suddenly sober, practical, once more scheming. Another stab perhaps at poor ineffectual Himmel and all those others, like Pristie and Jared and maybe even Magda herself, who profess to be artists. "It's a remarkable opportunity, Natalie. Show us what you're really made of."

Magda knows and she doesn't know. What it means to be angry, speechless, not-quite-seventeen . . . to have been chosen but not to have chosen . . . to grow up, finally and resolutely, too early and against one's will. I see myself burning in her eyes, reflected back, on the verge of dancing inside a powerful image—one that puts everything I come from exactly in its place. Come to me, Natalie, she could say, and together we will remake the past, rise above the poverty, bury your father and all the old men. We are new women in a new world. Whoever he is, whatever he stands for, he'll never find his way inside you again. But she doesn't say these things, and she doesn't really know.

I don't either. Past, present, old, new: how to sort them out? I still have to live with myself, don't I? If I abandon him to die alone—and that is how, finally, Henry will see it—will I have turned against myself? Will I be left holding a meaningless thing, something hollow, like Pristie's antimusic or Jared's body parts or some other shapeless vacant idea? The guilt, the love, the shame: they're all mixed up together. Magda will see my indecision as an artistic weakness, slavish adherence to conventional morality. I can easily be replaced: in China, in San Francisco, in her favor. She doesn't traffic in flawed merchandise.

So, if I go to China, I will truly join the body of dancers. Embraced by this elite old-world family of secrets, I will travel the Orient like Marco Polo, experimenting with new friendships, art forms, ideas. And when we return I will have, with Magda's blessings and support, a dressing room of my own. A real family, something to belong to, a clearly defined role to play, protection from the hostile civilians, a place to come home to. A new world, if not exactly a new woman. The past remade, the old men dead and buried. Except they aren't dead and buried, not yet, not for me. Suspended between the irredeemable past and the unforgiving future, I still don't know what I can, what I should, undertake. Because right here, now, in this dark room on this rainy night, an old man is dying, and, even dying, his shallow breaths come from his center, give life to his limbs, his features, his dancer's soul. Perhaps this is the only sure thing, what I will carry to the end.

Fran was sitting on a fire hydrant next to her illegally parked van. Toby and his leash were wrapped around both the hydrant and her legs, but she was oblivious, vacantly staring at the sidewalk. She looked up almost bewildered when I walked over to her. "Mind if we go out to Henry's studio?" I said. "Linc says it's flooded."

"Yeh, sure, what the fuck." She listlessly handed me Toby's leash. Even after I unwound him, she just sat there, her hair carelessly stuffed under a red kerchief, deep crevices rising from her eyes like exclamation points.

"You look like hell," I observed. Grateful to be free, Toby lifted one of his three legs and marked my boot. Fran shrugged, motioned for me to get in the van. "Anything wrong?" Ignoring me, she pushed herself off the hydrant and trudged over to her door. I climbed in the passenger side after Toby. "Then we'll head south, okay? It'll take about a half-hour."

"Sure, whatever." She dumped a road map in my lap, then wrapped her hands around the steering wheel, as if bracing her body against some invisible force. The van whined and rattled before lurching forward. Fran was always so difficult to read. I wanted to pierce her mood, get her to talk, but I knew it wouldn't do any good. Eventually, the silence would work its way through her and she'd lighten up or get to what was bothering her. So I hung my head out the window next to Toby's and closed my eyes to the wind. I didn't open them again until Fran made a fast turn and hit the curb before straightening out again. We were passing one of the spires of Henry's hospital. He was probably sleeping. It was, the nurses told me, about all he did between my visits.

"I'm sorry, Nat," Fran said suddenly. "I shouldn't have done it."

The hospital disappeared, was gradually replaced by functional clusters of labs and doctors' offices. "Done what?"

"Brought you to Armand. I used to do that for him. Before you."

I knew that. Where was she coming from? "Hey, I found him myself. And you stopped him. What does that matter now anyway?"

She leaned into the steering wheel, wiped at the front window. "Planet exploded."

"Your husband—?"

"Threw me out." She jerked her thumb back over her shoulder. I turned around, stared at the cluttered back of the van: an orange fringed lamp shade covered a stack of books; coathangers and photo albums were propped against bare canvasses; Toby's water dish was wedged under a patchwork quilt. Clothing was spread out everywhere. "Forty-two years old. Practically everything I own is right here." I faced front again, stared down at the map in my lap, tried to follow a thin red line, as Fran slipped angrily between two delivery trucks. "Looks up from the TV last night during a commercial and says calmly, 'Frances, the boys and I need a full-time mother.' Not 'mother and wife!' Just 'mother.' 'I did that, Arnie,' I say. 'Now I'm gonna paint.' 'Not a passing phase then, Frances?' 'No, Arnie, that was mothering you and the boys. This is my life.' "

We were moving awfully fast, changing lanes abruptly. "Slow up, okay?"

"Don't dawdle on freeways, get yourself killed."

I held up the map over Toby's body, close to Fran's face. "Looks like it's the green sign after the whatsa-thing."

"Jesus, Natalie." She pushed the map away from her. "What's that mean?"

"You know," I said, "the turn-off." I watched the passing overhead sign carefully.

"Yeh," she said, pulling into the wrong exit lane. "I know." She squinted under the dangling visor. "Says he'll get custody of the boys."

"He can't do that, can he?"

"He can." We'd somehow gotten off red and were following a blue bar. "And he will."

"Maybe you should pull off to the side, Fran."

"That's what I said. 'Give me time, Arnie. I gave you a chance to get started.' 'Maybe I can wait, Frances, but the boys can't.' He's right, of course."

She'd finally slowed down, squeezed between cars in the far right lane. "And then the commercial was over, and so was our marriage. Presto. Like he'd changed channels. And, you know, the funny thing was, the whole time he was talking I was watching the commercial, thinking about light and proportion and maybe taking a shot at lithographs."

I wanted to comfort her but I wasn't sure how. As we curved around Western Avenue and a string of clothing warehouses, she stuck a hand out the window, opened her palm, felt the air. "Thought it was supposed to be raining."

"So did I. Come to think of it, we haven't had any rain all the way out here." I leaned out the window and stared at a row of slow-blinking red lights. Henry's studio wasn't too far off. I pointed to the BART station. "Make a turn up there."

She reached up, adjusted the rear-view mirror. "You know, I don't even have a bank account in my own name."

We were creeping silently up toward the studio, under the redwoods, alongside the hedges. Suddenly, it hit me. "You won't go to Armand, will you?"

"Nope. That's over too. Started ending a while ago." Her voice was quiet, almost apologetic. "When you came."

"We just passed the studio," I said. She slammed on the brake and the van shuddered slowly to a stop, the stuff in the back shifting and clattering.

## Act Three, Scene Three

"Would you look at that," Fran said in her familiar sardonic voice. In an otherwise clear sky, one low-hanging grey cloud hovered over the building like a stage prop. A few drops of rain dotted the window panes, small proof there'd been some kind of storm. And then, hugging the emergency brake, she said it once more, but now her voice was quiet and apologetic again, as if she were seeing a natural wonder. "Would you look at that." And, as Toby started whining and wagging his tail in my face, I realized that I'd forgotten to tell her about the China trip.

Dr. Lovett, as sterile and orderly as an operating theater, has already made his duty call. His message is brief, blunt, irremediable. Spreading false corridor light over this night, he furtively motions me out of Henry's room, leads me down the hall to the glassy nurse's station, where starched-white voices whisper behind my back, as though chanting a nursery rhyme: "Old man's dying, old man's dying." And he tells me, methodically blinking his sad professional eyes: "Some discomfort, not much of an appetite, a lot of sleep. You'll see to him, I'm sure." But will I? Have I any vote in this? How can he be so certain I'll give up everything for Henry? Or that I should? And then, lowering his voice, the doctor says: "You know, we've been friends a long long time." Yes, I've heard these words— first in Henry's voice, now in Dr. Lovett's—and I've finally seen what they mean. Together, these two old men inhabit a different San Francisco, a city unscarred by earthquakes and radicals and cancer and other angry vigorous acts of God. Just the two of them, meeting for dinner and drinks at some small neighborhood Italian restaurant near the foot of Telegraph Hill, lovingly recreating a time, a place, a way of life, that never really existed. There is no place for me in this fraternity of two, this righteous bond between men—at least, not a me that I choose to be. I can see myself reflected in the well-meaning Dr. Lovett's tired eyes: another nurse-in-the-making, an old man's dying fancy, a pliant adoring girl destined to serve still other men.

And so I sit here in the cool astringent dark of Henry's room, avoid his collapsed face, struggle against this permanent intersection of my life with his. I can't make up my mind. I want to escape but I don't know how to get from here to there, wherever there is. I don't even know if a 'there' exists. My skin is tightly drawn, anchors me to my bones, to Henry's blood, to something I don't wholly want. Why must I stay behind, care for Henry? Why must I do the responsible thing?

True, in his own way, Henry has cared for me. I owe him this much. He has offered me his heart, his studio, his talents—places of refuge. He has shown me how to work low from my center, how to get on top of the music in order to remain inside it. He has taught me other, less important things as well: how a dot of red lipliner in the corner of each eye will make them larger, how a light coating of powder keeps the paint from running. He has also shown me, over and over again, how courageous a thing it is to get beyond the mere movements. But he was dying when I met him, and he did not tell me.

And he will not tell me now. When all this has ended, he will leave me what remains of his estate; up to his last breath, he will force me to pretend that we're a family; the whole time he will act as if art and life are things only old men really understand. Maybe I'm only sixteen, almost seventeen, but I've fought hard for my career, paid for it again and again. Why must I ask permission now to do something I've earned many times over? There was always something inside him, cutting close to my own dancer's soul, trying to stop me. Yes, old heart, you may do it. But will you? Should you? Must you? Right from the start he spoke so easily of our going away, of my leaving the Company before I was even in it. And then, after I did get in, he so readily wanted me to have the baby. It didn't matter that he was dying or that I was a teenager or that my dream, my dance career, would end. No, he believed, like so many of them, that my real role, my true function, was simply to be an extension of him, a reflection of his worth. In some ways, I guess, it's what I believed too. How can I forgive him this? I will, I should, I must; but may I?

Well, it's no good pretending that my father isn't somewhere mixed up in this, lurking in the shadows, whispering: "Be a good girl, Natalie, be a good girl." He's still there, undead and unexorcized, showing up in the damndest places, haunting everything I do. He's got more guises than I can even imagine. I try to resist, but it's so hard. I'm burning inside, terrified he'll go to Magda, as he threatened to go to Mrs. Pike, and tell on me once and for all. But that doesn't matter, not really, not anymore. Magda is willful, nothing breaks her down. She will say: "Go back to your grave, old man, it's where you belong." And because his voice is, after all, just one more thing I have to bury, I will join Magda. And I will be a good girl, or not a good girl, but on my own terms.

One thing I do know: I won't get down on my knees, scrubbing and praying like my mother, wringing out the disease and blood with my bare hands, swallowing back secrets and despair. Nor will I hold Henry's hand against the nightmare fears consuming him, all the while staring at the bedroom walls, wishing to God there were some way out and wondering if I exist except in the indirect light of a man's approval. Because, finally, I cannot live comfortably inside his lie: there is no room for me there. If I stay, it will be because I have loved him in my own way.

Whenever I look back at it, that afternoon in Henry's studio, passed under the influence of that solitary little grey cloud suspended so stubbornly and so improbably above us, seems like an interval of almost unlimited possibility. It was, after all, the last suspended moment before I found out that Henry was going home to die. Nothing was ever to be the same again. How could it be? Of course, I didn't know this at the time. I was thinking mostly about the China trip and Fran's homelessness. Henry was still in the hospital; I planned to visit him later, assumed we would read poetry, sneak sips of brandy, celebrate the news about China. At the time, that visit to the studio was just another distraction in an already distracted day, a duty call to Lincoln. But it became more, much more, and if I couldn't know it then, I do now. In a sense, I suppose, I've been within the ambit of that unlikely little cloud ever since. Strange things happen there: people are, well, . . . transformed. Lincoln felt it first, then Fran. It took me longer.

Lincoln's metamorphosis occurred before we even got there. When Toby, Fran, and I found him in the quadruple-mirrored main studio room, he was costumed in Henry's old galoshes, a cap with earflaps, a red rain slicker, yellow rubber gloves, and a pair of goggles. He looked like a huge alien insect. Although he was pushing a mop back and forth across the wooden dance floor, there were, oddly, no signs of a flood. No puddles, no water stains: he didn't even have a bucket with him, and his mop was dry. He peered at us through the mirror, straightened up, leaned on the mop handle. "Welcome, earthlings," he intoned, "it was written that you would come."

Fran bowed from her waist and responded in a voice of almost reverent amazement, " 'I have anticipated thee, Fortune, and entrenched myself against all thy secret attacks.' " They were the very words Henry had used the first day I had come to his studio. How did she know them?

"Fran," I said quietly, "where'd that come from?"

She shook her head in confused bewilderment. "I'm not really sure." And then, as if listening to something neither Lincoln nor I could hear, she tilted her head away from us and walked slowly, hands held out before her, toward the gold ribbons of light flowing under the little grey cloud and through the large picture window. "This is really something," she said. "Don't you feel it?"

I looked at Lincoln. He'd pushed the goggles to the top of his head, and smiled now as he watched Fran's dreamy progress about the room. She was running her hands along the wall-*barres*, pausing every few feet to close her eyes and sniff the rosined air. Toby hobbled after her. "What is she talking about?" I asked him. "Do you feel it?"

"I do not, terran bunhead," he said, pulling off his yellow gloves. "The Great Flood has done made me senseless."

"What flood?! This place is drier than I've ever seen it."

"Come," he said, his boots squeaking across the floor toward the unlit reception area. He stopped at the doorway and pointed the mop toward the waiting room. "There, space voyager, is your future."

I stared into the waiting room. It was deluged with opened boxes, tape measures, costume bags, pincushions, packing foam, crumpled receipts, bits and tatters of fabric. The stuff completely covered the floor, was creeping up toward the ceiling. I was confused. "What is all this shit?"

Lincoln leaned into the room and took a clipboard off the piles of papers on the desk. He read from the yellow-lined pages in a grim business-like tone. "This shit, as you so eloquently put it, includes—and I give you but the highlights—20 tutus, 31 canes, 2 dance belts, 14 spangled leotards, 47 green headbands that are supposed to be yellow, a box of tamborines that ain't even here but got sent to Fresno by mistake, and a parachute."

"A parachute?"

"A parachute."

And then, at some vague unwelcome level, it began to register. Every spring Henry ran a recital for the whole school. All this stuff had been ordered, and paid for, months ago. He'd probably been rehearsing the students in their routines since January. The hall was rented, parents and friends had already bought tickets, the costume companies had been shipping things in here for weeks. "Linc, we've got to call off the recital!"

"I hate to contradict the very first executive decision of my esteemed boss lady, but, seeing how she's gone and got herself a major dose of the flop sweats, I must, respectfully, dissent. It's *way* too late to call it off. The show, my empty bunhead, must go on."

"Oh God, Linc, I'm going on the China tour next month. Magda just told me."

"Good, then you've got time for the recital. It's in three weeks."

"Oh no."

"Oh yes." He switched on the overhead light and gestured toward the desk with the mop. "Not only that, but we got bills coming in. Gas, electricity, phone, insurance. Kids stop in here every day after school to try on costumes, the answering machine's clogged with honky mommas reporting ticket sales, and there's a big scary lady named Crystal—you know her?—" I shook my head, "who's gonna whup my pretty black ass if she don't get in here twice a week to teach tumbling. That's the blue rubber mats." He pointed to a looming mass in the corner. "She and Henry got a contract?"

"I don't know."

"Course you don't. You don't come out here. You don't answer phone messages. You be running off to Japan."

"China."

Fran suddenly appeared in the doorway, massaging the grainy wood frame with the palms of her hands. "God, this place has super vibes." She looked like a cat rubbing up against a rough surface, purring, delighted, calculating. "Feel it, Natalie. Wow!"

"Feel what? What is *it*?" But she wandered off down the hallway, lovingly straightening the pictures of Henry's former students. "They don't hang right, Fran, they never did," I called after her. But she ignored me.

"It's a mess at the front desk, that's what it is," Lincoln said, as if in response to my question to Fran. Those were Magda's words the day she took over Himmel's class, the day I started becoming her Dream Girl. What was going on here? Was everything anybody had ever said in my presence suspended like water droplets in that little grey cloud? Was it all recirculating now, about to rain down on me? Still, it was true. I'd forgotten the recital, ignored Linc's phone calls. It was all Henry had and I was letting him down.

"Okay, where do we start?"

Lincoln put down the mop, took off his rubber gloves and rain slicker, and pointed behind the desk. A pile of boxes blocked the path to it. "How—?" He pointed to the floor. I crawled under the desk and emerged on the other side. Next to the blinking answering machine were piles of opened and unopened mail, a jar of pencils and pens, a bowl of hairpins and rubber bands, a desk calendar still turned to February, the attendance books, a stack of messages and notes in Lincoln's handwriting, Henry's checkbook, and a hard-backed green ledger. It was all so confusing. Magda said I'd have to get a passport. Did I have a birth certificate? I'd call my mother, she must have one.

"Nat!"

"Yeah?"

"Jesus, you faded out again."

"I'm sorry, I . . . I was in Japan, I guess."

"China." He shook his head. "Look, bunhead, I think that's great news, I really do, you deserve it." He reached across the desk and placed his hand on my cheek. "But you're not there now, you dig?"

Fran wandered by. "Okay if I bring a few things in?"

"Sure, whatever," I said over Lincoln's shoulder. "Look, Linc, I'm really sorry I stuck you with all this. Just tell me what to do."

He opened the ledger. "Crack the code." Debits on one side, assets on the other, column after column of Henry's shaky red and black mystery numbers. Each time I'd think I'd figured something out, Linc would dismiss it. "C'mon, Nat, that's not the way to do it." He grumbled and fretted a lot, but, really, he took to the business almost joyfully. It gradually began to occur to me that Linc didn't really need me. He had his own ideas. He just wanted to be authorized, given the okay. Good thing too: that was about all I had to give. Every once in a while Fran would lumber past the desk carrying a box, her orange-fringe lamp shade balanced on her head. Whenever I'd start to ask what she was doing, Linc would shove another document in front of me. "Work," he'd say, "work." We sorted through bills, wrote out checks, forged Henry's signature, argued the various problems surrounding us. I even composed a letter that explained Henry's illness and assured parents that the recital would still go on under the supervision of Lincoln Freeman, Professional Dancer, Bay City Ballet Company. "More like 'Professional Apprentice,' " Lincoln muttered but he didn't dispute the billing. "Good for business," he said. Finally, we agreed he'd take over a reduced schedule of classes, keep the studio temporarily running until the recital was over, pay himself a small salary. We were only looking at a few weeks. "You know," he said, "always wanted to do something like this."

"You did?"

"Yep." Linc licked the back of an envelope, slipped it neatly on top of the growing pile. "This crazy old Hungarian lady, Madame Lenya, comes by the Oakland Community Center one day, looks in at our dance class, sees me. I'm sixteen, goddam near living there 'cause the streets are full of dope and shit. She feels my thighs, looks at my feet, says it's kinda late but she'll train me if I'll help out in her studio. Answer the phone, open the mail, do the books. I was with her two years, 'til the Company took me."

I closed the ledger, stuck it between the roll books. Fran walked by with a bunch of clothes and hangers. The lamp shade was still on her head. "She's moving in, isn't she?"

Linc looked back over his shoulder. "Sure looks that way."

I leaned forward on my wrists. "Her husband kicked her out."

"Straight men," Lincoln said softly. "They don't get it, do they?" He shook his head. "She okay?"

"I'm not sure."

Lincoln straightened up and stretched. "We need a break. I'll order a pizza." He patted my head. "You done good work."

"Thank you, massa." I climbed carefully over the neat little piles on the desk and walked across to the studio doorway. Perhaps it was the soft grey and yellow afternoon shadows pulsating in the studio room. Maybe it was the warmly odd domestic scene before me: a woman leaning into her easel, brush clasped between fingers; a dog dozing in a sunbeam, fur covered in rosin; around them, like a faery circle, piles of boxes, clothes, and unmatched house furnishings; a room of mirrors doubling these images again and again. Whatever it was, it was different and unexpected, a moment neither here nor there nor anywhere, and finally, whatever it was, I felt it.

I began drifting toward the center of the room, away from the bills and rolls and ledgers, away from the world of strict accounting and custodial responsibility and life-support monitors, drifting dreamily, as if harnessed to that parachute in the waiting room, floating ever so slowly downward through the little grey cloud and into the mirrors and reflected lights. I don't know how long I was adrift in that moment, a micro-second, a light-year, but the next thing I knew I was in the middle of the dance floor holding out my arms in a classical pose and there was Lincoln, emerging out of the mirror, simultaneously behind me and in front of me, his hands outstretched, his leg extended behind him in a long *arabesque*. I curtsied to his reflection; he bowed gallantly in turn. We didn't speak, there was no need to. And then we began to dance, together and apart, touching and not touching, following a pattern of steps almost intuitively.

Oh, sure, it was something we'd learned long ago in Himmel's *pas de deux* class—one of those classroom dances that you never forget and never want to do again. But this was different, it was between us—just a quiet secret homage that only Fran and Toby would see. Turning away from the mirrors, we faced each other and began moving unfettered by choreography or reflections, a free dance inside a spontaneous luminous empty space. My hair tumbled down in my face and my body rocked gently—no counts, no music, only the movement. I lifted my arms, touched fingertips with Linc, then let them drift through the air, tumbling, curling, falling like snowflakes. As I twirled and leapt, Lincoln's graceful body seemed to lift us both from the floor and out of the dark labyrinth of too much training. We were on our own, outside time, inside a silent unbounded space of liberated movement. It was so beautiful and peaceful, a moment of almost pure being.

And then, slipping beyond Lincoln, I caught a sunbeam and whirled away by myself, across the floor, past Fran and Toby, through the window of framed light, out among the breathing redwoods and red-berried shrubs and northern air, drifting ever upwards, past that solitary grey cloud and all the things that anybody had ever said to me, until I was looking at the curvature of the earth, the horizon stretching from Indiana to China. It was, I knew even then, too much for me to see all at once. I had felt it; that was enough. Later, when I fell to earth, Linc and Fran and Toby and I shared a pizza. Even later, when I went to see Henry at the hospital, it finally started to rain, cold, hard, and steady. I felt that too.

# Act Three, Scene Four

It will help if you think of the dance as a whole, not
just as a succession of traps and tests. The dazzle
of the big steps depends on the quiet mastery of
the little ones, and during quiet passages you can
get your breath and take stock of the physical
situation about you. But do not think of these
periods as rest and just let go.

–Agnes de Mille, *To A Young Dancer*

I've gotten off the bus in the heart of weary frayed
Haight-Ashbury, an expiring counter-culture of dispirited hip-
pies and aged beats, bruised punk rockers and drugged Western gurus. I carry a blue ceramic urn. It is late May and very
warm; everyone is outdoors; Henry's dead. I'm still not sure it
really happened. I haven't been able to let go of him. I've
obsessed over the urn fourteen days, carried it from one room
in his apartment to the next. I've boxed up papers and photos,
old programs and clothes. I've made phone calls. I've cried a
lot. I've even started believing he will rise from his ashes,

177

magically reappear, his old heart suddenly young again. I can't sleep as long as this possibility exists. Henry would want me to get on with my life. He would want me to find a place for him. A final resting place.

But this is not it. Spectral hawkers crawl the streets, ply bewildered tourists with marijuana sticks and spiked steel collars. Packs of teenage ghouls run the avenue like starved dogs, ribs plain and sharp beneath ripped black T-shirts, hips pushed inward as though hiding tails. Their skin is pale and gauzy, their eyes dark and hollow. The papers call them another 'lost generation.' What am I doing here? This was never one of our places. I just got on a bus, then transferred, then on another, then off. I'm wandering. Henry would hate this place. No real art, no authentic freedom, nothing but a graveyard of the living dead. I hug the urn more tightly, try to shield it with my body. I'm terrified something will happen to the ashes before I've had a proper chance to say goodbye.

At the intersection of Haight and Masonic an old bearded man with long fingernails and rings in his nose is handing out pamphlets about Christ. His lips are the color of raw liver. I turn sideways, my body wrapped around the urn, scurry past him. "Gonna burn, gonna burn, gonna burn," he yells. Running from these daytime horrors, this squalid center of the modern city, I turn onto a quiet street of Victorian flats and slow-moving cars. Henry's still safely between my hands. I feel a little better now. The urgency is settling into resignation. But I still don't know where to go.

It was the end of March when I told Magda I wasn't going on the China tour. I wanted to make it brief, no long explanations or lies, just a succinct statement: "I cannot go." I knew this wouldn't be good enough for her, it never was, but I'd made up my mind, was determined to hold my own. As usual, I went to her studio dressing room, and, as usual, she made it hard for me.

## Act Three, Scene Four

She was sitting at her writing desk, a pair of reading glasses crouched on the end of her nose. She tilted her forehead toward me and peered over the glasses. "My dear, hiding from the Mafia again?"

I hadn't been to class for almost a week, since I'd gone home with Henry. I stood in her doorway, reluctant to step inside. "A friend of mine is very ill," I explained, already betraying my original decision not to give her any unnecessary information.

"A friend?" Her eyebrows met together almost viciously. This was going to be even harder than I thought. I stayed in the doorway, said nothing. Magda stared at me a moment, then took a folder off the top of her desk, opened it, offered me a mimeographed sheet of paper. "Your itinerary, dear." She wasn't even looking at me, had already turned back to her work at the desk. The mimeograph dangled listlessly at the end of her outstretched arm.

So this is what it came to. I could just make out some of the printing: two columns, events on the left, dates and times on the right. It was so easy, so tempting. All I had to do was step into her room, take that sheet of paper. Instead, I took a deep breath. "No one else can care for my friend," I said. "He's dying." Magda said nothing, didn't even look up from her folder. Perhaps she hadn't heard me, perhaps I hadn't said it. "I . . . I really wanted to go." Still no response, yet this time I was sure something had been communicated. I had that cold tingling feeling I usually got when I knew Magda wasn't pleased.

She took off her glasses, turned slowly, and looked up at me. "Do you really believe, Natalie, that you can pick and choose what you will and will not do in this Company?" Her voice was steady, her eyes never shifted. I remained in the doorway, uncertain how to respond to a question that had only one answer. Magda watched me carefully, then placed the folder behind her on the desk and extended a hand. "Come," her voice still steady, "let's clear up this confusion."

I hung back, did not take her offered hand. "I can't. Someone's dying."

*179*

"My dear, someone is *always* dying." Sighing theatrically, she stood up, swooshed across the floor, then sat down again on the edge of the divan. "Didn't we go through this once before? Wasn't there already a death this season?"

"That was my father," I said quietly.

"Dying again, is he?" Her face was placid, unrevealing. Only her mouth had that familiar ironic twist to it.

I could feel myself coloring over. "No, not really. This is . . . someone else."

Magda sighed again, but this time as if genuinely annoyed, and leaned forward on the divan. "Natalie, let's drop the games. Why don't you want to go to China? What are you afraid of?"

I was still standing in the doorway. I couldn't answer her questions, at least, not in the way she wanted. "I've thought about this a great deal," I said, "really, I have." Magda's eyes pulled together, like two dark magnets. She wasn't impressed. "But I decided staying here was more responsible—"

"My dear," Magda intoned in a cutting voice, "you've got it wrong. You're under contract."

"Yes, I know, but—"

"But you're a dancer, Natalie." She paused. "Not a nurse." She crossed her legs sharply, pushed a bracelet up her arm. Her words drew me a couple of steps into the room, but I stopped short of the empty chair across from the divan. If I sat, I would sink. "Of course," Magda continued, "I could be wrong."

Could she be? Suddenly, it hardly seemed possible. She was always so sure of herself. She had no way of knowing that my mother was a nurse, yet, as always, she was driving straight for the heart of things, as if she had a roadmap to my soul. "I'm still a dancer," I said tearfully.

"Yes?" She gazed past my left shoulder, as though waiting for the real me to come through the door. She didn't really know about Henry either. Without being quite aware of it, I'd been steering him away from her clinical gaze ever since the parking lot outside the theater, when we'd surprised her talking to Simon. I'd only thought then, in my embarrassed adolescent hurt and confusion, that Simon mustn't see me. What I didn't begin to understand, until much later, was how much more threatening it would have been if Magda had seen Henry. Simon had been merely indifferent to my feelings; but Magda didn't want me to have any, at least none that she couldn't control.

I tried the one thing I had left. "I have to do the right thing."
"Of course, dear." She was impatient, derisive. "We all do."
"Wouldn't you do the same?"

Magda emitted a champagne laugh, threw back her head to reveal the white of her throat. "I *always* took the job," she said emphatically, flicking her hand ever so slightly. "It's what *you* must do." The lines around her mouth were now tight and set, like the reinforced seams on a costume.

I stared at one of the posters of Magda framed on the wall behind her head. It was a remarkable face: young and hard, staring confidently through the camera into the future. It never had, never would, look back. But, as much as I'd once wanted to wear that face, I realized now that I couldn't. Not if I always had to take the job. I knew what it was like not to be free to choose. Even then I'd tried to set something aside, something that was mine. "I'm sorry," I said, "but I'm not going." I remember when I said it that my steady voice surprised me. I didn't know then where it came from and I'm still not really sure, but I'd like to think it was there all the time, just waiting for me to make an authentic statement. In the elusive memory of my mind's ear it sounds like the voice I used when my father threatened the trip to Indy with Mrs. Pike—except that time it said I *was* going.

I guess Magda heard it too, because she looked at me in a way she never had before, as if we weren't dancers anymore and there wasn't a Bay City Ballet Company. Suddenly, and unexpectedly, we were just two women in a room, one sitting, one standing, two women who had never been friends and now never could be. Once upon a time we had shared something: call it a dream. But we had woken up—and discovered that, after all, we inhabited different bodies. Sure, I still wanted her respect, still needed her approval, yet now she knew that no matter how hard she squeezed my heart, dug her polished nails into the valves, it was still mine. For better or for worse, and I really wasn't sure which it was to be, I would choreograph my own life.

She rose from the divan, a monstrous exquisite woman, just beginning to fade into a reluctant old age. I backed up to the doorway. I didn't want her touching me. "You're not going to change your mind, Natalie, I can see that. Forgive me: I misjudged you. I thought you were . . . ," she paused, as if searching not for a word but a tone, and when she found it, it was angry and sad and wistful all at once, " . . . *different*."

"I'm very sorry," I tried to say, but Magda placed a finger over her lips, shook her head, then abruptly dropped her hand. "Let us not tarry over regrets, Natalie. You have made your choice. Go care for your dying friend." She threw a dismissive hand in the air, then turned and followed it back toward her desk.

"It may take a while," I said to her retreating figure.

"Yes, it usually does," she muttered sardonically over her shoulder.

"May I come back?"

She stopped at the desk, turned and faced me again. "You must come back." Her voice was matter-of-fact, business-like. "You have a contract. I expect you to honor it."

"Does this mean—?"

"It means nothing," she said curtly, then sat down and put on her glasses again. She was already hard at work when I stepped back into the hall and closed the door.

I walk listlessly among the fume-speckled pigeons and boxed yews that surround the now gurgling granite fountain in the middle of the Civic Center plaza. Almost a year has passed since I posed here as a living half-formed statue. Somehow, I'm still with the Company, still holding an impossible *arabesque*. Once again I think of how Henry and I would sit on our bench, feed the pigeons, wait for the rain. But now I remember something I always used to try to forget. He'd want to leave when too many other people showed up. "Why do they come here?" he'd say. "Why don't they leave us alone?" I guess he was afraid I'd just disappear into the crowd, a secret tourist, gone forever, like so much else in his life. Who knows, maybe he was right. I came to him on a whim: riding the BART line, clutching a sheet torn from the Yellow Pages. There wasn't much holding me down. I could have been swept up and carried away so easily. In fact, I almost was, several times. But he never lost faith in me and, finally, I found my way back to him.

So now I sit on the fountain edge, hug Henry to my chest, wait out the panic. The weather is beautiful; there are people everywhere; I have nothing to give the pigeons. An easy wind brushes the grainy concrete. A few feet in front of me is a man dressed in a nun's habit. He's giving away black balloons and bumper stickers that read 'Sex without Sin.' He's one of the Sisters of Perpetual Indulgence, a local phenomenon, drag queens with a social conscience and a political agenda. They raise money for charities, feed the homeless, campaign for gay rights, do the can-can on the footpath across the Golden Gate Bridge. One of them—I think it was Sister Bang-Bang or Sister Coitus—ran for City Council. He didn't get elected. I run my hands over the urn. I wonder if they ever get the bodies confused. "This is really crazy," I whisper, "what am I going to do with you?"

# THE BODY OF DANCERS

As Lincoln pulled back the curtains onto the empty high-school auditorium, I squinted into the bright incandescent wing lights. My head felt thick and tingly from too little sleep; the lights were making me dizzy. "How is it now, bunhead?" Lincoln was behind the lightboard in the wings, fiddling with the dials when he wasn't shouting at me.

I stumbled toward the downstage corner, where Fran was propped behind her easel. "Very yellow."

Abruptly, the stage was washed in sharp green streaks and cool smoky-blue shadows. "This make a difference?"

Fran peeked around her easel. "Hey, Linc, cut it out! Can't see anything." She wore a T-shirt spray-painted with the words 'Giving De Gas to Degas.'

Linc darted out of the wings, his eyes shining like two white bulbs. "Listen up, you two, doors open in twenty minutes!"

Rubbing a piece of red charcoal across the canvas, Fran looked up and narrowed her eyes at Linc, as though warning him to behave. They'd both been like this for weeks, carefully letting me off the hook, eying each other when they thought I wasn't looking. They were trying to take care of me. I guess I needed it. "Blue's better than yellow." My voice was vague, fuzzy, almost incoherent. I was just too tired to contribute anything worthwhile.

"Wash out most of the green," Fran said firmly, "and add a little pink." Linc nodded and dashed back into the wings. "It's Okay, Nat," she whispered hoarsely. "Why don't you go backstage for a while?"

I straggled through the wings, headed toward the dressing room. The two of them had been here all day, suffering the usual disasters of a dance-recital run-through. By the time I'd come in most of the problems had been forgotten, remedied, or ignored. The only tales still being repeated were about a coed intermediate jazz class which had contrived to lock itself into a closet, some tap dancers who had shuffle-ball-changed their peanut-butter sandwiches into the dressing-room floor, and the pre-ballet kids' discovery of a box of fake eyelashes and a pot of glue. But I had a hard time getting excited about any of this. I'd been looking through Henry's fading eyes for too many weeks now. All that really counted in my narrow little world were the daily routines: boiling the hand towels in a cracked-white pasta pot; keeping track of the medications; turning the heat up, turning it down; inching the sweat-stained sheets out from under him; feeding him; emptying the bedpan; sitting with him as the room got darker each day. It was all I had to believe in. I was trying to hold on to him, but he just kept slipping away. And so I boiled the towels and changed the sheets and rubbed his legs, and waited—for the drugs to kick in, for sleep, for Fran to spell me a few hours in the late mornings.

The noise in the dressing room was unbelievable, like a vat full of bumblebees. I circled aimlessly around the room, bumping into parents and children, trying to remember why I was here. But life was buzzing crazily on all sides, and I was desperately disconnected from everyone. Then I saw the check-in sheet taped to the vanilla-colored wall. It seemed to offer something solid: another routine. I peeled it off and began calling out names. Most of the kids ignored me. I tried a different approach. "Tumblers! Where are the tumblers? You're on first." A knot of girls and boys wearing red glittering tanktops and white tennis shorts twisted around me. Each clutched a blue mat. Their pudgy arms and painted faces bobbed up and down. "C'mon," I said irritably, "make a line." They stared at me, didn't move. I stared back, uncertain what to do next. Suddenly, one of the parents reached over my shoulder and snatched the check-in list from my hands. "That's not the way to talk to them," she snapped. I turned on her, startled and trembling, just as Fran rushed forward. "It's okay, Natalie," she soothed, "everyone's on edge." She pushed me gently away from the squirming tumblers and irate mother. I was still trembling. Everything here seemed to be slipping away too. "Isn't there something I can do?" Fran grabbed one of the pre-balleteers by her pony tail. "Take this one to Lincoln, he must be looking for her."

When I got backstage, Linc was arranging the pre-ballet kids in a row. They were going on after the tumblers and tappers. "Hey, bunhead," he said, "you're doing good work." But I wasn't, and we both knew that. I delivered the little girl to him silently, then crawled on a stool by the wings. There were too many sounds cluttering my head: the audience outside filing into the auditorium, the rustling of programs, the children's chatter, Linc's soft playful commands, backstage parents scurrying to and fro. I couldn't remember when I'd last slept.

During the night Henry was always restless. He complained that his legs were drawing, that he had bad dreams. And he kept calling out to me. Sometimes he got me confused with Fran, and then I'd wonder why I'd bothered to stay behind to take care of him. What was the point of this if he couldn't tell the difference? "It's me, Henry," I'd say, "your old heart." But it would be sometime deep in the night, a moment when names don't always signify. He'd reach out, grope for my hand, mutter, "What time is it, Fran?" I'd get so angry—not at him, it wasn't his fault—that I'd squeeze his hand real hard. "Henry!" Then he'd move one of his legs outside the covers, bend it at the knee, say again and again, "there's a pain inside, there's a pain inside." And I'd rub and I'd rub, trying to get that hurt out of his leg, knowing I couldn't and the best thing would be if he could just sleep through. But he wouldn't—almost refused to—because it was black all around us and he was scared to die in the dark. Finally, he'd remember it was me and he'd go to sleep. I'd watch the minute hand on the clock trace a tiny arc in the endless circle—and then he'd cry out and it would start all over again. By the time Fran had taken over the vigil, he was ready for a real sleep.

"You seen a pink tutu anywhere?" Linc's voice startled me. I leaned forward on the stool, stared into his glowing eyes. "What?" Linc patted me on the leg. "Little girl," he said calmly, "fat belly and ribbons. The one you delivered to me. She's missing." I swiveled around, looked over my shoulder. "I don't know." Linc squeezed my knee. "Course you don't. It's okay. If she comes wandering by, just send her this way." He pointed to the wings where the pre-ballet kids were waiting. I could just see the tumblers making somersaults across the stage. Some kind of ice-skating music was hollering from the walls. "Sure, all right," I said.

Suddenly, the tumblers were all holding hands, bowing from the waist, beaming under the lights as the audience clapped. A mob of tappers wearing black headbands and silver leotards thundered past me. "Go get 'em, metal-toes!" Linc called out, as though cheering on a football team. I grabbed my head, closed my eyes, opened them, tried to keep from sinking. A few days earlier I'd gone out to do some grocery shopping, left Fran with Henry. When I'd returned, Linc was sitting on the edge of Henry's bed, talking as though they were lifelong friends. Fran was gone. I hid in the doorway, uncertain what I should do. Henry hadn't shown much interest in the studio since he'd come home, seemed satisfied to know a "nice young man was running things for him." Linc, on the other hand, had wanted to meet Henry. He had a lot of questions to ask about the studio. I'd told him I didn't think it was a good idea. I don't really know what they said, what took place between them. But afterward Linc seemed less worried and Henry was pleased. "A very serious young man," he said, "good head for the business."

Fran was in front of me, bent over the tape machine, punching buttons. "Can I do anything?" My voice sounded weak and powdery. I wasn't even sure I'd spoken. "See my boys anywhere?" she whispered. I looked straight across the stage to the other side. "They're with the bunheads," I said. Fran backed away from the machine, peered past the vibrating on-stage tap dancers, who'd fallen out of pattern and were turning off-rhythm. "How about that," she said quietly. Her sons had started taking the BART over to the studio soon after Fran had moved in. At first they'd just wanted to ride their skateboards out front on the pavement, bounce basketballs against the outside walls, tease the girls, pester their mother. But then, as though the studio magic had gotten inside them too, they'd started trailing after Linc, asking questions, watching ballet class out of the sides of their still-wary eyes. I guess they'd never seen a real male artist before. Now the younger, Brian, wanted to take ballet, as long as he didn't have to wear anything pink.

The tappers scurried off into the wings. I watched Lincoln walk the tutu-girls out onto the stage. I wondered if the lost one had ever turned up; I'd forgotten to look for her. Linc carefully arranged each one in her set position, then turned and bowed gallantly to the audience. A loud communal chuckle, then some applause. I got off the stool and wandered backstage. Fran was setting up her drawings in the dressing-room hall-way. For weeks she'd been sketching the kids at the studio; now she hoped to sell the pictures during intermission. The parents were getting a deal, even if they'd need labels to recognize their own children. The sketches were really pretty good: Fran had seen something authentic. She'd concentrated mostly on the older dancers—captured the hard work, the sweat, the struggle against the body. There wasn't anything soft or romantic about these drawings. She really had turned Degas inside-out, taken his muted soft fantasy and streaked it with pain.

I meandered down the row of pictures, tried to focus on them. But my eyes were heavy and the colors seemed to be floating together, drifting in and out of the tinkling jewelery-box music. "You okay?" Fran asked. I nodded sleepily. "Not much longer to go, Nat." Her voice was soft and kind, like a great big pillow. I put my arms around her, rested my head against her solid body. "Just want it to end," I said quietly. Fran hugged me, then walked me back to the stool. "It will," she whispered, "too soon."

"Shit," Linc said, "wouldya look at that." The missing pre-ballet kid had suddenly reappeared, just as her group was finishing its dance. She'd run straight across the stage to our side, sobbing and gulping, her ribbons flying behind her. The other kids onstage had stopped moving, were pointing their fingers at her. Linc jumped into the wings, urged them on. "Take your bows now, c'mon, take your bows." The crying child ran onto the stage again and stood in bewilderment beneath the lights, tears rolling crazily down her rouged cheeks. Linc cupped his hands over his mouth, called out to her: "That's it, make your pretty curtsey." She looked from side to side, like a stunned wild animal. "You can do it," Linc coaxed, "I know you can." Suddenly, the little girl smiled, gathered up her stiff short tutu at the sides as though it were a dress, and offered an awkward wobbly bow. As the audience clapped in relief, the child curtsied again. Finally, Linc had to go onstage and get her. Even then she was reluctant to leave.

Out front of the Cannery, Armand whines French love songs, plucks the guitar strings with his tobacco fingers, squints morosely into the lukewarm sunlight. He's got himself a real money-making crowd today, it's raining nickels and dimes. Sitting at his feet is a barefoot girl wearing a tattered sweater, a freckled American face. She's stringing beads with her small dirty hands. I hover outside the circle of strangers, even consider giving Armand a dollar to do the Woody Guthrie song again. But his charm, whatever it is, no longer bewitches me. For a brief moment my body blocks the sun and he glances over, his black eyes glaring. But I'm just a dark shape outlined against the light and he doesn't realize it's me. He never did.

Still hugging the urn, I move away, weave aimlessly through a maze of rickety oyster stands, five-dollar museums, double-jointed freaks. I glide unevenly, like a broken sailboat. My head is whirling, my body empty. Stretched out in the fogless day, the Bay shimmers and beckons. Ahead of me are the piers, a small cold distance to Alcatraz. I still don't know where to go. All I know is that I can't keep this urn. From now on, I travel light. It's enough that our memories are buried in my heart. I'm almost seventeen, I need to be free.

I've wandered up to the ticket booth on Pier 43. Without thinking, I hand over a soiled $20 bill, wait for my change, watch the clock hands move slowly toward two. And then, swept up by the crowd of tourists, I find myself on board the Alcatraz boat. Rocking and sailing westward beneath the sun, I start singing to Henry, rubbing my hands back and forth over the smooth cold ceramic vessel balanced in my lap. The prison-bound passengers shift away from me, huddle on wooden benches along the backbone of the boat. All they want is a postcard picture to take home, a gruesome story, three minutes in black solitary confinement somewhere inside the dead damp prison. I'm ruining it for them, but I don't care.

I get up from the bench, wobble over to the boat's railing, peer down into the roiling ice-green waters. Alcatraz is closing in, a dark looming island, a bad dream from which there is no escape. Hugging Henry to my chest, I sway inside the light and waves, hum softly the familiar cadences:

Rock of Ages cleft for me,
Let me hide myself in thee;
Let the water and the blood,
From thy wounded side which flowed,
Be of sin the double cure,
Save from wrath and make me pure.

I'm crying real tears, the kind I'm not afraid to hide. I guess I didn't know it, but I was headed this way all along. The Rock and the water: a double cure: so be it.

I wait patiently until the deck is clear, until everyone's gone to the other side of the boat to get a better view of the approaching prison. Then I open the urn, fling it as far into the Bay as I can. The boat's slowing down before it docks at the pier, but even so, I quickly lose sight of the place where the urn enters the water. Instead, I watch as the birds courageously circle the sky, plunge down into the foam, reappear, shoot gracefully upward, like small gleaming rockets. When the boat finally stops, I don't get off. I've already taken that tour. I know what's inside.

It wasn't easy taking care of Henry in those last weeks. Mostly I just went through the motions. There were plenty of books on how to cope with death, how to be an efficient cheerful nurse. They all seemed so impersonal and glib, had nothing to do with who I was or who Henry had been. After a while I stopped checking them out of the library. I began to sense that it was just a matter of time until none of this counted anyway. The clichés would set in soon enough, leave me feeling as bereft as my mother must have felt when my father died. Except, of course, I didn't really feel it: not then. So I still kept busy during the day, doing the routine things. It was only at night, huddled in the corner chair of Henry's closed dark bedroom, that I'd begin to worry. Where was the Company tour now? What was Magda going to do to me? Why hadn't I called my mother for so long? Was there really a God? The voices in my head were relentless, I felt powerless to stop them.

I couldn't actually see Henry from where I sat but I knew when he was up and stirring. Sometimes I would get to him before he'd even call out. Tonight was different. I think I'd finally worn myself down, was almost asleep, when suddenly his voice drifted through the darkness, startled me. "How about some brandy, old heart." I peered through the shadowy room to his bed. All I could make out was a lumpy motionless shape wrapped in a quilt. Maybe I'd been dreaming. I got up from the chair, trailing a blanket after me, then reached out my hand and rested it on his shoulder. "Henry?" He took my hand, squeezed it. "Something to warm us." I wasn't sure he should be drinking, but somehow that didn't seem to matter. If this was what he wanted, I would get it for him. "Okay," I whispered.

## THE BODY OF DANCERS

I stumbled through the dark into the living room, wandered around in the silence, searched numbly for the brandy and a glass. When I finally returned, Henry was propped up in the bed. "Let's have some light," he said softly. I started for the wall switch. "Candles, Natalie. Light the candles." There was something strong and insistent in his tone, as though he'd finally emerged from this nightmare illness. I couldn't really believe it, but I wanted to.

I went over to his bureau, felt around for matches, then lit three candles. I brought the red one over to the trunk-stand by his bed. "Our favorite," I said. He gave me his sliding-board smile. I uncapped the brandy, poured out some of the dark gold liquid into the tumbler. I handed it to him and sat on the edge of the mattress, rubbing my hand across his leg. "What are we celebrating?"

Henry held the glass out to me with his good hand. " 'Love's mysteries in souls do grow, / But yet the body is her book.' "

I wrapped my fingers around his, took a sip of the brandy, watched the candle's jagged flame cast a shadow on the wall behind his head. "Who wrote that?"

"Oh, it doesn't matter. A poet. He died a long time ago." He squeezed my hand. "Anyway, I changed it a little. Poetic license. In your honor, old heart."

I crawled under the quilt next to him, leaned my head on his thin shoulder. "I love you, sweet man."

We sat like that for a while, sharing the glass of brandy, watching the candle wax drip slowly down onto the bruised-black traveling trunk. It was so warm and quiet, just the two of us, so intimate. I guess I should have known this was the last stretch before the end, something I would return to again and again, as though searching for some clear sign which said: He's going now, this is only his goodbye. But I didn't know. I wanted so much to believe this was a miraculous recovery, that the flush in his face, the steadiness of his hand, the poetic allusion meant that he was coming back to me. I felt if we could only stay this way until the morning sunlight burned through the drapes we'd have outwitted the illness, deceived it with love.

I should have known something was wrong. It was the first time since he'd been ill that he hadn't mentioned the baby. Maybe he never really believed in it, or perhaps he believed in it just as long as he needed to. And maybe I did too. It's hard to say. But later, when it shouldn't have mattered anymore, I felt the loss. What I remember now is that, as we settled back on the bed, he started humming something familiar from one of the traditional sentimental ballets, either *Swan Lake* or *Les Sylphides*. Whatever it was, it was pure and light and magical. And just as we'd often done in the early days, we gently began tracing our movements in the muted light, willingly surrendered ourselves to the softly flickering candle flames. I lifted an arm, pale and long, let my fingers waft through the air, waited for Henry to follow. And he did, great dancer that he was, raising his good hand up to mine, partnering me inside our private special music. We were both smiling and humming, rapidly flitting our fingers about, delighted, as we'd always been, at the crazy beautiful dances we could bring to life, how easy it was to be boneless and free, making love out of shadows, candles, breath . . . between us, our flesh, our love. It was the only dance that counted. And then it was over, as though I really had dreamed it, or we'd dreamed it together.

# Act Four

You finish, walled safe by light. And there are the
faces and the noise, and it was all over so fast, this
thing you prepared ten years for.
  –Agnes de Mille, *To A Young Dancer*

*I*dentity is contingent upon broken dreams. Tonight, as
on every Tuesday, Friday, and Saturday night throughout the
summer, we dance *Swan Lake*, the greatest, most tragic, most
classical ballet of all. Bound in feathered bodice, tight-fitting
headpiece, hard pink war-shoes, I dutifully circumnavigate the
tape-marked rosined stage with twenty-nine other trembling
white swan-maidens. Running on the balls of our feet, we try
to create the illusion of flying around a blue-white lake, itself
a beguiling concoction of dry ice and colored light. We stab our
boneless arms into the air, rotate our shoulder blades in endless

194

circles, resound inside the musical crescendos with small exact insignificant breaths. This could be the role of a lifetime, the role I was born to play. It's my seventeenth birthday. I'm in the *corps*.

The assembled guests of Act One have already emptied the stage wine-bottles, danced in mock celebration of another birthday, young Prince Siegfried's. He's doomed, perhaps cursed, to choose a beautiful wife before the evening is over, before the curtain falls. He must do it, he has no choice. This is the way this story always comes out, night after night, before audiences around the world. Boy meets girl, boy loses girl, boy finds girl. Always the same old story, the familiar patriarchal plot, reenacted again and again in ballets, operas, plays, movies, sit-coms, and soaps. Love triumphs, closes the anxious circle of women's projected lives. So I ripple fifth in a double-diagonal assembly-line of birds-in-waiting, peer furtively through mascara eyes to center stage, to the spotlight that can never now be mine. Relegated to the background in the story that never changes, I am indistinguishable from all the others, from the body of dancers.

The *corps de ballet* is a writhing pit of jealousy, disillusionment, and resignation. Magda has sent me here, stamped my timecard with her cold disapproval. She does not speak to me anymore, but every night it's as if I hear her unforgiving voice: "This is what it's like for most women. You had your chance. You made your choice. Now live it." Banished and humbled by her unspoken words, I hold my head at precisely the same angle as the next girl, breathe, hop, and sweat in synchronized measure, wear a practiced expression of hollow relief upon my exposed powdered face. "You made your choice. Now live it." And so, with the other swans, I complain about blisters, rehearsals, stage lighting, diets, tempos, broken shanks—the traditional pre-approved topics for *corps*, no different really from what women have always talked about. Monthly cycles, the latest fashion, self-analysis, flattering settings, hidden illusions. We pass the time this way. Most of us will eventually lose faith: it's why there's always room for another body.

Stage-night is falling on Act One, the curtain will soon be lowered. Harps, strings, oboes: a swelling theme of doom: a brief entrance, an exit. Posed in the shadows of the stage, just another object in the general gaze, I drift off, remember something that may or may not have happened, something I've patched together out of memory and fantasy, the past, my life, another kind of death. Once more I enter the dark red-brick house in Indiana, creep quietly past the front-room door of my father's secret fragmented world where the confused knotted images of childhood twist around us both, like angry coils of TV static. I see and don't see the opened black-leather Bible, the pair of scarred cowboy boots, the blinking Zenith set, the brown metal furnace shaking against the peeling wall, the spilled vodka and stale cornbread, the bloodied rags stuffed along the baseboards. Is he here? Am I? Where am I going?

Suddenly, I feel it, the slow irregular pulse vibrating along the floor. It's coming from the cellar, from the dark secret place beneath my dancing feet. Of course. A young woman alone in a haunted house. Where else would she go? That's what they want to see, isn't it? The frightened eyes, the thin dress, the pale skin, the creaking floorboard, the dark staircase, the horror lurking at the bottom of things. That's what they want: to know what happens to the body of dancers when the lights go out. So be a good girl, Natalie. Find the cellar door.

Prince Siegfried prowls the stage with his crossbow and lighted torch, suspended between midnight and dawn of his twenty-first birthday, searching for a swan to kill or tame. Doesn't matter which. It's all the same to him, to Simon. He's been gifted from the beginning with male indifference, with the power to murder or create. Backstage, between acts, he passes me in a flurry of invincible color and curls: blue-vested tunic with two evenly spaced bands of gold, clean white tights, burgundy-painted lips. His theater-face is the same one I slept with. He never looks at me. Why should he? I'm only a sad flightless female bird of the night, eyes downcast, emerging from the theater of water and sky. I'm not even really here.

I reach for the huge spherical cellar doorknob, twist it with both hands as though turning the dial on a safe. But it won't open. Of course not. I must try harder, must show how willing I am to descend to the depths, to plunge my body into the unknown. And so I search until I find it, the familiar grating in the door, the one that opens from the inside, the one the young woman puts her hand through and tugs from the outside until its rusty hinges reluctantly give way. I stand now at the top of the stairs, on the edge of the abyss. A slow-rising stream of moist decayed wood drifts up from the impenetrable darkness. There's no light to carry me down these rickety splintered steps into the rottenness below. Doesn't matter. The show must go on. We must move our body into the next position.

I change my arms, set my fingers, assume the proper attitude. Lowering my eyes so that I'm staring at the turned-out tormented feet of the dancer next to me, I listen to her heaving breaths, her own tale of abjection. The Indiana summer's swarming with clouds and insects, she tells me, the whole sky's boiling in rage. Momentarily reconnected across the narrowing expanse of the country, we speak beneath the words, around the point, the double-talk of mother and daughter. A lie that should fool neither of us displaces a truth known to both of us because we're determined to deceive ourselves. "Henry died," I say, trying for a flat even tone. "You know, my coach." It's only a name to her, but she knows, must know, what my voice conceals. "I'm sorry, honey. Were you close?" A pause. Too long: the silence tells all. Then, finally, a faltering statement, never meant to be completed, that hurts us both, "Well, you know . . ."

A stage-left girl is on the wrong foot, but there's nothing she can do about it without disrupting the pure motionless line of swans. I can see the panic in her slow blinking black-lined eyes.

# THE BODY OF DANCERS

Down there, in the darkness, the audience rattles programs, tries to get inside the ballet's story-line. Prince Siegfried's hunting party of bachelors is traipsing across the stage, pursuing the *corps* of long-necked swans. We *bourrée* in place, maintaining still the illusion of movement. I reach out, touch the wet mildewed walls on either side of the cellar staircase. They are my only guide down into this labyrinth of darkness where only my fears are distinct. I descend the creaking wooden stairs slowly and carefully, shivering in the ever cooler dampness, brushing past unseen cobwebs. With each step I hesitate, uncertain if my foot will come down again on creaking wood or the hard-packed earth of the cellar floor—or nothing. My wings are aching against the imaginary wind. I don't believe I can hold them in place much longer. The faceless feathered girl on the wrong foot drifts and flutters in her line, marks time until the music changes.

All this week Fran's been painting Henry's apartment, stripping layer after layer of history away from the present, as though she might finally, miraculously, find herself beneath the multiple surfaces. She and Linc are going to live here now. I can't: too many memories. Whenever she slaps her paintbrush on the freshly spackled walls, she screws her face into a fierce pout, shakes her scarved head from side to side. Betrayed by language, men, machines, she works furiously inside the colors. It's taken her over forty years to shed her own good-girl skin. Now she's all blood and nerves and tissue, an artist, stripped to the bone. A mournful violin: the cue to bury my face modestly in mythical feathers. We're in the forest scene, the beginning of the Second Act.

The Swan Queen leads us on stage; the Prince sees her, steals away from the hunting party. Love-struck, he steps forward, reveals himself. The Swan Queen is frightened: that big bow, those sharp arrows. Not to worry, little bird, he gestures, I wouldn't stick *you*, and casts aside his weapons. Reassured, she mimes her misfortune. As Fran says, it gets pretty complicated here, lots of flapping feathers and mournful posturing, lots of running in and out of the forest, lots of squinting at the fine print in the program, but, in its nutty fairy-tale way, it's familiar enough and everybody soon gets the message. An evil sorcerer has transformed her into a swan, the lake is really a swamp made of her mother's heartbroken tears, only a good man can break the spell and make her a real woman again. Siegfried welcomes this news. What ambitious fairy-tale prince wouldn't? If he breaks that spell, he'll be a hero. Will *she* be grateful! Even better, she must be valuable and virginal: evil sorcerers don't waste nasty spells on unclean serving girls. Big dowry there, maybe a kingdom. All this Siegfried realizes in an instant of mythical time, so fast we don't even notice. What we see is Simon getting down on one knee, hand on his breast, pledging his eternal love. The Swan Queen—Valerie, of course—reaches out to him, he rises, and they run off into the forest. The delighted swan-maidens—that's us—fly around the stage again, find a pose, preen our feathers. Then the Swan Queen and the Prince return, begin to dance. We watch. Intently. After all, Valerie's dancing for us too. We're her ladies-in-waiting, transformed along with her. Simon could also make the *corps* real women again. Will he expect all of us to be grateful?

"Where you gonna go?" Fran asks me. Stretched out on Henry's old sofa, I stare up at the ceiling, imagine those boiling Indiana clouds, the blooming summer flowers, the languid heat, the cherry trees rotting in the soil. Simon triumphantly lifts Valerie above his head. Her legs slice the air, clean as glass. It's an *adagio* of submission, we all know she's going to pay for being good. I'm controlling the counts, straining to see beyond the sister torsos, the feathered caps, the penetrating lights, the dry ice swirling upward from the lake. I'd like to join a parade, a huge unruly mob of mocking marchers led by the Sisters of Perpetual Indulgence: all the misfits of the world, banded together in a carnival of difference, spilling haphazardly through the city streets and across the Golden Gate Bridge, waving banners and flags and signs. "Across the Golden Gate Bridge," I whisper, still staring at the ceiling. Fran slaps her paintbrush on the wall, shakes her scarved head. "Great. Then where will you be?" I don't answer. "Marin County," she says, "that's where."

The Prince weaves in and out of our protective lines, touches each swan-maiden on the shoulder. He's searching for his Queen; she's disappeared into the wings, lured back to the dark safety of the evil sorcerer. It's not turning out to be as easy as the Prince thought, unless this is just a game, a little mating ritual. I see him coming, striding purposefully among us, thirty swooning yearning females with arched necks, taped-down breasts, girdled spirits. It makes no sense, yet, despite everything, I carry inside me this hope, this belief, this burden, that Simon will choose me. Something—a certain look in his eyes, a lingering hand—will indicate that I'm the special swan, the one he should be dancing with, the one he'll marry in the end. I'm pressed against the sweating cellar wall, still posed on the decaying steps, listening to the wind rattle above me. I turn around and peer up the staircase, just as the door slams shut. One cold finger of light slips through the metal grating.

Four charming cygnets appear, arms crossed and linked, legs and heads jointed in solo spectacle, like marionettes controlled by invisible strings. It's a rapid brief famous *pas de quatre*, joyously heralds us closer to the end of Act Two. On the hardwood shiny floors of Henry's legacy, Lincoln moves barefoot among a new generation of dancing fools. Sun burns the windows, plants sprout in every corner, music rains through the gaps in the wall-paneling. "Take it," I say from the doorway. Linc walks slowly toward me, rolls his wet chocolate eyes, holds out his hands. "Bunhead, you done gone crazy." But I know this is right, for both of us. Perhaps it won't betray him; I'm pretty sure what it will do to me. "I mean it," I say, "the studio's yours now." Over his shoulder I can see the parachute.

## Act Four

We never could figure out where it came from and nobody ever sent us a bill. So Lincoln's unfurled it and draped it decoratively across the reception area, as if he really has just dropped out of the sky into foreign territory. Alerted by the rippling music, the lowered lights, I join the swans in full flightless protest. We run like this until the second-act curtain falls.

We fly down the cement stairs from the stage to the greenroom to the dressing rooms. In this act, the third, we do not dance. We've been reduced to our essence, a representation of our virtue, a half-dozen plastic mechanical swans appearing occasionally beneath a spotlight, drawn back and forth across the stage by wires and stagehands. Momentarily enchanted with an impostor Black Swan—Valerie, again—Siegfried has forgotten all about virtue and fairy-tale heroism. Don't worry, he'll be forgiven. Dual role, dual standard. Meanwhile, we keep the homefires burning. In the dressing room, between the acts, we pound our shoes with hammers, soften the boxes so we can glide silently across the stage floor, darn our satin toes to keep from slipping. Our arms rise in unison, our hands and backs ache from the work, our faces are stitched and sweating with the same hard-earned fear. We come from a long line of seamstresses: centuries have passed and still we hold a threaded needle between our arthritic fingers. There are three pink balloons pinned to my mirror, a party streamer on my make-up case, a hard glossy toe shoe with my name stenciled in red. The *corps* has remembered my birthday. There's even a cake, but so far only Carabee has had a piece.

I plaster Saran Wrap around my ankles to keep them insulated, draw it tighter and tighter against the tendons, then cut myself a piece of cake, eat it quickly in this room of disapproving eyes. When I look up, the other girls glance away. I take another piece, slowly fork the chocolate river into my mouth, feel it melting in my throat. The mirrors double my identity, my size, while the gasping *corps* girls stab their shoes with needles. Some nights Pristie comes backstage, a silent apparition lurking in the shadows of my phantom life. He still thinks I'm unique, surveils me from the darkness with his cold parrot eyes, calculates the moment to approach me again. Futile ambition, watchfulness debased. He's willing to wait. Someday he'll lead me back to the semi-tonic solitude of the white piano-room. The *corps* senses the danger: the other girls hover protectively about me, braid their pale white arms around my back. In these moments we are bound together, an impenetrable body of fear and loathing.

His apprentice class has already ended, but Himmel remains, still rapping his counting cane against the sweat-worn floor, as though searching for a rhythm that constantly, almost deliberately, eludes him. Between classes and rehearsals I wander hallways. At night, it's the streets. I don't sleep much anymore, have to keep moving. I pause in the open doorway, watch this solitary figure tapping cryptic messages on the smooth floor of an empty room of mirrors. He senses my presence, turns to see who it is. "Miss Barnes," he says, as if he's been expecting me, his sad angry voice wrapped around a conspiratorial whisper. "Mr. Himmel," I murmur, averting my eyes. This is one mirror I will not look into. "Couldn't we—," he begins, but I'm already turning away, walking briskly down the hall. I don't look back: he might be gaining on me.

Upstairs, beneath the cold dazzling light of Act Three, the Black Swan's angry dance is seducing Siegfried and the audience. Everybody's already forgotten about the White Swan's virtue and her mother's tears and the feckless swan-maidens perched before their dressing-room mirrors, carefully dabbing their faces, necks, and arms with foundation-caked sponges to hide the natural skin color. I'm still groping around in the cellar, searching for a light. I don't know what I expect to find or what I'll do when I find it, but the conventions of this journey insist that I be afraid, that something terrible and grotesque is waiting for me. I slide my hands along the damp cement wall on my right. It's only fitting that my father should be here, buried alive, a heap of putrefied flesh and rotting bones. Or better, more true to life, he's lurking, full-bodied, behind the water heater. He's waiting for the last dance. I paint my lips so they're bloodless, adjust my feathered cap, rub some flesh-colored pancake over the straps of my swan's tutu.

The dressing-room ceiling lights blink on and off, a warning that we should prepare for Act Four, once more don our blank white faces. By now Valerie has plunged into a sharp variation of relentless cutting *fouetté* turns, whipped her arms and legs in tight swift triumphant circles. This is a famous dual role for a ballerina: she can be pliant and strong, needy and willful, technical and passionate, good and evil. It's a division of self we've all been trained to embrace. Luring the Prince into her steely arms, the Black Swan will suddenly pull away from him, project all her self-sufficient contemptuous charm into a defiant but short-lived *arabesque*. I've studied this pose in books, films, rehearsals. It's supposed to come like a breath, something fleeting, even angry—a flash of dignity that only the evil swan can reveal. The White Swan's sustained poses are always soft, boneless, on the edge of dissolving. Wouldn't it be nice, just once, to bring the two roles together, same body, same act? Wouldn't it? Well, so much for fairy tales. In this docudrama the Prince will do as he always does: abandon the dark side of his beloved and embrace the ethereal passive light. The White Swan will make a good wife, she'll be grateful—even if she must die for her cause.

I can just barely touch the white string hanging above my head in the center of the shadowy cellar. I think I hear something, but it's probably only the door trembling and creaking at the top of the stairs. Holding my breath, I tug on the string. Dull dim light fills the room. An old chair leans against the water heater, its rusty springs and foam spilling onto the dirt floor. Some broken wooden crates are stacked under the stairs. Otherwise the cellar's cleaner and emptier than it's ever been. There's nothing else here—just my own fears twirling around in an endless mocking echo. Aside from the expectations of popular narrative, there was never any reason to come to this place. The monsters aren't buried down here.

As the hideous theme of the abandoned White Swan screams through the black wall-speakers, the *corps* is singing "Happy Birthday" to me. Between nervous adolescent giggles they promise me champagne, salad, and tired companionship. "Girls' night out!" they squeal, shimmying inside their feathers. Carabee bursts through one of the doors, followed by the third act's eight heaving mazurka dancers. "Outta my way, birds, outta my way," she snaps. We flap our clipped wings, roll our eyes, lope toward the open door.

I'm calmly walking up the stairs now, out of the damp dark cellar, away from memories and fantasies that aren't my own, never were, never will be. I'm defying the cinematic plot: still alive, still clothed, still whole. My father once told me that no matter where I went he'd find me, that I'd never get away because there was nowhere to go, no way of getting from here to there, even if a there existed. I don't really know yet if this is true or not. So I keep climbing the steps—of the theater, of the cellar, of my life. I must believe, have chosen to believe, that there is a way out of the darkness. Up the cellar steps, past the front room, out the door into the thick Indiana summer heat, around the side of the house, all the way to the farthest reaches of the backyard. Weeds have grown up around it, nearly cover the nailed-over planking. But it's still there. Somehow, I knew it would be. This is the place where the bodies are really hidden. My father, myself, perhaps all of us, are buried here.

I dance with the other girls around the betrayed White Swan, enclosing her in a safe cocoon, in this choreographed fairy-tale written over all our wounded female bodies. It's the wistful *tableau* of the old last act: grieving music, tender soft lighting, fresh batches of dry ice smoking in the wings; pathetic swan-maidens clustered in groups of three, a *corps* of hybrids, a collection of body parts, grounded little birds. Valerie's marriage plans have failed, the sorcerer's pissed, and now, of course, only death can release her from his curse. A few token black swans have joined us, symbolic reminders of how far we've come. In one way or another, we've all been betrayed by the ballet.

The stage darkens. It always does at this point, right before, first, the jilted White Swan and, then, the fickle Prince drown themselves in the illusive glittering lake. They do this, the program tells us, because only in death is there freedom. Grieving and trembling, the *corps* poses on one knee, hands crossed, heads bowed. I kick open the door of the shed, let the beautiful hot sunlight scald the shadows, burn straight through the rotted wood. Light is streaming between the cracks in the boards, winding around my body like white surgical gauze. The apprentice girl behind me, a last-moment replacement for an injured regular, is counting under her breath. She's got the counts wrong, but I can't just turn around and tell her.

I've been here often, it almost seems my entire childhood is contained between these four uneven wood walls, pressed against the earth floor, rocking and crying inside the diffused light, the pain, a tormented childhood. I want to whisper, "It's okay, bunhead, follow my movements, the ballet's almost over," but another voice drums against my throat, "Mommy, my ears are breaking open." I'm curling my fingers around myself, thinking if I just play dead, he'll go away, he'll stop hurting me. But it doesn't end, it can't, because he's so much bigger, because he's the adult male and I'm the little girl, because he's my father. "Please, Daddy, I'm breaking open. Please, Daddy." But he doesn't stop, it never ends. I open my eyes. The white-blue stagelights are dancing straight up into the ceiling. "Please, Daddy." After two intermissions and too many drinks in the lobby, the audience is restless for its ending, for the mutual miraculous resurrection of the virtuous woman and the treacherous man. You can hear the anticipation in their season-ticketed silence.

# THE BODY OF DANCERS

The music reaches a surging climax. We fly together across the stage, our warshoes barely grazing the floor, arms and heads moving in different directions. We are destined to circle the drowned stars, again and again, until, finally, they rise intact from the waters, clasped together in a staged embrace. Then Simon and Valerie will take their curtain bows, triumphantly gather their dethorned flowers, throw powdery kisses to the conductor, pretend to be unworthy of the bravos offered by the gleaming flushed audience. Behind them, the *corps* will join hands, curtsey in unison, share a little in the glory. This is what's supposed to happen.

Except that tonight is different. When the curtain closes, I'm leaving. I don't know where I'm going, how I'll get there. It doesn't really matter. I gather with the other swans next to the lake, take my place fifth in a double-diagonal line, cross my arms to the side. Carabee's in the wings, straightening up the huntsmen from Act One for their curtain call. She's got safety pins dangling from her puckered mouth. The apprentice girl's still counting, as though saying a prayer. Somehow she's finally found the tempo. Strips of light are breaking across my body. "You've made your choice. Now live it." This time it's a real voice, startles the swans in my line. Fingers stiffen, feathers tremble.

It's just a storage place after all: rakes, hoes, my mother's potting soil; an old wash bucket with a Raggedy Ann doll stuffed inside it, a torn schoolbag, a pair of ballet slippers; a box of empty canning jars, a shredding phonebook, my father's welding torch. I begin punching the roof's splintered slats, kicking through the walls' rotted wood planks. Dust, dry ice, maggots, shards of glass, feathers, sun-bleached weeds are flying around me. The theater is crackling, nervous, and dark. I *bourrée* out of line, heading for center stage, away from the *corps'* gasps, toward the spotlight and the front-row darkness beyond. Unaware of my transgression, the symphony thunders on, swells violently inside its own music. I have broken the one solid law we live by. I'm bringing down the walls around me, hammering my body against the lie I've been forced to live. Carabee's voice travels from the wings, follows after me. "What in the hell's that girl doing?"

Pounding my toes into the stage floor, into the earth, I wrap my fingers around another decayed board, pull on it until it rips and crumbles. The shed's breaking open, tumbling down around me: rusty nails, the dated Yellow Pages, my old twice-dyed ballet shoes, my father's naked skull are already buried beneath the falling wood. I'm only vaguely aware of Valerie and Simon, who have dropped their embrace, glare at me with frightened hostile eyes. The backdrop is rippling behind me, the *corps* whispering, the stagehands groaning in the wings. "What is that girl doing?" I'm moving inside the music, phrasing the counts in angry breaths beneath the bright dazzling theater lights. Lifting from my center, I step out of the destroyed shed into the full sunlight, pull my back up against my extended leg, abandon myself to a strong defiant *arabesque*. I feel as though I could hold it forever. Focusing my eyes on that unseen spot beyond the red-brick house, somewhere deep in the heart of the darkened audience, I give my boneless arms an edge—reaching out, as far as I can, from the body of dancers.